GATHERED FROM THE NORTH

BLOOMS OF THE BITTERBRUSH
BOOK THREE

BARBARA A. CURTIS

WILD HEART
BOOKS

Copyright © 2025 by BARBARA A. Curtis

All rights reserved. No portion of this book may be reproduced or transmitted in any form or by any means—photocopied, shared electronically, scanned, stored in a retrieval system, or other—without the express permission of the publisher. Exceptions will be made for brief quotations used in critical reviews or articles promoting this work.

The characters and events in this fictional work are the product of author's imagination. Any resemblance to actual people, living or dead, is coincidental.

Unless otherwise indicated, all Scripture quotations are taken from the Holy Bible, Kings James Version.

Cover design by Evelyne Labelle at Carpe Librum Book Design. www. carpelibrumbookdesign.com

ISBN: 978-1-963212-43-3

O magnify the Lord with me, and let us exalt his name together.

— PSALM 34:3 KJV

Let the redeemed of the Lord say so, whom he
    hath redeemed from the hand
of the enemy, and gathered them out of the
    lands, from the east, and from the
west, from the north, and from the south.

                        — PSALM 107:2–3 KJV

CHAPTER 1

Boise, Idaho
January 1945

All Beth Calloway had to do was smile. Stretch out her hands, pretend she was happy to hold a baby.

"Thank you for filling in." The Boise Foundling Home director placed a crying infant into Beth's arms. Mrs. Martin's silver-streaked dark bun and black suit matched the solemn occasion. "All of the paperwork is complete, and the Donaldsons will be right out to take Annabelle home. Summon me if you have any questions."

"Yes, Mrs. Martin."

The director turned and headed down the hall, the click of her sturdy-heeled pumps underscoring her departure.

Beth stared at the babe she held. If the Donaldsons had come on time this Monday morning, she'd be at her desk typing, as she was supposed to be doing, not having to hold Annabelle. But now it was feeding time, and all the nurses were busy with the other babies.

Oh, please, can't just one nurse walk by and take her?

Annabelle was so light, so fragile. What if Beth dropped her? She was the last person who should be holding this little one. She touched the infant's face, screwed up in a howl.

"Shh." Beth tightened her hold on the child and shifted from one foot to the other, rocking, the way she'd seen the nurses do. "It'll be all right, Annabelle. You'll have a home now. A mother and father to love and care for you." Beth trailed a finger along Annabelle's cheek. "Always obey them. Make them proud of you." She adjusted the baby. "Do you like music?" She hummed a few measures of a song her mother had sung to her and her siblings, and Annabelle's cries became quieter. "You do like music, don't you? I'll sing it for you."

> "Little one, look above
> to the Lord—for He is love.
> And as He watches over you,
> with tenderness, He'll gently woo."

Annabelle stopped crying. She curled a small finger around Beth's larger one. And smiled.

"Oh, Annabelle." Beth leaned down to the baby's soft skin and kissed her cheek. "See? You'll be very happy with your family."

Soft clicking echoed through the hallway as the Donaldsons approached to claim their child. Beth turned to greet them. All she had to do was loosen her grip on their baby, hand her over to her new parents. But Beth drew Annabelle closer, letting the smell of freshly washed baby fill her soul. She'd forgotten the feel of a baby, as she hadn't held one since her sister, Susannah. And that was three years ago since...

"There she is, Edward." Mrs. Donaldson stepped alongside Beth and leaned over, cooing into her baby's face. "You're beautiful, just like your name means—Belle."

Beth touched Annabelle's hair. Would the peach fuzz grow

into honeyed ringlets the color of Mrs. Donaldson's? Or turn dark and thick like Mr. Donaldson's?

"Is she all ready for us?" Mrs. Donaldson spread her arms the perfect width to accept Annabelle.

"Yes, she is." Beth trailed her hand along the baby's cheek. Even through typewriter-roughened fingers, she could feel the softness of newborn life. Transferring Annabelle into her mother's care would make one more crib available for another orphan at the Boise Foundling Home. She'd seen how the nurses did it effortlessly. But this was the first occasion she, the secretary, was the one to cradle a smiling bundle and place joy into hearts that would give her a home.

Annabelle was beautiful in the frilly pink store-bought dress the Donaldsons had an employee drop off yesterday to take her home in today. A dress all her own. And the purple velvet collar on the tiny winter coat made her look like royalty.

Her smile in place, Beth handed the little princess to Mrs. Donaldson. "God bless you with this addition to your family."

Mr. Donaldson beamed. "Thank you so much. You've no idea what having Annabelle means to us. Do you have any further instructions for us?" He glanced at the paper Beth had typed up that morning.

Beth reached over and retied the strings of Annabelle's hat. "You have her eating and sleeping schedules, a list of what to feed her. So just love her. Call us if you have any further questions. And be sure to bring her by to visit us sometime." The parting speech she'd heard Mrs. Martin say countless times tumbled out.

Mr. Donaldson shook hands with Beth, tucked his arm through his wife's, and ushered his family out the door. As soon as the door clicked shut, Beth's smile vanished. She stepped to the window and lifted a corner of the drape. Snowflakes smacked the sidewalk as Mr. Donaldson removed his coat and

3

sheltered Annabelle and his wife under it as he shepherded them into their black Packard.

No one else heralded Annabelle's victory in finding a new home, not even the commanding face of Uncle Sam on the nearby recruiting poster. The only passersby who stopped to look were a lady with a long brown coat, a black scarf wound around her head, a market basket in one hand, and a little dark-haired boy, maybe four, reined in on the other. Within moments, the Donaldsons' car pulled away, taking with them a life that Beth would never have. For she was unworthy of being a mother.

"Did you get Annabelle off all right?"

Beth turned at the director's voice behind her and stepped back to her metal desk, the place she belonged.

"Yes, I did. But, please, Mrs. Martin, I'm just a typist. You know I'm not good with the babies." She'd seen that truth in her mother's eyes the last three years. Beth placed a sheet of paper into the typewriter and rolled the platen until the paper stuck out two inches, ready for her keystrokes.

"When we're shorthanded, everyone has to pitch in."

"Yes, Mrs. Martin." Beth clicked away on the keys, feeling the director's eyes on her.

"Beth."

She met her boss's gaze. "Yes?"

"Come with me into the kitchen and have some soup."

"Yes, ma'am." Had she done something wrong? As it wasn't break time for her.

Beth rose and smoothed her apple-green skirt, the one Mama had styled and added pockets to, even during war time. The one that brought pleasure with each step as the gores in the gabardine swished and swirled around her knees. Except there was no joy today as she trailed behind Mrs. Martin down the hall, following the enticing aroma of chicken broth.

As they passed the infant room, Beth shut her ears to the

cries of the babies still in the foundling home. Why weren't more people like the Donaldsons lining up to claim each one of these children? By tomorrow, Annabelle's crib would be filled, and they'd be back to looking for homes for twenty-five children again. Some of these babies had been here so long that they were able to eat the chicken soup.

At the kitchen, Mrs. Martin opened the door and held it, allowing Beth to scurry through. "Pearl?"

The gray-haired cook standing over the stove swiped her forehead with her arm.

"May we have two bowls of soup, please? I'll take mine to my office. Beth, you stay and eat here. Enjoy a few minutes of an extra break."

"Yes, ma'am. Thank you." Beth sat at the small table. So maybe she wasn't in trouble, after all?

Cook Pearl ladled the bowls and handed one to Mrs. Martin, who left with a nod to Beth.

"Here you go, Beth." Pearl slid the other bowl to Beth with a smile. "Are you staying after work for Chester's birthday party? Already two. I made a cake for him and the staff. Though it's quite light on the sugar, he still deserves a celebration of his birth."

Oh, the sweet boy certainly did. He was the oldest of the children, but she couldn't get attached to any of them.

"No. I'd best be heading home after work." She gestured toward the window. "All this snow, you know."

"It's sure a doozy of a storm out there." Pearl nodded. "But if you change your mind…"

"Thank you."

Sweet Pearl always included Beth in invitations to gatherings and celebrations but seemed to accept Beth's answer was always going to be no. How could it be anything otherwise, given her history? And there was no point in getting too attached to anyone.

∼

*T*imothy McPhearson shivered in the wind as he leaned against the rail of the troop transport ship as it lumbered into New York Harbor. Home. Except his future was as empty as the vast ocean now separating him from the fighting in Germany. He tuned out the incessant laughter and talk from other returning soldiers crowding around the railing, all most likely with someone waiting to welcome them home.

Once the ship docked, a private sidled into the now-empty spot beside Timothy, scanning the crowd waving onshore. "You got a girl out there waiting?"

"Me? No." With her arm raised in the midmorning sun, the Statue of Liberty had been the only one welcoming him home.

"I sure hope mine is. When I find her—there she is—Viola!" The man waved his arms furiously, then slapped Timothy on the back. "I hope you find someone like her one day."

Unlikely. But he wished all the best for this guy and the shoving soldiers making their way to their screaming gals.

When the gangway lowered, he slung his duffel bag over his shoulder and joined the other soldiers as they disembarked the ship returning from Germany, some with visible wounds, others with unseen ones. He had both.

People clustered in groups, girls craning their heads, jumping and yelling when they spotted their sweethearts or brothers. Mothers exuberantly greeted their sons.

He dodged couples kissing just to get to the street. Once he made his way to the apartment of Mr. and Mrs. Jackson, friends of his parents, he'd greet them, then be on his way. More of an aunt and uncle to him, they'd welcomed him into their home after the tenement he lived in had burned, taking his parents and most of the other fifth-floor tenants with it. They'd been his anchor until he was old enough to join the army. So of course, he had to stop and visit before heading to Grandmother's house in Boise. She and Great-aunt Cora up in Sandpoint were the only family he had now.

As soon as he knocked on their door, Auntie Georgette and Uncle Eugene flung it open, and he was engulfed in the Jacksons' arms.

"Timothy. What a joy to see you." Auntie Georgette's hugs were as sweet as his own mother's had been. "Your letter said you'd just be passing through, but we have an early lunch prepared for you. At least stay that long with us?"

"Of course. Thank you so much."

"Then you're heading out to be with your grandmother?"

"Yes. This afternoon, leaving from Grand Central." Hopefully, his letter to Grandmother would arrive before he did.

"Then sit, sit." She ushered him to the table already laden with food. "I'm sure Bea is anxious for your arrival. I imagine she has certainly missed your family living out there for a few years before moving back here to aid your other grandmother when her health declined."

"Both of my grandfathers were gone before I was born, so Mama and Papa made sure their mothers were cared for as they aged."

Auntie Georgette patted Timothy on the shoulder. "Your folks were good people. We miss them, as I know you do."

His throat clogged, so he simply nodded.

"Let's ask the Lord's blessing on our meal and Timothy's travels, then we can eat as he catches us up." Uncle Eugene reached out, and Auntie Georgette and Timothy completed his circle of prayer as they joined hands.

After the amen, Auntie Georgette passed a platter of sandwiches. "I'm sure there are many things you don't wish to speak of, but can you tell us about your discharge? Medical, was it?"

His discharge. Not exactly medical, with the stigma of *Combat Fatigue* inked across his record. Now he was deemed

7

unfit to even scrub the floor of an overseas hospital. Sent home to—what? Recover?

But battle fatigue had nothing to do with his actions when he'd sat up in that hospital bed and heard the truth—or lack of it—from the private in the next bed. His shaking hands, tears so close to spilling out, "overreacting," and his attack on PFC Roland Johnston, trying to choke the answers out of him, weren't symptoms of combat fatigue or anything else the army wanted to call it.

They were the actions of a man wanting the truth. And he'd get it from the soldier he'd vowed to track down after this war was over—Roland Johnston, the man who was there when Timothy's best friend, Stanley Tomaszewski, was killed. The man who knew what had happened in that moment Stanley was shot.

"My buddy Stanley and I were advance scouts on a mission. There was gunfire, and in the process, the door of the abandoned apartment building we were in splintered, and a piece landed in my eye. While the surgery was deemed successful, my eye just needs time to heal." Probably he should still be wearing the patch the doc had recommended. "The vision is returning, even the pain is decreasing, but the surgeon said the main thing to watch out for is irritants, especially smoke."

"Then you will follow his advice, yes?" Auntie Georgette gave him a firm nod.

"Yes, I will."

They chatted a while, then Timothy stood. "I need to head on over to Grand Central to catch my train. It sure was good seeing you both."

Auntie Georgette wiped tears from her eyes, then clasped Timothy into a hug. "We're so glad you stopped to see us. May God's grace walk with you."

"Thank you, Auntie."

She loosened her grip but reached for his hands. "Do you remember those words?"

"That's what Mama used to say."

"She did. That was her prayer for everyone she met, but especially for you. Never forget them."

"I promise, I won't."

He exchanged an embrace with Uncle Eugene, then headed to Grand Central to catch the 20th Century Limited. By the time he reached Boise, he hoped to have a plan in place to track down Roland Johnston. And this time, combat fatigue or not, he aimed to get the truth—one way or another.

CHAPTER 2

At five o'clock, Beth gathered her purse and shrugged into her coat. From down the hall, she could hear Chester's party getting underway with the nighttime staff, but with the snow falling heavier now, she didn't dare stay even had she wanted to change her mind.

Please, Lord, give sweet little Chester a real home.

"Beth"—Mrs. Martin's pumps clicked up the hallway in her staccato fashion—"before you go, here are your wages from last week. I'm terribly sorry the money wasn't available on Friday. If you met any hardship due to that, let me know. But here." She held out an envelope to Beth. "I'm glad I can give you this today."

"Thank you, Mrs. Martin." Beth reached for it before the thought of where the money had come from registered. If it hadn't been available on Friday, how was it in the foundling home's account on Monday? "But where—"

Mrs. Martin closed Beth's fingers over the envelope. "You do a good job for us. And here"—she thrust a thin, wrapped package into Beth's other hand—"Pearl cut you a piece of

Chester's cake. Now off with you before you miss your transportation."

Beth walked outside to the bus stop, clutching her handbag tightly. Mama always said to hang on to it. She brushed snow off a bench and sat down. Only on a day like this, when most people had left for home early, did she get a bench to herself. Few cars were on the road with the snow falling harder. A Ford, a truck, a Packard. Just like the Donaldsons' car.

Annabelle must be in her new crib now, dressed in nightclothes all her own, not those passed around among fifteen baby girls. Maybe right now, Mrs. Donaldson was rocking Annabelle to sleep. Mr. Donaldson might be tickling the tiny little feet. And Annabelle would give them a big smile, just as she had given Beth. The feel of the baby in her own arms had been...wonderful, flowing straight into her heart.

But she was just a typist. Nothing more.

Where was that bus? The few people who were out scurried past, heads down as they battled the wind and snow. Something dark at the edge of a nearby brick building moved—a lady with a black scarf and market basket and little boy, the same two who had been outside the foundling home witnessing Annabelle's departure hours ago. Were they homeless?

Beth laid her purse down and bent to retie her boots. She didn't want to trip on the laces as she climbed onto the bus. If it ever came. As she started on her second boot, a lumbering engine huffed down the street. She jumped up and hurried to the corner to check. If the public transportation didn't come soon, it'd be dark by the time she got home. But Mrs. McPhearson had promised she'd leave the porch light burning before departing on her trip so Beth wouldn't be unlocking the door in the dark. And hopefully, her landlady had also turned up the heat, wasteful as it was. Beth rubbed her arms. Tonight she'd need a nice toasty house.

She stepped off the curb for a better view. Yes, it was the bus—but in her haste, she'd left her purse on the bench. How could she have been so foolish? She turned, and yes, it was still there. Just as she took a step back to the bench, the little boy against the wall dashed from his mother's side toward the bench. He grabbed her purse and took off running.

"Hey! Come back here!" Her boots slipped on the packed snow. "Stop!"

The boy handed the purse to the lady with the black scarf. The woman glanced at Beth with an almost apologetic expression. Then, with a cough, she stashed the purse into her market basket, grasped the boy's hand, and scuttled behind the arriving bus. The last one of the day.

"Come back!" The squeal of the brakes drowned out her words, even if the lady was listening.

Beth's wages were gone. Her identification also.

The bus door opened. "Are you getting on, miss?"

Beth dug into her pockets. *Thank You, Lord*, her keys were there. And enough coins for bus fare. She nodded, handed the driver her money, and boarded. Oh, she was so foolish. Why hadn't she heeded Mama's warnings? She'd learned a long time ago what carelessness cost.

The bus was almost empty. Once settled into a seat, Beth leaned her head against the cold window, watching the snow swirl outside until it became too dark to see. She had to learn to think before she acted. To be more cautious, alert.

Finally, her stop came, and she walked the two blocks in the darkness that had set in so quickly. Not even the promised porch light emanated from her landlady's half of the house. Beth fumbled with her key and at last got inside and switched on a light. Snow had blown right up onto the porch, covering even the neatly stacked wood by the front door. Indoors, she shuddered in the air just as frigid as outside.

Beth left her coat on. The pale buttery-yellow Christmas

gift Mama had sewn had been protective enough in the snow outside, but what had happened to the heat? She'd have to try to light a fire in the fireplace. But the only logs were the ones on the porch, now snow covered. In her haste to leave for northern Idaho today, Mrs. McPhearson must have forgotten her promises, as well as to cover the wood.

After using most of her matches trying to light wet wood, Beth gave up and wrapped her coat tighter around herself, pulled out an extra blanket, and cocooned herself in her bed in the back room, where the covers helped seal in her body heat.

Little Annabelle would be warm and toasty this evening, safe in her new home. What would it be like to be Mrs. Donaldson tonight, in her warm, cozy home, singing her sweet baby girl to sleep with a lullaby? Wrapping her in a lovingly stitched blanket?

The wind howled outside, and Beth drifted off to sleep. She dreamed Mrs. Donaldson came and got Annabelle, then couple by couple showed up, each taking a baby. But one was crying, wailing his little heart out to no avail. Chester? Why had no one taken him? Was he calling to her?

Beth sat up in the dark, yet the wails from her dream continued. She climbed out of bed, put on slippers, and crept to the living room, where the sound grew louder. She turned on the porch light and opened the door, only to be slapped by the bone-numbing air and ear-piercing cries.

The light stopped at the edge of something lodged against the wood stack in the corner.

Beth searched the surrounding darkness, then stepped over to the wood pile. The crying was coming from a market basket. It couldn't be...

She yanked back the blanket covering the contents. A baby! A little red face screwed up in distress, and a tiny fist flailed.

She hastened inside with the basket, set it on a side table in the living room, and pulled out the baby dressed in a pink flannel gown with a heart-shaped locket around her neck. Underneath the child's worn pink blanket were square cloths—for diapers?—another gown, and a bottle with white powder in it. And tucked into the side of the basket, her own purse, with a note on top.

Cradling the baby, she read the block printing.

You are a good woman. I give to you this baby. I know you will take good care of her.

Someone trusted Beth Calloway to tend this gift from heaven? She'd love to.

The only problem was…she couldn't.

Thankfully, this poor baby girl didn't have to worry about Beth doing anything more than just getting her through the cold night. In the daylight, Beth could take the little girl—maybe two months or so old—to the children's home. Annabelle's crib was empty, as if prepared just in time for this little one. Beth set the child on her sofa and surrounded her with pillows in case she moved.

Now she had to start a fire. How long had this infant been out in the cold? Were the scarfed lady and her little boy homeless? Maybe they needed a place to stay as well.

Beth peered out the window in the door, where moonlight danced on the snow. If they were lingering nearby, she'd invite them in and ask the lady about the baby. She opened the door.

"Hello? Ma'am? Are you still out there? Please come in and warm yourself and your son."

No answer came. She grabbed a couple logs off the woodpile within reach, dusted snow off, and brought them inside, quickly closing the door against a further draft. Maybe the wood from earlier had dried a bit. There must be something in the house she could use for kindling. She'd managed most of the night without heat, but now she had the baby to care for. If

Mrs. McPhearson were home, she'd know what to do for heat... and for a baby. But she was gone for two weeks, visiting her sister up north in Sandpoint.

Beth scouted around, even rummaged through the cabinets. Nothing to burn. Only... No, she couldn't. The sweet letters from Lawrence. Her love letters. What would Lawrence even think when she told him a baby had been left on her porch? He didn't even like Beth working at the orphanage.

"Don't worry." Beth smiled over at the baby. "Someone will take you right away." Who wouldn't be drawn by this sweet child's inquisitive blue eyes and silky tufts of blond hair?

I give to you this baby. I know you will take good care of her.

If only that could be...

Beth shook her head. "No, this will be the best thing for you, little one. You'll have a real home one day as Annabelle does with the Donaldsons. But until I can take you to the orphanage, you need to be warm."

She retrieved her letters and untied the pink ribbon bundling the stack, then reread the last one.

Dearest Beth, I cannot wait to discuss the future when next I see you. You are the one who supports my goals. As a team, working together, we will succeed in life. Until then, Lawrence.

Even though it wasn't as romantic as the poems Papa wrote to Mama, they were words from Lawrence's heart. She couldn't burn his letter. Not any of them.

The baby whimpered, and Beth turned to her.

"You're cold, aren't you?" Beth picked up the letters and pressed them tight against her chest. "I'm sorry, Lawrence. I'll keep your words down deep in my heart, though."

The possibilities of her future with him were enough to add warmth to her soul right now.

She struck a match to the corner of the top letter and tossed it into the fireplace, aiming for the log with a stub sticking up. The letter went up in a flame. The stub smoldered, then glowed. She tossed another letter onto the flicker of fire. Then another. Until the fire was blazing.

Thank You, Lord. Thank You.

Beth scooped up the baby, set her in the market basket, and placed her close to the fireplace. And as the heat encompassed them, the infant cooed.

Beth tucked the pink blanket tighter around the little girl. "I'll be right back. I'll warm some milk for you." She hadn't done this since she left home. But she knew the steps. Plus, how many times had she typed the words when a baby was sent home with a family? *Heat the milk on low, then test it against the wrist before feeding it to a baby.* And this child had even come with a bottle tucked inside the basket.

Once the milk was ready, Beth picked up the infant and cuddled her as the girl sucked on her bottle. "Would you like a lullaby? Mama says every baby should have a special song to go to sleep by." She tucked the girl closer into the crook of her arm as she sang.

> "Little one, look above
> to the Lord—for He is love.
> And as He watches over you,
> with tenderness, He'll gently woo."

Deep blue eyes locked with Beth's...as if thanking her.

"You need a name. Not that I could actually keep and raise you, but you deserve the dignity of a name, even if you're just staying overnight. A beautiful name. If you were mine, I'd call you Elizabeth. Elizabeth Rose. It's a family name. There was Great-great-grandmother Elizabeth Rose Roberts, Grandmother Eliza, and my mother, Lizzie. And me, Beth. See, it's a name of a good lineage. Elizabeth Rose. Of course, that's much too long for you right now since you're such a tiny girl." Beth fingered the pieces of hair making a halo around the baby's head. "You need something short and spunky for a nickname. Like Elly. And Rose says that you're beautiful and delicate. Yes. You'll be Elly Rose."

Elly smiled as if approving.

Beth unclasped the heart-shaped necklace from Elly Rose's neck and fingered the inscription on it. *Psalm 107:2–3*. A Bible verse. Such a delicate piece of jewelry. It even resembled real silver, which would've cost a lot of money. But if her parents had money, why hadn't they been able to keep her? Could it be that the lady with the small boy and market basket was her mother? And the engraving meant they'd spent even more money on it.

Beth pulled out her Bible and flipped to the psalm, the words Elly's parents had wanted her to remember all her life.

> *Let the redeemed of the* Lord *say so, whom he hath redeemed from the hand of the enemy, and gathered them out of the lands, from the east, and from the west, from the north, and from the south.*

If this family had both faith and money, what was Elly doing on her front porch in the early hours of morning?

Beth turned the locket over and discovered another engraving.

Liebe.

She stared at the word.

Liebe. German for *love*?

Was Elly a German baby? She did have pale blond hair cropping in, blue eyes. But so did a million other babies.

"You sleep, Elly Rose." Beth refastened the necklace around Elly's neck and tucked the blanket snugger around her. "And today you'll come to work with me, and then you'll have Annabelle's bed. I'm sure you'll find a new home quickly too."

In the morning when Beth arrived for work with the market basket on her arm, Mrs. Martin was in the reception area, giving several nurses instructions.

"Did you bring us cornbread again, Beth?" Mitzi came over and pulled back the blanket covering the basket. "Oh my!" She gaped at Beth, then back at the basket.

"She was left on my doorstep during the night."

"What are you going to do with her?"

"I'm..."

Mrs. Martin, again in her black suit, also stepped over and peeked inside the basket.

"Mrs. Martin, this baby—Elly Rose—was left on my doorstep overnight. She can take Annabelle's crib and—"

"Oh, my dear. No." Mrs. Martin shook her head. "Annabelle's crib has already been filled early this morning. A baby was left on our doorstep also. I'm afraid we have no room for her."

"But—"

"I'm sorry, Beth. There's absolutely no room for even one more child." The wails coming from down the hall echoed her point.

Beth peered at Elly, just waking up in the basket. Elly trusted her. And Beth had failed already in providing safety for her.

"She could sleep next to my desk in the basket during the day, and I could take her home at night until a bed opens up."

Mrs. Martin laid a hand on Beth's arm. "I am so sorry, dear. I know you want to help this little girl, as I do also. But a basket in an office is no place for a child. A crying baby would interrupt your work, and our nurses are overworked as it is with the other infants. We don't even have enough milk for one more mouth." Mrs. Martin shook her head again.

"But someone needs to care for her." Panic rose in Beth. What would become of Elly Rose?

"Of course, but we can't possibly take on another mouth here. I'm so sorry, but the answer is still no."

"But what should I do with her?"

"If someone left her for you to find, I believe they wanted you to take care of her."

"But if she'd been dropped off here during the night, if you had two babies, you would have taken both of them, wouldn't you?"

The director gave a slow nod. "All right, Beth. We'll try this for today. For the rest of the week. Maybe someone will adopt her—or one of the other children and open up a bed. Put her down, take off your coat, and get to work."

"Oh thank you, Mrs. Martin!" Now Beth could breathe, could make her fingers type.

The director waved her off. "This war… I don't know what we'll do…" She strolled away, muttering.

Beth smiled at Elly. "I'll put you right here next to me, and you'll get to see what I do all day."

With each passing day, even though the nurses were busy and Mrs. Martin still made a point of scowling, every one of them, including Mrs. Martin herself, continued to stop by to hold this mystery baby whenever she woke up. Pearl managed to fill Elly's milk bottle throughout every day, and the little dress Annabelle had often worn mysteriously appeared on Elly one afternoon. And clean diapers were always tucked into the basket at leaving time.

At the end of the week, Mrs. Martin didn't say anything about Elly's trial being over, nor anything about being low on diapers or milk. Hope surged in Beth that Elly was loved and welcome here, with or without an actual bed.

On Friday evening, Beth trudged home from the bus stop and up to her front door of the two-family house with Elly Rose in the basket on her arm, as usual. Since nothing had been said to the contrary, Beth would take Elly to work again next week. And the day would surely come when someone did want to adopt the little girl, though Beth couldn't think about that.

In the meantime, Elly filled the loneliness of the night hours with her sweetness. And it wasn't just her company Beth relished. Elly made her feel like she was important to someone.

The doorbell rang just as Beth settled Elly Rose in front of the fireplace. She lifted an edge of the front window curtain to see who was there. Lawrence. She hurried to the door and swung it open.

"Good evening, Elizabeth."

She'd given up telling him that only her parents called her that, and rarely. "Hello, Lawrence." She ushered him inside. Tall and blond and handsome, the catch of any girl, but he'd chosen her.

"It's cold in here. Doesn't your landlady give you any heat?" He rubbed his arms and nodded toward the fireplace. "You do know how to start a fire, don't you?"

Elly let out a loud wail.

"What—?"

Beth hurried over to Elly and picked her up.

"What is a baby doing here?"

She motioned to the couch. "Sit down, and I'll explain."

Lawrence remained standing, his arms crossed. "Go ahead."

"Well, I—"

Elly cried out again.

"Excuse me. I have to fix her a bottle."

"What do you mean, you have to fix her a bottle? I demand an explanation."

"All right." Beth rocked back and forth, trying to soothe Elly. "Someone left her on the porch during the night on Monday. Now I have to warm her milk for her." She turned and scurried into the kitchen.

"Elizabeth." Lawrence followed right behind her. "I understand your kindness. But you'll be taking her to the orphanage—when? Tomorrow? They're open on Saturdays."

"They have no room." She turned to face him. "If no one comes for her..." And in that moment, the decision—firm and right—was made. "Then I'll keep her."

"You'll what? You can't. What did you think this would do to us?"

"I thought maybe, that we'd..." She snuggled Elly tighter.

"That we'd what?"

Lawrence's eyes no longer held his usual earnestness, his take-charge leadership, but a chill she'd never seen before.

"I thought...maybe...we'd get married and be a family."

He stared at her.

"I named her Elly Rose."

Lawrence shook his head. "You really thought... You have to choose between me or her. I'm not going to be this baby's father."

The words struck like a slap. Beth bent her head against Elly's pink blanket to discreetly wipe away tears slipping down her cheeks. "Lawrence—"

"Elizabeth. I'm in no position to be getting married now."

"But you said we'd discuss our future—"

"And you thought..." Lawrence laughed. "Oh, Elizabeth. I said we'd discuss *the* future. My future."

What was he saying? He didn't want her either? "I'm all Elly has until someone takes her."

"With the war and rationing, you know no one's going to take her. You said even the orphanage won't." He pulled his coat collar up. "Warm her bottle. I'll find my own way out."

And he was gone.

Beth braced one hand against the stove. What had she done? Now she had no hope of a father for Elly. She wasn't beautiful like other girls who had men swooning over them—or even pretty like Mama with her curly dark hair and chocolatey brown eyes. Beth had ended up with the Calloway plain brown hair and plain brown eyes. Plain, plain, plain.

Tears dropped and soaked into the blanket. She was abandoned. Just like little Elly Rose.

Elly cooed, and Beth rubbed a hand along her soft cheek.

"You're right, Elly. Neither of us is truly alone. We have each other."

※

At last, Timothy stood in front of Grandmother's house. But the only light shining was from the side he'd lived in years ago with his parents. Grandmother's side was dark.

The door to the lighted side flew open, and a man stormed out and slammed it behind him. In his haste, he rammed into Timothy on the sidewalk and glared. "Move aside."

This obviously wasn't a good time to knock on the door of Grandmother's renter—a Miss Calloway. But a spinster lady might be in some trouble—or could at least use a kind word. He'd check on her after making sure Grandmother was home and safe.

No one answered his knock, though, on Grandmother's side. Where would she be at night? Unless she had fallen? He'd tried calling at each train stop en route, but she hadn't answered.

Timothy moved to the renter's door and knocked. A porch light came on, and the door opened.

"Lawrence—" A dark-haired young lady holding a baby stared at him, eyes wide, apparently realizing she'd opened the door to a stranger. She abruptly yanked on it.

"Wait—please, I'm Bea McPhearson's grandson, Timothy McPhearson."

She stopped tugging on the door with just inches to spare before it slammed in his face.

"I'm sorry to intrude. I'm looking for my grandmother, Bea McPhearson. She didn't answer her door, and I was worried something happened to her."

"She's not home."

"Is she all right? Do you know where she is?"

She studied him—oh, hopefully, Grandmother had spoken of him to her. Maybe showed her the picture he'd sent of him in his uniform so she'd know he was telling the truth?

"I just got discharged from the army and returned stateside. I wrote Grandmother that I was coming to visit and tried calling several times, but I guess the surprise is on me."

"She's visiting her sister."

"Great-aunt Cora in Sandpoint." Adding that seemed to increase his credibility, as she nodded.

"Yes. Could you hand me Mrs. McPhearson's mail from her box?"

"Of course." He reached into the black receptacle she indicated and pulled out a stack of mail. She riffled through the correspondence and held one up. His handwriting on a VE letter. No wonder Grandmother wasn't here waiting for him. But with the letter in hand, the young woman opened the door wide. "Well, come on in out of the cold."

"Um, thank you, but"—he gestured down the sidewalk though the man no longer was in sight—"was that your husband? I'm not sure he'd like me being here while he's gone."

She swiped at her eyes. "No, he's not."

Timothy pointed at the babe in her arms. "Then—?"

"I'm not married."

Heat filled Timothy's cheeks, probably blotching his face red all the way to his ears. "Oh." He glanced at the baby. "I... see."

She pulled the pink blanket across the baby's face, as if shielding her from Timothy's assumptions.

"Um, is Miss Calloway—Grandmother's neighbor—home? Perhaps I could speak with her—"

"I'm Beth Calloway."

No, that couldn't be right. She was the neighbor Grandmother had written of in passing? So much younger than he'd expected of the woman who brought Grandmother homemade bread and soups, who shoveled her porch in the winter, who did her marketing for her, who checked on her nightly. And, yes, though he tried not to notice, pretty, even with her brown eyes shadowed with accusation.

"Miss Calloway, I'm sorry."

"Beth. And Elly Rose was left on my doorstep a few days ago."

"An orphan? You took her in by yourself?"

"Well...yes. She needed care. And someone to love her."

"And you gave her that."

"Everyone needs to be loved." Beth bent her head and kissed Elly Rose on the cheek. "Mr. McPhearson, since your grandmother isn't here to welcome you after your trip, would you at least like to stay for supper?"

He eyed her for a moment. "If you'll have me after my rudeness, yes."

"Of course. As Mrs. McPhearson's grandson and for serving our country, how could I not?"

"Thank you."

"Follow me." She stopped to pick up a basket and led the way into the kitchen. "I had just started to warm some stew."

"It smells delicious."

Beth settled Elly in the basket, then ladled two bowls of stew, placing more broth in her bowl than meat, and pulled out some bread and set it on the table.

"May I say grace?" Timothy asked once they were seated.

"Of course. Thank you."

"Lord, thank You for Miss Calloway's hospitality in offering this meal—and for her compassion in taking in a baby. Please bless them. And Grandmother. Amen." He smiled at Beth, then filled his spoon with stew. "I used to live here, you know."

"Oh...you... Of course. Mrs. McPhearson said her son, daughter-in-law, and grandson had lived here for a while, quite some time ago."

"I was about ten when we moved back to New York City."

"I'm assuming you were planning to stay here with your grandmother?"

Timothy set his spoon down and finished chewing. "I did, but now..." He shrugged. "Maybe I'll just head up to Sandpoint myself for a few days."

"Do you want to use my telephone to call her? I have the number."

"Yes, thanks." He stood and followed Miss Beth Calloway to the phone table in the hall. When she turned to smile at him, hope swept through him that he might still be able to stay at Grandmother's

CHAPTER 3

From the kitchen doorway, Beth watched Timothy. He settled on the cushioned telephone chair with a curved writing desk. For a moment, he traced the jagged scratch on the desktop with a finger, as if he was familiar with it, perhaps had put it there. Most of the furniture was Mrs. McPhearson's, so very likely Timothy did remember it. Then he pulled the phone from the deep shelf underneath. After he read the operator Miss Cora's number, the switchboard employee put the call through.

This was the grandson Beth and Mrs. McPhearson prayed for weekly? The twinkling eyes and big smile of the uniformed soldier from Mrs. McPhearson's framed photograph were missing. But the short blond hair, hazel eyes—shadowed surely by sights unimaginable, with one looking sore—and the mouth like Mrs. McPhearson's, though set in a straight line—yes, he definitely was the soldier in the picture. But here in person?

She picked up the contented baby from her basket, needing a cuddle herself after Lawrence's visit. "What do you think, Elly?" With Timothy arriving on the heels of Lawrence, she'd barely had time to shed more than a few tears. "I was so foolish, thinking Lawrence loved me. And I'm sorry he treated you as if you didn't matter... But I promise you, I'll do everything I can to make sure you end up in a home where you're loved."

She set Elly back in the basket and cut two pieces of a pie she'd made in hopes of Lawrence stopping by sometime.

"Beth?"

Timothy stood in the doorway. "Grandmother would like to speak with you."

"Of course." She scurried to the living room and picked up the telephone receiver lying on the desktop. "Hello, Mrs. McPhearson."

"What a wonderful surprise that Timothy is there. Thank you for taking care of him and welcoming him. Could you give him the key to my side of the house? I'll be arriving as soon as I can—hopefully on Monday."

"Of course." Had Timothy told her about Elly? "Mrs. McPhearson—"

"I'm so excited. Could you put Timothy back on the phone, please? And I should see you soon."

"Yes, ma'am." Beth held out the receiver. "Timothy?"

"Thank you." He spoke softly to his grandmother, and Beth went back into the kitchen and pulled the key from a can on a shelf. After measuring out coffee, she lifted Elly.

When he stepped into the kitchen, she handed him the key. "Before you go, I have a cherry pie if you'd like a piece. And some coffee too."

"Why, yes, thank you."

She set the coffeepot on the burner and turned it on.

"Do you need any help at all, seeing you're rather one-handed?" He gestured to Elly snuggled against her.

"No, I can manage. After watching the nurses at the orphanage, I've figured out how to do things with one hand pretty well."

"You work at an orphanage?"

"Yes. For almost three years now."

"They must have hired you on the spot. It's obvious you love children and are so good with caring for them." He nodded at Elly, perfectly content.

"I'm just the secretary there." She didn't mean to clatter the spoon against the plates, but maybe that'd cover up the pounding of her heart.

"That's an important job too. I'm sure something will open up for you eventually with the—"

"I don't want to work with the children." She kept her back to him so he wouldn't see the tears forming.

"But you seem to know what exactly to do for—"

"I know *what* to do. I'm the oldest of six—four boys, then the youngest is another girl—Susannah, who's three and a half now. When I left the family farm in Caldwell, this was the only job I could find. Not one I was looking for. I'm...well, the truth is"—she shrugged as if the words didn't hurt—"I'm not good with children. Babies, anyway."

"Not good with them? You know just what to do for Elly Rose. You're a natural."

Beth smoothed Elly's tufting hair. "I enjoy the office work." Maybe he wouldn't hear the catch in her voice.

He crossed to the counter, reached for the coffeepot, and poured two cups without speaking. Almost as if he understood some wounds went too deep for words. After placing the coffee on the table, he took his seat, the silence lengthening. Yet a companionable quiet settled between them, rather than something uncomfortable.

When Beth snuck a glance at him, his eyes were on Elly cuddled against her, a smile tweaking up his lips.

"She looks very peaceful. I think she's found her home."

"No—" But the word didn't come out as adamantly as Beth meant it to. "I mean, when a bed opens up at the orphanage, she'll have a home there."

"That's too bad. She looks very content right where she is." And now he full out smiled.

And there was the laughter in his eyes from Mrs. McPhearson's photograph. But she dared not look into them too long. The mischievous twinkle held too many things she longed for—compassion, kindness, acceptance despite his initial judgment. All things that matched Mrs. McPhearson's stories of him as a wonderful man.

But for all she knew, he could be exactly like Lawrence.

∼

Sometimes things just needed to simmer. That's what Mama used to say.

As Timothy sat eating his cherry pie in the quiet of the room, that's exactly what seemed to be called for. Apparently he'd said something else amiss, but he was clueless as to what. But somehow he had offended this striking girl with the mother's heart a second time.

He'd only spoken out loud what he observed. *"It's obvious you love children and are so good with caring for them."*

"I'm just the secretary there."

Then the clatter of a spoon against the plates.

The clink of cups.

The sound of coffee percolating.

He rewound the words. Everything he'd said was complimentary, wasn't it? Then why was she silent? And he'd caught her wiping at her eyes now and then.

Was she ashamed of her position? Miffed that she wasn't assigned to work with the children? That couldn't be, as she'd added words to the contrary. *"I don't want to work with the children."*

But her clipped tone had cut off even the first of the questions he had. Even now, her every smile and coo to Elly contradicted her words. She *was* good with this baby and clearly enjoyed caring for her, no matter what she claimed.

"Beth." His voice seemed to boom into the stillness. "Are you expecting your gentleman friend"—if that was even the correct term for the arrogant man who ran into him outside— "to return today? I don't want to intrude or cause a problem by my presence."

She barked a huffing sound. "Lawrence. And no, he isn't coming back."

Her tone indicated a finality, not just this evening. "You said he's not your husband. Is he your beau?"

"Not anymore."

"Oh... I'm sorry."

Beth wiped her eyes, then dipped her head and kissed Elly on the cheek. "I'm not. He had no regard for Elly Rose. I'm glad I found out before..."

Before what—she married him? Timothy didn't even know the fellow, but one thing was obvious. The man was undeserving of Beth Calloway. And of this baby. "May I refill your coffee?"

A startled gaze of her dark brown eyes landed on him. Had this Lawrence never offered to help her?

"Why, yes, I think I would like a bit more." She scooted her chair back. "But I can get it, as well as a refill for you."

Timothy waved her down. "There's no need to disturb Elly. And"—he winked of all things—"remember, I used to live here, so I know my way around."

"When you were what—ten or so?—you served coffee?"

Timothy laughed out loud. "Probably not. But I can walk from here to the stove and back." And, oh, he should stop basking in how her eyes changed, her smile adding golden glints to those brown depths. How, when she tried to hide that smile by tucking her head low over Elly Rose, those rich brown waves cascaded over the bundle in her arms.

She lifted her head. "The coffee, Mr. McPhearson?"

"Oh. Right." With her eyes filled with merriment, he stumbled over to the stove.

"The cups?" She held hers out.

"Yes. Of course. The cups." He reached for her flowered one, and their fingers met on the handle barely big enough for hers alone. At her touch, he jerked away, but she held onto the cup while his fingers still tingled. Never had brushing hands with any of the USO hostesses affected him like this. Ever. Beth must think of him as such a schoolboy.

He held out his hand palm up so she could simply set the cup down there, and he grabbed his own cup as well. After he refilled both cups, he returned them to the table. "There you go."

"Thank you." She kept her gaze on her coffee, but had her cheeks turned red?

He gulped his coffee, ignoring the burn all the way down. Now the silence was awkward. "Well." He scooted his chair back and stood. "Thank you again for your hospitality, but I'd better get on over to Grandmother's side."

Beth stood as well, Elly Rose peacefully asleep. "I'll walk you out."

At the door, Beth ran a hand along Elly's cheeks. And the crazy impulse darted through his own fingers. What would it be like to caress Beth's cheeks like that? He grabbed the knob at his back before his hands took action on their own. "Good night. I guess now that we're neighbors I'll see you around."

"Yes. And let me know if you need anything before Mrs. McPhearson returns."

He nodded and hurried outside, stopping only long enough to listen for the click of the lock behind him. Then he let himself in to Grandmother's side of the house—her big and very cold house—and turned the lights on.

The first thing he did was set a fire blazing in the fireplace.

Maybe instead of picking out a bedroom upstairs, tonight he'd sleep right in front of the fire, the only warm place for now.

Everything was exactly as he remembered, as if Grandmother hadn't moved or changed a thing since his own family moved away a good ten years ago. The furnishings were a decade older now, but still neat and tidy. There were no decorations to speak of except three framed photographs on the mantel. The older man with his arm wrapped around Grandmother was his grandfather, who had died long before Timothy had been born. But his portrait still held its place of honor. A wedding picture of his parents was in the middle. And then the one Timothy had sent Grandmother of him in his uniform. Almost laughing.

That was the day he'd spent a few hours in Paris with Stanley on their way through to Germany. Stanley had been standing behind the photographer, making goofy faces, and Timothy had done his best to not burst out laughing. But the camera had caught the merriment of that one moment. A photograph that seemed appropriate for Grandmother to think of him during the war rather than by the horrors most days contained.

"May God's grace walk with you." The blessing Auntie Georgette had spoken over him as a benediction rang true with this photo. That had been taken when Timothy had been sure God was walking with him.

But with Stanley gone and the pain in his eye flaring up now from the fatigue of traveling, some days it was hard to hold on to that blessing. Yet, it seemed a blessing was right next door. That Grandmother's neighbor had not only had enough rationed ingredients to make a pie but that she had shared such an extravagance with him said something about Beth Calloway. Besides the fact of her caring for a little orphan baby. Kind, compassionate. Pretty. Very pretty, indeed.

Yes, the twinkly-eyed soldier was gone. All that was left, that kept him going, was finding the truth about what happened that day with Stanley. Once he was settled here, he'd start by writing a letter to Roland Johnston at his troops' last APO box.

Then maybe he'd have the luxury to ponder the girl next door. Was it possible he hadn't been the only one who had felt something?

But she was his grandmother's renter, barely broken up with her boyfriend. And for the foreseeable time being, came with a baby.

Though once he found Roland and got the truth out of him by whatever means, someone like Beth Calloway wouldn't be interested in him, anyway.

CHAPTER 4

In the pre-dawn of the January day, Beth bundled Elly Rose in her basket and stepped onto the porch against a blast of icy wind. Timothy McPhearson's footprints from Friday night had been erased with the wind sweeping wisps of snow across the porch. Would that the vision of his kind but haunted hazel eyes be wiped from her memory as cleanly.

A quick peek toward Mrs. McPhearson's front window revealed no movement inside, no early Monday lights on.

Beth pulled the door shut and locked it. "Enough of this dillydallying, right, Elly Rose? We have a bus to catch, and I have a job to do. There's no time to speculate about Mrs. McPhearson's grandson."

The only interaction she'd had with him on Saturday and again last night was when she'd knocked on Mrs. McPhearson's door and offered him a bowl of chicken soup and a slice of bread. Though he hadn't invited her in, his hazel eyes had spoken volumes in addition to his few words, at least in her imagination. That he was astute enough to realize no baby with her meant she needed to return quickly. That he appreciated not only the food but having a friendly face in his grandmother's absence. And that he particularly liked having her as his neighbor.

The cold, jostling bus ride to the foundling home froze Beth's nose, fingers, and toes. But once inside the building, she was at last thawing out.

"Dear Lord," she whispered as she set Elly beside the desk, "please go before us. Guide us. Maybe touch Mrs. Martin's heart that Elly can stay? Or open up a bed?" Though that last part was getting harder and harder to pray as Elly wove her sweetness and innocence deeper into Beth's heart. Elly had already thrived under her care this past week—so what if it were possible that Beth could truly care for this treasured babe?

Though Mrs. Martin hadn't mentioned anything last Friday about Elly's trial basis being up, would she be welcomed back today? Her very presence would remind Mrs. Martin that a decision was yet to be made.

Mid-morning, with Elly Rose sleeping soundly and no nurses lingering around her basket, Mrs. Martin approached and stopped beside Beth's desk.

"Beth, I wish I could say we have a bed for your little Elly. I was hoping by the end of last week someone would have come to say they were looking for a sweet little girl." Mrs. Martin smiled sadly down at Elly Rose. "But there's still no extra crib, and she's getting too big for the basket. In addition, our food supply is low, and I think you'd agree that a busy office is no place for an infant. But she, unlike these other babies left here, has someone to care for her. To love her." Mrs. Martin turned glistening eyes to Beth and cleared her throat. "You'll have to find something to do with her by the end of this week. I'm sorry. Terribly so."

One week? How could Beth find anyone on her typist salary

to watch Elly? That wasn't possible. But Mrs. Martin's tone brooked no argument this time.

"Yes, ma'am." Beth leaned over and smoothed Elly's silky blond tufts as Mrs. Martin's heels clicked away. "Oh, Elly. I don't know what we're going to do. But I'll figure something out. I promise."

Elly opened her blue eyes that already held trust and—could Beth hope?—love.

But what if the lady in the brown coat came back for Elly? Or a couple came to adopt her? Just the thought of empty arms was colder than any wintery sting.

Oh, Lord—please—

She didn't even know how to pray. Pray for a bed and a chance of a real home for Elly? Or pray—yes—that somehow she could keep this precious baby? But to be able to do that, God would have to give her the gift of being responsible, if He entrusted a baby to her care.

And a job, come the end of the week. What else could she do? Maybe find a cleaning position. But who during this war could afford to hire a housekeeper? And one with a baby she needed to bring along?

Her hoping was foolish. Of course, she wasn't able to properly care for a baby, to provide for her on her own. And she wasn't about to depend on a man who might turn out to be like Lawrence, even if one did show up.

And yet...God had chosen her porch for Elly Rose to be left on.

"We'll trust Him, then, little one. That's what we'll do."

A shadow crossed the side window, blocking the light. When Beth raised her head, there stood the lady with the long brown coat and black scarf and her little boy, noses pressed to the glass, their pale blue eyes staring in. Right at Elly.

Beth jumped up, ran to the door, and flung it open. "Wait!" she called after the twosome now running down the street.

Her heart pounded as the lady and boy rounded the corner. Surely, the woman wanted to see Elly—but if she did return, would she take Elly then and there? Beth closed her mouth to any further call.

"Beth!" Mrs. Martin called behind her. "Close that door."

"Yes, ma'am." Beth stepped inside and hurried back to her desk.

"And take the baby to the nurses. It's feeding time. On second thought, never mind. We have a family coming in a bit looking for an infant, so they might as well see this child along with the others." Mrs. Martin took Elly from Beth's arms and handed her to the nurse walking by. "Mitzi will handle feeding her. Welcome the couple when they arrive, then bring them immediately to my office."

"Yes, ma'am," Beth squeaked out past her constricting throat. What if this couple fell in love with Elly Rose? And why wouldn't they? Elly was a happy, cooing baby—one who drew smiles and cuddles from all the staff.

She took her seat in front of her typewriter and was clicking away, deep in her work, when an older couple, along with a two- or three-year-old boy, entered.

"Good morning, miss." The man was tall and commanding. "I'm Judge Woodrow Garrison. We're here to meet with Mrs. Martin to discuss taking in a child."

"Yes, sir. Ma'am." Beth nodded to his wife and stood. "Please follow me. Mrs. Martin is expecting you."

"As she should be. We have an appointment. Promptness is to be observed at all costs."

"Yes, sir."

The little boy ran around behind Beth and kicked Elly's empty basket at the side of the desk.

"Gentle, gentle," Beth said softly.

"Miss!" Judge Garrison grabbed the boy by the scruff of his collar and hauled him to his mother's side. "Clutter in the middle of the floor is unacceptable. My boy could have been hurt over this tripping hazard."

"It's not—"

"You're all right, Lionel." Mrs. Garrison wrapped her arms around the boy. "You're all right."

"Are you ready, miss?" Judge Garrison pulled a watch from his pocket and glanced at it. "We will be late if you continue to dally."

"Yes, sir. Please follow me." Beth led the way to Mrs. Martin's office. Elly lay cradled in Mitzi's arms, her eyes brightening when she spotted Beth.

"That's all, Beth," Mrs. Martin said pointedly. "Thank you for bringing our guests in."

Beth nodded and headed back to her desk, leaving Mrs. Garrison reaching for Elly Rose and murmuring soft words. Of course, Mrs. Garrison would want Elly. Who wouldn't? But, surely, Mrs. Martin wouldn't consider handing over any child to the judge.

Oh, Lord, please protect Elly Rose.

By the time the Garrisons came back through the office area, Mrs. Garrison was holding a sobbing Lionel in her arms.

"No baby!"

"Shh. Of course, we want the baby. You'll have a little sister."

Judge Garrison steered his wife and son through the office, all but pushing them along to the door. "That baby had better be a quiet one." He didn't even bother to lower his voice. "I will not abide two crying children."

"No baby!" Lionel screeched and pummeled Mrs. Garrison on the shoulders as the family exited.

Beth swallowed hard so she wouldn't sob right along with the little boy.

Mrs. Martin returned with Elly and handed her to Beth. "You will be very pleased, Beth. The Garrisons were delighted with Elly Rose and wish to adopt her. Mrs. Garrison was so gentle with her. And"—she chuckled—"Judge Garrison held her like a fragile doll, as though he was afraid his size would intimidate her. Very sweet. By the end of the week, she'll have a good home, and you'll still have your job. So now you don't have to worry. Everything worked out wonderfully." She smiled and stroked Elly's hair. "Fine, upstanding people they are."

"Mrs. Martin..." Did she dare speak up about the harshness of Judge Garrison? About her concern for Elly with Lionel's rough antics, hitting his mother, kicking the basket? What if Elly had been in the basket at the time?

No—that wasn't her place. She wasn't the interviewer of families. And should the typist be casting aspersions on a well-to-do family? Perhaps even a donor to the orphanage?

"Yes, dear?" Mrs. Martin smiled at Elly. "You'll lack for nothing with them, Elly Rose, and you'll have a big brother to protect you. You can get the forms and paperwork started, Beth."

Beth pulled Elly tighter against herself. Safety aside, it couldn't be a harmonious home. "I want to keep her." With the words out, she didn't have to think twice. There would be no retracting them.

"Beth, whatever are you saying? Surely, you don't think..." Mrs. Martin shook her head. "How will you support her? There is absolutely no room here—and I explained to you we cannot continue to have a baby in the office in a basket. That would mean you must leave your position. I know you love her. But think of her welfare. With the Garrisons, she'll have a home. Loving parents. Even a brother."

The image of Lionel kicking Elly's basket knifed through her heart.

Yes, this was the right decision. "I'm sure, Mrs. Martin." She lowered her eyes. "I can pack up my belongings now if you need me to."

"No...no, the end of the week is fine. But I must get word to the Garrisons. They'll be sorely disappointed."

Maybe not as disappointed as Mrs. Martin might think—though Mrs. Garrison probably would be. She dared not suggest one of the other babies, even if that meant a bed opening up for Elly. No baby deserved to be under Judge Garrison's influence.

"Yes, ma'am. Then at the end of the week, I'll leave."

Without God's intervention, however, Elly might not be any better off with her.

~

Timothy didn't know what time Beth would return from work—assuming that's where she'd gone early this morning with her market basket swung over her arm, trotting off down the sidewalk as he'd watched from the dark behind a curtain. In preparation for Grandmother's return from her visit with Great-aunt Cora, the least he could do was stock her cupboards and refrigerator and have supper waiting.

With the bright sunlight and smoke from neighborhood woodstoves, his eye was acting up, irritated and starting to throb. He pulled on his patch and walked in the direction Beth had taken. If she were headed to a bus stop that way, hopefully, a market wouldn't be far off either. After two blocks, he spotted both a bus stop and a little grocery. And—*oh thank You, Lord*—a *Help Wanted* sign in the window. *Delivery and Stock Boy Needed Immediately.* He could do that.

He walked inside, thankful that this market offered the thing he needed most. Hope. And it was so close to Grandmother's house. Maybe there'd be a discount on food, even. It was perfect.

A few people milled around the counter chatting about the war while a man in a white apron rang up purchases. Timothy filled Grandmother's shopping basket with a few potatoes, carrots, onions, a small package of meat, a loaf of bread, eggs, and a bottle of milk and joined the line. He'd even found Grandmother's ration book in case it was needed, though this was new to him.

At his turn, Timothy placed his items on the counter. "Sir, are you the proprietor?"

"I am." The man weighed the produce and wrote totals down on a slip of paper after each item.

"I just arrived in Boise and saw your *Help Wanted* sign out front and would like to apply for the job. I'm a hard worker and strong."

"Hmm." The man stopped his sorting and ringing and eyed Timothy up and down, his gaze lingering on the black eyepatch. He crossed his arms. "Actually, I've already had a candidate in today. I think I'll go with her. She seems quite capable."

"But..."

The proprietor totaled the purchases, scooped up the items on the counter, and dumped them into the basket. "Here." He handed the paper to Timothy. "Don't hold up the line."

The line of one elderly woman behind him. Timothy counted out his money and scuttled out. At least he'd bought enough this trip that he wouldn't have to return right away.

Was this the reception he was going to receive at every job opportunity? Maybe if he didn't wear his eyepatch...but then folks would think him a shirker. Besides, it was too late to yank it off now.

Timothy trudged the two blocks back home and up his grandmother's steps.

No new footsteps had imprinted the porch since he'd left.

He let himself in and set the basket on the table with a cherry-patterned tablecloth. Thinking of cherries...what he wouldn't give for another slice of that delicious pie Beth

Calloway had fed him upon his arrival on Friday. Interesting, that girl.

She had backbone. Courage. Compassion. She hadn't wilted under his wrong assumption of how she came to have a baby in her care. Oh yes, the grocer's once-over and assessment of Timothy's eyepatch had mirrored the same kind of self-righteous judgment Timothy—and how many other people?—had aimed at Beth without knowing the truth.

So maybe he shouldn't fault the man for refusing him a job. He was exactly like the grocer.

He opened Grandmother's cupboard and pulled out a soup pot, clattering pans against each other so loudly, he almost missed the sound outside on the porch. He stilled. A *clump-clump* up the steps. Beth? His pulse quickened. He did have her washed soup bowls he could use as an excuse to knock on her door.

But no, she was light footed.

He slipped to the front window and discreetly lifted a corner of the wispy curtain.

A little boy tromped onto the porch, followed by a lady with a long brown overcoat. The black scarf wound around her head accentuated her pale, gaunt face. But—upon closer examination—perhaps she wasn't but a few years older than he was. Friends of Grandmother? Or Beth?

The lady stopped at Beth's door.

But no knock followed. The woman furtively glanced around, up and down the street. Then reached into her coat pocket, pulled out a white paper, and jammed it in the crack between Beth's door and doorframe.

She turned the boy around, and in that moment, the face of the little girl hiding under the table in the German apartment swam before him. The lady's furtiveness made him look at her again. Closely this time. And a shudder ran up his spine. Pale blue eyes. Wisps of blond hair poking out around the edges of her headscarf. Full face. So similar to the woman in the smashed portrait in the bombed-out building in Germany where he and Stanley had hid. And to the peasant women in other villages they'd marched through.

He was sure of it. The woman leaving a note for Beth was German.

But what dealings would Beth have with a German woman? Was she bringing the enemy right to Grandmother's own house?

Once they left and walked quickly around the corner, he let the curtain fall back into place. He hadn't a clue how to find out from Beth what the paper said without flat out asking—but what if he snuck a peek at it? Before Beth arrived home? All he'd have to do was cross the porch, pull the note out, read it, and stick it back in the door. It'd be so easy—

But dishonorable.

He could mention it to his grandmother, though, see what she thought about it. And who knew, maybe Beth would bring it up on her own.

He went back to the kitchen and peeled some potatoes and carrots and started the soup. At least for now, he had one thing he was capable of doing—welcoming his grandmother home.

CHAPTER 5

At the end of the day, Beth's steps grew slower and slower once she stepped off the bus and made the two-block trek from the bus stop to her home.

What had she done? And if Mrs. McPhearson had returned home today, how would Beth explain this whole situation to her? A baby now living in the house—and no job. How would she ever pay the rent? Or would she be jobless and homeless?

But no matter what, Elly Rose could not go to the Garrison family.

Lights were blazing on the other half of the house when Beth traipsed up the porch steps. Mrs. McPhearson's door burst open, and Timothy stuck his head out.

"Beth. Grandmother posted me here to watch for you. She's home and wants you to join us for supper. Please come in over here."

With no time to think of how to explain the baby in her basket—unless Timothy had forewarned her—Beth was tugged inside and engulfed in Mrs. McPhearson's warm embrace.

"Mrs. McPhearson, I'm so glad you're home."

"And who do you have here, dear? Timothy told me about your surprise delivery." Mrs. McPhearson pulled back a corner of the blanket across the basket. "Oh, such a sweetie. Tell me all about her. I'm sure Timothy left out details." She winked at Beth.

"This is Elly Rose." Beth questioned Timothy with her eyes, but he just smiled.

"Elly Rose. What a beautiful name. May I hold her?"

Mrs. McPhearson barely waited for a nod before she reached in and pulled Elly out.

"I..." Beth breathed deep. "I've decided to keep her. To adopt her."

"You what?" Timothy's tone clearly stated at what he thought of her announcement.

"Hush now, Timothy. Where are your manners?" Mrs. McPhearson wagged a finger at him. "Of course, she loves this child."

"I know she does." His hazel eyes widened as he turned them on Beth. "But your job—"

Beth reached over and stroked Elly's hair. "I gave it up. Elly is more important."

"What are you going to do?" Timothy edged closer.

"I'll look for a housekeeping position. One that will allow me to bring Elly along."

"And in the meantime," Mrs. McPhearson added, "I will help care for her as you make job inquiries."

"Oh, Mrs. McPhearson, would you truly?" Tears sprang to Beth's eyes.

Timothy's grandmother drew Elly tighter and smiled down at her. "I would be delighted to."

Timothy stared at Beth, as if he couldn't begin to fathom her decisions. Finally, he nodded. "I don't know anything about babies. Never even held one. But I'll help, too, if there's anything I can do."

"Then we'll be safe, Elly," Beth whispered to the baby. "Mrs. McPhearson, Timothy, thank you."

After a supper of hearty soup and good nights, Beth departed for her side of the house. When she unlocked and opened her door, a slip of paper fluttered onto the porch. She stooped to retrieve it, then stepped inside. She turned on a light and set Elly's basket down in front of the sofa. Mrs. McPhearson had gotten the furnace going again, and the house was warm and cozy. Beth took off her coat and sat on the sofa, Elly at her feet, and read the note.

Meet at bus stop tomoro.

Whatever did that mean? The bus stop two blocks away or the one by the orphanage? What time? And who was she meeting? The lady with the little boy?

And most importantly—was someone wanting Elly Rose back?

Beth scooped up Elly. "No. No one's taking you away. Not the Garrisons. Not the lady in the scarf. Unless—is she your mother, Elly? Is she who you truly belong with?"

After tucking Elly in for the night, Beth unfastened the necklace and studied it again.

Liebe. Someone loved her. She wasn't abandoned out of neglect. And apparently, Beth had been chosen to care for her out of everyone. Because the lady in the brown coat could have left the basket on the doorstep of the foundling home just as easily.

And the verse...

> Let the redeemed of the Lord say so, whom he
> hath redeemed from the hand of the enemy,
> and gathered them out of the lands, from the

east, and from the west, from the north, and from the south.

Oh, Elly had some story—if only Beth could find out what it was. This verse was one that Elly's parents wanted impressed upon her life.

Dear Lord, help me to be the mother Elly needs. To live up to the privilege and blessing You've given to me.

Since Elly was now here to stay, Beth placed the necklace in a box and tucked it into her drawer for safekeeping. She dropped a kiss on Elly's silky hair before climbing into her own bed for the night.

Liebe. Love. What Beth wouldn't give to be loved by someone who truly wanted her as his own. And who would love Elly Rose too.

Not Lawrence. Definitely not him.

And perhaps no one. Still, she would never change her mind about keeping Elly.

The next morning as the sun crept over the horizon, Beth followed her daily routine of preparing for work, plus getting Elly up and fed. Just three more days after today and then… She sighed and opened her door to step out into the cold with Elly snug in her basket. And there was Timothy.

His face lit with a smile and, my, when he smiled, he was a duplicate of the soldier in Mrs. McPhearson's picture—handsome and dedicated. And with that twinkle in his eye, even if not long lived, she had no coherent words.

"Good morning, Beth. Elly Rose. Would you mind if I accompany you to the bus stop?"

Would the note-writer show up if she was in the company of a man? Or maybe it'd be safer to have Timothy with them?

"Well—"

"I need to start looking for a job."

"Of course." She locked her door. "What are you looking for

in particular?" All she could picture him as was a soldier in uniform, ready to serve his country. But he must have had some special training, a useful skill, even in the army.

"I don't know." He reached for the basket and carried Elly down the steps as easily as if there was but a loaf of bread inside. "Anything that someone will hire me to do. I seem to be competing with women for jobs."

He kept the market basket in one hand and took Beth's elbow with the other. "Something with history would be interesting. I love reading biographies and learning of the past. I'm glad I was able to be part of the army since I wanted to make history as well as to serve."

"Maybe something at the library, then? Or with the newspaper?"

He nodded. "Those would be good places to start."

"My uncle Sammy is a reporter at the *Caldwell News-Tribune*. Maybe he has some connections with someone at the Boise paper, if that would help." Mama's youngest brother, more like a cousin than an uncle, had fulfilled his dream of leaving the family Double E Ranch and being a newspaperman.

"Thanks. Anything would help."

As they approached the bus stop, Beth scanned the area. No lady with a scarf and a little boy. No stranger peeking from behind a building. Nobody other than the usual few people who caught this bus.

But Beth's heart couldn't quit pounding yet. What if the person was waiting at the other end of her route, in front of the orphanage, ready to snatch Elly? Or what if the note-writer would be waiting for her to get off work? Or to return to this stop tonight?

One by one, the riders nodded to her, a few speaking an early-morning greeting before the bus chugged to a halt alongside them. The group boarded, and Timothy sat in the seat beside Beth and set Elly and the basket on his lap. They must look like—Beth caught a gasp before it escaped—a family.

And what would that be like? A family for Elly. A family for Beth. Something she rarely dreamed of anymore. Not for the last three years, with the exception of Lawrence.

She brushed the ludicrous longing away. But a niggling thought snuck into the empty spot remaining. Would Elly not benefit from having both a mother and a father? Maybe instead of trying to avoid whoever was seeking her, Beth should take the initiative to find the person and to hear her—or him—out.

And to be willing to do what was best for Elly. No matter the cost to herself.

~

*G*randmother's neighbor was delightful, full of surprises. Spunky. Determined. And loyal. With Elly on his lap staring up at him, Timothy could feel Beth's eyes on him also. What would she think of him if she knew the real reason he was in Boise? Discharged from the army, declared unfit to defend his country. Jobless, without even an inclination of what he should be searching for. All he knew was the army. And a love of learning. But no one paid for that.

Beth leaned over, brushing his shoulder. "Timothy…"

Judging by her tone, she'd already spoken something to him. "Yes?"

"This is my stop."

"Oh." He stepped into the aisle, still holding Elly.

"There are a few shopkeepers in this section of town, or you might have better success one stop up."

"Oh." He gathered his wits along with words. "I'll get off here." Though she reached for the basket, he gently guided her forward instead, following close behind her with Elly. Once they'd exited the bus, he walked a few steps toward the orphanage with her. "Um, may I meet you here after work and escort you home?"

She stopped in the middle of the sidewalk. The tips of his ears burned even in the windchill of the morning. He'd never be suave—her hesitation proved it. And the way her eyes were darting around—was she embarrassed to be seen with him? An army-aged man seemingly healthy to the passerby yet standing here as though he had no care in the world?

"Why, yes. That'd be nice. Thank you. I get off work at five."

"Five. I'll see you both then." He handed the basket with Elly to her, and she headed for the orphanage.

On the doorstep, she stopped, her gaze darting past him up and down the street, before she turned the knob and entered. Was she searching for someone?

Could she be hoping Lawrence would come to his senses and beg her forgiveness? And why wouldn't he? She was so attractive with her silky brown waves and eyes full of determination and her oh-so-sweet spirit. A fellow would be mighty lucky to have her. And her little one, as it was obvious they were inseparable.

Timothy was so focused on the traits of Beth Calloway he almost missed it. He'd only been off scouting detail not even a month, but already he was losing his sharpness. He'd missed the original movement, but the back of a woman—tattered overcoat, scarfed head, and a little boy in tow—scooted around the side of the orphanage. The same pair who had been on Beth's porch the day before, who'd left a message for Beth? The Germans.

Was that whom Beth had been looking for? Waiting for?

Keeping his distance, he headed in their direction. Maybe now he'd find out why Beth had Germans standing on her porch, furtively wedging a message into her door. Just an innocent visit from a neighbor or friend? Perhaps. But his training had taught him to be alert, to look beyond the surface of seemingly innocent events.

More than anything, he wanted to clear his suspicions about Beth in his heart. And following this woman and her boy might provide that.

The lady stopped along the side of the building and flattened herself against the wall below a window. Shushing the boy and motioning for him to be still, she inched her eyes above the window sill and peered in. Quickly, she ducked back down, grabbed the boy's hand, and started walking again. Back toward the bus stop.

Timothy dug in his pocket for a coin for bus fare. He'd only brought enough for lunch and the return ride home, certainly not planning on an extra ride. But the two continued past the corner. Keeping his distance, his pace steady, occasionally stopping to peer into a shop window when the lady slowed down, Timothy kept them in sight. All the way to an alley between a dress shop and a bakery. She ducked into the opening as though she'd been there before and stopped in front of a garbage can. Timothy stood at the entrance to the alleyway, peeking around the bakery wall as neither the woman nor the boy was looking his way.

The woman thrust her hand into a can and rummaged around. Pulled out a bag, checked inside, and tossed it back in. She stuck her arm in again, deeper. With a smile, she withdrew a half-eaten bun and handed it to the boy. He devoured it in two gulps.

"*Danke, Mutter.*"

"You're welcome, Nicholas." She covered her mouth and coughed, then sank onto the snow-littered ground. "Come, Lieber. Dear one." She pulled the boy onto her lap, rocked him back and forth, and wept.

"Mutter?" The little boy ran his hands along the woman's wet cheeks.

Mutter. All Timothy could hear now was the voice of the little German girl under the table calling out for her mother, her father. *"Wo sind Mutter und Vater?"*

Would this world's suffering never cease? He'd been discharged, but the war had followed him home. And even if this German woman was a spy or somehow in cahoots with Beth, little boys—and even their mothers—weren't exempt from hunger or sorrow.

Timothy stepped back, then slipped inside the bakery. Coffee percolating smelled wonderful. They probably even offered a tiny bit of sugar for a price. And milk, even if not cream. The still-warm scent of baked bread that had followed him inside led him straight to the counter. He hadn't had a good slice of hot, fresh bread since the last loaf Mama made the night before the fire. Her cinnamon swirl.

"Good morning," the woman behind the counter greeted him. Her white apron barely covered her girth. "What may I get you?"

Timothy fingered the coins in his pocket. He needed to save enough for his bus fare home after Beth got off work. "Two cinnamon rolls. And a sugar cookie, please."

The lady bagged them up.

"And a cup of coffee." He fingered the coins again. "With a spoonful of sugar."

The baker's eyes widened as if he were a rich man, or she'd at least not had anyone ask for or be willing to pay for sugar in some time.

"There you go." She slid the purchases toward Timothy and accepted his money. "Thank you."

"Thank *you*." Timothy took the bag and his coffee into the alleyway and walked past the lady and boy. She scooted back as if frightened.

He set the cup on top of an empty crate, then shook his head as if in commiseration. "If you want good coffee, don't go in *that* bakery." He motioned with his thumb to the shop around the corner. The aroma of the bakery's sweet-smelling cinnamon swirl and warm yeast bread wafted into the alley, following him, tantalizing him, making his resolve falter. But he tossed the unopened bag into a garbage can and walked away.

The sounds of rummaging in the garbage and a paper bag crinkling as it was opened filled his ears and heart as he rounded the corner.

Hopefully, his stomach wouldn't complain until he got back to Grandmother's tonight.

But even the woman's exclaimed "Danke, *Gott*!" didn't absolve her from still being suspect.

Timothy walked around the neighborhood shops, scanning each window for a *Help Wanted* sign. He came across a total of three. One for a seamstress. One for an electrician. And one for a delivery boy.

The man looking for a delivery boy did not want him. "I'm looking for a boy. A young lad. Try an armament factory." But with precision needed around the machinery, factories weren't even an option for him—at least until his eye totally healed.

He kept shuffling along outside, and eventually, the noon whistle blew. Through windows, Timothy could see people pulling out lunches, sitting to enjoy a break and food at counters. He kept going, ignoring the rumbling in his own stomach.

After walking block after block, inquiring at stores that didn't even post a *Help Wanted* sign, Timothy sat on the bench back near the bus stop by the orphanage. He had no money left to take a bus another stop until Beth got off work, and neither the library nor the newspaper was anywhere near this stop. He was tired and hungry. And his only hope now was that Beth would be out right at five o'clock so he could go home and eat —and that maybe Grandmother had baked some fresh bread.

CHAPTER 6

At five on the dot, Beth bundled up, tucked Elly snuggly in the basket, and stepped out the orphanage's front door. Apprehensive. Hopeful.

But no one was about on the sidewalk. That should have been good—no one following her, ready to take Elly from her. No more problems to deal with.

And no Timothy.

Why should that matter? He could hardly be expected to wait all day to ride home with her. Even though after he said he would be here and she'd anticipated it all day.

She was foolish. Dreaming of yet another thing that could never be. War, realities, mistakes, Lawrence...had they taught her nothing?

Beth walked to the corner bus stop. Though the bus wasn't due for a few minutes, already the bench was taken. A man sat slumped over, head bowed—whether against the cold or in despair, she couldn't tell. Perhaps both. Despair invaded many a man these days.

Yet his build was not of an old man but of someone muscular. Perhaps not old at all. He raised his head, and she sucked in a breath. Timothy. Hopelessness blanketed his shoulders.

"Hello, Timothy." She stood in front of him, though her heart pleaded for her to sit beside him, clasp his hand, and comfort him.

"Beth." He reached for Elly's basket and placed it on the bench beside him and motioned for Beth to sit. "Did work go well for you today?"

"Yes, thank you." She sat on the other side of the basket and folded her hands, crossed her ankles, patted Elly's blanket, all the while wanting to do nothing more than ask Timothy about his job hunting. But his eyes, dull with the light gone out, said it all.

And in the silence, she remembered her note. She spotted no one lurking about, either down the street or up the sidewalk the other direction, waiting to talk to her. Unless, once again, the person didn't appear with Timothy there. Or maybe the note meant the meeting would occur at her final bus stop on the way home from work. She'd know within a few minutes, as the bus lumbered up the street and stopped.

Timothy hooked the basket on his arm and stood, ushered Beth up and onto the bus, and again seated himself next to her. He kept Elly on his lap, absently stroking her head as little Elly Rose smiled up at him, the way Beth wished she could.

At their stop, Beth exited with Timothy and Elly and walked the two blocks home. Though no one spoke to her at the stop, a peace settled around Beth. How nice to have someone to walk with. To carry Elly now that each day she was getting heavier. To have someone grip her elbow on the snow-covered sidewalk. Someone to make her feel cared for. If only she had words to share to comfort Timothy. She couldn't very well invite him to stay for supper again, not with Mrs. McPhearson home now and expecting to feed Timothy and have his company for the evening.

When they climbed the porch steps, a rapping on the window made them look over to where Mrs. McPhearson was motioning for them both to come in. She met them at the door as she opened it.

"Beth, won't you and Elly please join us again for supper?"

"I..." Of course, she wanted to—especially at the glimmer of light in Timothy's eyes. But she couldn't impose. And she needed to change Elly. And feed her. "I'd love to. Thank you. May I bring something over?" Not that she had anything to offer, really. And then she smelled it. Bread baking. "A jar of strawberry jam, perhaps?" She had two left. Not that she'd been saving them for any special purpose, just to keep a splash of color—and hope—on her cupboard shelf.

"Yes, that'd be wonderful. Now, come in, come in." She reached for Elly. "I'll take care of her while you go fetch the jam."

"And milk."

Mrs. McPhearson waved her words away. "I have plenty. Timothy stocked me up on the essentials."

"Thank you." Beth scooted out before she burst into tears. Tears for what she longed for, for those she sorely missed—her family. Her father and siblings. And her mother with the closeness they used to share. Mama would be just like Mrs. McPhearson, caring for Elly, loving her, holding her. If things were different, Beth would be married, living near the farm and ranch, and giving her mother grandchildren to dote on.

Yes, if things were different, the way she wished they were.

Beth backed out the door and dashed into her side of the house before her heart suffocated.

From the cupboard she pulled out a jar of jam she'd made last summer after picking berries from her Victory Garden. She'd cut way back on the sugar added, saving her rations up, but it'd been worth it to have this special treat over the winter. And one more thing she needed—her jam spoon from Mama.

A moving-to-Boise gift. With her contribution to dinner in hand, Beth opened her front door. And tripped.

A small jar of milk lay at her feet.

From the scarfed lady?

Beth bent and picked up the milk. "Ma'am?" She hurried to the railing, searching the sidewalk in both directions. "Are you out there? Please come in. Wouldn't you like to see El—the baby?"

No answer.

"Please."

Mrs. McPhearson's door opened, and Timothy stepped out. "Beth—is everything all right?"

She glanced from him to the street. "Yes. I—I'm just bringing some extra milk along."

He followed her gaze to the street, too, then his landed on the jar of milk in her hand. Had he seen anyone? He opened his mouth, then closed it. Just nodded instead. "Okay. Come along, then."

"Timothy." Beth clutched the milk tighter. "Did you not find a job today?" Though she could certainly guess the answer, as the despair in his eyes at the bus stop had been a good indication of exactly how it had gone. But maybe it would help him if he shared his burden.

He shrugged. "Nothing yet."

"You'll try again tomorrow?"

"Yes. I plan to take the bus another stop or two and see what else is up that way."

"There's a candy store not too far from the foundling home bus stop. Brighton's Candy Shop. My mother knew the original owner from way back—and Gideon Brighton too. That's Mrs. Brighton's grandson, who now owns it. Maybe he can help. Look for the man with the red hair."

"Thank you." He smiled, but his eyes still didn't look hopeful.

At least she'd offered a lead. "I hope you find just the right job. And that there will be some to choose from." Because come next Monday, she'd be out looking for one herself.

∽

*B*eth Calloway might be a puzzle, but she was a lovely one, scurrying about with the finishing touches of supper while Grandmother beamed with baby Elly in her arms.

Timothy loved watching Beth. Her deft movements said she was comfortable in Grandmother's kitchen, that she'd been here enough to know exactly where things were—and apparently, how Grandmother liked things done. She heated milk for Elly, then handed the bottle to Grandmother, who cooed and sang to the baby as she fed her. When yesterday's soup was heated, Beth ladled it into bowls, breathing deeply with a smile, as if the aroma was heavenly and fresh. Not leftovers from the day before. And when she sliced the bread—still warm from the oven—with a soft "mmm," Timothy almost chorused right in.

And if that wasn't enough to stir Timothy's soul, Grandmother set Elly down in her basket as they all sat at the table. "Let's join hands." And there he was, clasping Beth's hand. Petite. Strong. Molded perfectly into his.

"Timothy, would you ask the blessing?"

He would, if he could get words out. He cleared his throat, pushing down the song that wanted to burst out. "Heavenly Father, we thank You for Your blessings, for Your care of us throughout the day, and for this provision of food. Please bless each of us. And may we serve You with our whole hearts. Amen."

And Beth's hand was still in his.

She seemed to realize it at the same moment he did, as she

jerked her hand away and grabbed the bread basket and offered it to him. The jar of strawberry jam followed right behind.

"Timothy." Grandmother turned to him. "Tell us about your day." Her eyes gleamed, and she smiled, clearly expecting good news.

He shook his head. "Nothing to report. I wasn't...qualified for the few jobs I did see posted. Tomorrow I'll search in a different part of town."

Beth perked up. "The library, perhaps? It's only one more bus stop past the candy shop. There's also a drugstore near it that sells books. You might enjoy that. Or the small bookstore. They might need help boxing up books to send to the men overseas. Did you ever receive one of the books from the shipments?"

"Books?" Grandmother eyed Timothy. "Do you enjoy reading, Timothy?"

"Um, yes." A warmth settled in his chest at how Beth knew a part of him already that even Grandmother didn't. He nodded at Beth. "Yes, I usually got some. Not very many of the men wanted the books of poems or history, so I could hold onto them for a while before passing them around. Sometimes I'd stay up at night discussing them with...my friend Stanley."

Yes, Stanley was the only one Timothy had been able to talk in depth with. To share his fears, his hopes. His dreams. And the Bible Stanley always carried. And that was how he knew Stanley was in heaven now—because Stanley had told him how he believed in Christ, his beloved, risen Savior.

The night before their last assignment, Stanley had sat with his open Bible beside Timothy, pestering him to memorize Stanley's chosen verses of the week.

"*Come on, McPhearson, you can learn a few verses. Say it again.*"

"Okay. 'They wandered in the wilderness in a solitary way; they found no city to dwell in. Hungry and thirsty, their soul fainted in them. Then they cried unto the L ORD in their trouble, and he delivered them out of their distresses. And he led them forth by the right way, that they might go to a city of habitation. Oh that men would praise the Lord for his goodness, and for his wonderful works to the children of men! For he satisfieth the longing soul, and filleth the hungry soul with goodness.'"

"You got it. Remember those words, Timothy. Through the war. Even after. Praise the Lord for His goodness. Hold on to that."

And that was what Timothy was trying to do. He could praise God for this night at Grandmother's, that he still had her. For Beth Calloway taking care of Grandmother and now Elly. For this fresh, warm bread.

Beth was looking at him now too. "What did your friend like to read?"

"Oh, that's easy. He was always reading his Bible and memorizing it. Making me memorize verses too."

"He sounds like a wise man," Grandmother said, and Beth nodded heartily.

Timothy took a deep breath, mentally wiping away his last sight of Stanley huddled under that German apartment table. "Some of the guys only read the cartoons."

Beth smiled. "Even those, I'm sure, brought some laughter into camp."

"You're right. Even they had value."

"Timothy." Her brown eyes seemed to see right into his soul. "Thank you for serving our country. Every man's efforts count. Every man."

He was captivated by this perceptive, sweet woman.

Grandmother bobbed her head, as if she also approved of Beth Calloway.

"What do you like to read, Beth?" Timothy pegged her as being widespread in her reading. Probably enjoying history and facts.

"I used to like to read mysteries when I was at home and had time in the evenings. But now I just read the copies of *Good Housekeeping* or *The Household Magazine* that patrons or nurses occasionally bring to the foundling home. I enjoy some of the articles in there."

"Which ones in particular, dear?" Grandmother passed the bread around again.

Beth's cheeks reddened. "Ones on homemaking. I mean—um, there are interesting recipes."

"Perhaps you could share some with me."

"Of course. I'd be glad to. In fact, why don't both of you join me on Saturday for supper, and I'll fix one of my favorites for you?"

On her last paycheck? Timothy glanced at his grandmother. What were they to do? They couldn't be ungracious—yet by then, she'd be without a job.

"That'd be lovely, dear. But I have an idea. You tell Timothy what you need from the market, and I'll send him to pick it up. Then I wonder if you would prepare the meal over here and show me exactly how to make it. So I can serve it in the future."

"But, Mrs. McPhearson, Mama and Papa said you're known in Boise for being an excellent cook. Back when you ran this whole house as a boardinghouse."

"Ah, yes, that's true"—she winked—"back when I had your mother's help in the kitchen and in serving the men. But it's been years since I did that and had to cook for more than myself. And I must say, I don't want to get any rustier. Plus, I could stand to learn some new-fangled dishes."

Beth cocked her head at Grandmother. Perhaps Beth saw right through her but was also weighing her options against needing to make her money stretch. Then she grinned. "Okay, if you'd like. I'd be happy for us to prepare it together."

"I would like it. Very much."

Relief filled Timothy. In four days, there'd be another meal with Beth and Elly Rose. What if she hadn't agreed, though? His heart pounded at the very thought. She and Elly blended in and brought such joy along with them. For the first time in weeks, he was looking forward to something with a hint of hope.

Beth thawed his heart so much that he certainly must resemble his army picture more each day. A man with something to smile about.

Until he remembered the lady with the scarf at Beth's door. And the appearance of a bottle of milk tonight.

CHAPTER 7

One split second later, and Beth would have missed it. Timothy's smile wavered, and a flash of something—suspicion?—crossed his eyes. No, surely not.

But what if it was? Secrets hid behind his haunted eyes. And then again, maybe she had imagined it. As he was smiling again, even leaning over to coo at Elly as Beth lifted her from the basket. Other than Papa, never had she seen a man coo at a baby. Lawrence certainly hadn't.

When Elly Rose smiled right at Timothy, his eyes softened so sweetly, and his smile grew. Yes, Beth had been wrong, assigning hidden motives where there were none.

But then again, she didn't even know what he had done in the army. Maybe he had been a spy. She pulled the baby tighter, until Elly squirmed her protest. Then with another peek at Timothy, she relaxed. Elly did not need protection from this kind man, whose eyes even now held a longing.

No, Timothy McPhearson was an honorable man. Even Mrs. McPhearson was nodding approval at his tenderness with Elly.

Beth scooted her chair back and stood. "If everyone is

finished eating, I'll take care of the dishes." She bent to put Elly in her basket.

"I'd like to say never you mind," Mrs. McPhearson said, "but if you insist, I'll let you—if you'll allow me to hold this precious bundle."

"Of course." Nobody could be loved too much. She transferred Elly Rose to Mrs. McPhearson's arms. "I'll put on the teakettle, too, while I'm at it."

With the clattering of dishes and running water to fill the kettle and Mrs. McPhearson humming hymns and Timothy looking on, Beth could think.

There was only one explanation for that jar of milk appearing outside her door this evening. It had not been there when she'd arrived, and she'd only be inside for a matter of a couple minutes.

Someone had followed her and planned exactly when to sneak onto the porch and set it there. And the who? She hardly would be jumping to conclusions to guess that it was the black-scarfed lady.

What did she want? Maybe not to snatch Elly back but to simply care for her as she could? To feel she still had a part in her child's life? For now Beth had little doubt but that the woman was Elly Rose's mother.

If only Beth could talk with the lady, to find out why she gave up her own baby. Why or even how she'd chosen Beth to receive such a precious gift. And how they could even work together in caring for and loving Elly Rose. Of course, that wasn't the baby's given name. But how could Beth think of her as anything other than the family name she'd bestowed upon this little one?

"Beth—the teakettle." Mrs. McPhearson nodded toward the screeching sound coming from the stove.

"Oh! Of course." Beth scooted over and turned the stove off, set the remaining dishes in the soap-filled sink, and gripped the counter as all the questions and obstacles of raising a baby poured over her.

"Beth, would you like to hold Elly now, and I can finish up serving tea? I just wanted a minute to cuddle her. You sit now and enjoy her."

"Yes. Thank you." Beth took Elly in her arms and sat, memorizing every feature of her tiny face. Her beautiful smile. Her deep blue eyes. And without even looking up, Beth could feel Timothy watching, studying her.

Finally, he stood. "I'll help you, Grandmother."

After Mrs. McPhearson poured the tea, he set the cups on the table, keeping Beth's far enough out of Elly's reach should she squirm. Then he added a generous dash of milk to hers— more than should be spared during rationing. "My mother used to say just a splash makes it not only creamy but adds a bit of comfort." Almost as if he understood exactly what she needed.

And in that small act, Beth registered something else about Timothy McPhearson. He noticed and filled unspoken needs simply and quietly, just as Papa did with Mama.

Timothy's sweetness carried Beth into the next morning as she settled Elly next to her desk and took her chair after another bus ride with Timothy. One of companionship, of him carrying the basket to the bus stop and grinning at passengers who stopped to smile at sweet Elly.

"Two more days here, Elly." Two more days for her to be warm and safe inside the orphanage during business hours— well fed, passed around to many doting hands—before Beth would be walking the sidewalk like Timothy, seeking a job. And if no one employed her, not only would she be homeless, but Elly Rose would be too.

Oh, Lord, please provide for us.

The door slammed open as the wind caught it, and Judge Garrison filled the entrance.

"I'm here to speak with Mrs. Martin. Immediately." His narrowed eyes skewered Beth, and he seemed oblivious to Elly's presence just the other side of the desk. *Oh please stay quiet, Elly.*

"Y-yes, sir." Beth scooted her chair back and scrambled to her feet. What if he grabbed Elly while she was gone? She hurried down the hall to Mrs. Martin's office, her low-heel oxfords making barely a sound in her speed. "Ma'am—"

"Yes, I know. I can hear him all the way from here." She stood. "Beth, are you sure of your decision? Of course, we'll hate to lose you here, and I'm so sorry there's nothing I can do since a bed still has not opened up. And with the Garrisons wanting Elly, I would have to give her to them, anyway. I know you love her. But are you absolutely sure?"

Beth nodded. "I am."

Mrs. Martin sighed. "Then send him in."

"Yes, ma'am." Beth stepped out of the office, but Judge Garrison was already barging down the hall and shrugged past Beth. He'd only been in Mrs. Martin's office seconds before his voice boomed out, probably all the way back to the baby rooms and even the kitchen.

"That child belongs to us. How can you give her to that unmarried snip of a girl? What kind of a home is that? She'll grow up shamed. We can give her everything money can buy. Even during wartime."

It wasn't a mistake in claiming Elly for her own, even when the Garrisons wanted her. But for Elly to be ostracized because of her—Beth couldn't bear it.

"Now, Judge Garrison..." Mrs. Martin closed the door with a soft click, and Beth could hear no more. Mrs. Martin wouldn't change her mind, would she?

Beth had just taken her seat at her desk when a door slammed. Judge Garrison stomped up the hall, pinned Beth with a glare—of hatred? revenge?—and stormed out the front door. Mrs. Martin wasn't far behind.

"You are right, Beth. Elly Rose belongs with you." She dabbed the corner of one eye. "Now please take her back for feeding time with the other babies."

If Mrs. Martin had been the hugging type, Beth would have hugged her good and hard. But Beth immediately obeyed and headed with a lighter step to the feeding room with her baby. *Her* baby, for truly, that's who Elly was now.

The nurses were abuzz with their opinions about Judge Garrison.

"I could have told you exactly what he was like." Mitzi reached for Elly and sat with her as she fed her a bottle of milk. "I was in Mrs. Martin's office the other day with this wee one when they came to visit, up until Mrs. Martin had me hand her over to them. Now Mrs. Garrison—she was a fine lady. But that little boy, Lionel...he and Judge Garrison were a pair. No, Elly, I don't believe you would have been happy with them. Not at all. You're blessed to have your mama." She nodded at Beth. "She truly is."

The other nurses, feeding their charges, agreed.

"Thank you," Beth whispered. *Lord, may it be so.* She allotted just a few minutes now from her lunch time to stay within Elly's sight before heading back down the hallway toward her desk.

"Beth," Mrs. Martin called from her office. "Please step in a moment. And close the door."

"Yes, ma'am." Beth's breathing came faster at the click of the door when she closed it behind her, as Mrs. Martin sat with her hands folded on top of her desk. "I'm sorry I stayed with Elly a few minutes extra. I'll make it up at—"

"Beth. Sit down. You're not in trouble." She took off her reading glasses and pinched the bridge of her nose. "At least not with me."

"Ma'am?"

"As I'm sure you're aware, Judge Garrison was very upset when I informed him that Elly Rose was no longer available."

"Yes." The fire in his eyes had terrified her as he'd swept out of the foundling home.

"He's a very influential man in Boise. And being a judge…"

"Would he be the one who would have to sign the legal papers for me to have Elly?" Because he would never do that.

"No, no. I sign them here. But I just want to make you aware that he may, shall I say, make life difficult for you. There may be repercussions, I'm afraid."

"I—I see." She was afraid to ask, let alone imagine, what those might even be. But the worst he could do would be to take Elly away from her.

"Do you want to change your mind? It's not too late. And no one would blame you."

"No. I want Elly Rose. No matter what it takes. Or whatever Judge Garrison—or anyone—may do."

Mrs. Martin smiled. "I thought so. Our prayers certainly will be with you."

"Thank you. Is that all? I have some letters to type."

"Yes. That's all."

Beth rose and walked out, head held high. She could feel Mrs. Martin's eyes on her, but she didn't look back.

At last, the clock approached five o'clock. When Beth got off work, she quickened her pace to the bus stop. Though Timothy hadn't said he'd be waiting for her after work when she got off the bus this morning, she hoped he'd be sitting on the bench. She had much to tell him about her day.

The bench was filled with waiting riders, but he wasn't among them. Nor was he standing nearby.

He had made no promise. Hadn't even gotten off at her stop this morning. She assumed he was going to the next stop to the library, drugstore, and bookstore. Maybe Brighton's Candy

Shop on the way back. Surely, something would open up for him so he could— Though she didn't want to admit it, her heart supplied the word. *Stay.* So he could stay next door with Mrs. McPhearson. So they could share meals. So they could...

All wishful, foolish thinking. He was such a gentleman, he'd be kind to anyone. She wasn't anyone special. And now she had a baby in her care. She didn't know a lot about men, but Lawrence had made it clear how men thought. No one would want her and Elly.

So it was a good thing Timothy wasn't here, so her heart wouldn't get any more attached than it already was.

The bus came, and she found a seat, missing Timothy sitting beside her, holding Elly. At her stop, she went into the market and selected a few items. They needed to last not only for tonight's dinner but for all of next week. Eggs and potatoes. That should do. Three nights of eating with Timothy weren't the normal. Just memories. Wonderful memories.

As she approached the house and saw a light on in Mrs. McPhearson's window, one last flicker of longing arose. But it was snuffed out as movement occurred behind the curtain, yet the door remained closed.

Maybe she'd just eat the last piece of cherry pie and save her eggs and potatoes for when she was hungry...and needed them.

CHAPTER 8

"Is that Beth and Elly Rose coming home, dear?"

Timothy dropped the corner of the curtain. "Yes, Grandmother. They went inside already."

She wiped her hands on her apron. "Well, if you aren't going to invite her in, then I will." She walked over to the coat-tree and shrugged into her coat.

"Grandmother." Timothy sighed. "I'll do it."

"Good. Now go."

It wasn't that he didn't want to see Beth. He did. But how could he face her again with no news about a job? He was a hard worker, willing to learn, ready to accept any job he was capable of doing. He needed to support himself and Grandmother. Not be a burden, just another mouth to feed.

Dutifully, he went next door and knocked. Beth pulled back the window curtain in the door, and her eyes widened when she spotted him. She opened the door but didn't invite him in. Didn't even smile. In fact, something was definitely wrong.

"Timothy. Did you need something? Is Mrs. McPhearson all right?"

"She's fine. She sent me over to invite you and Elly for supper tonight."

"I—"

"Please don't refuse. She has her heart set on you coming. And seeing Elly."

"Oh. But I don't have anything prepared to bring—"

"You don't need to bring anything. Just come. She has supper ready to dish up."

"I... Well." Then she nodded. "All right. Thank you. We'll be right over."

"That'll make her very happy." He added a smile to prove it —and to see if she'd return it. Which she didn't.

He walked back to Grandmother's side. Maybe Beth needed cheering up more than he did. Well, Grandmother was just the one to do it.

By the time Beth arrived with Elly Rose for supper, she showed up with a smile, though obviously forced. But who could stay truly sad around Grandmother and her joyous welcome and embrace? Coming home to her warmth and love each day helped hold him up.

After supper, Beth insisted she clean up and do the dishes. Grandmother agreed again only in exchange for holding and feeding Elly. Timothy grabbed a dish towel and made himself useful as well and also set coffee on to percolate this time. Regardless of Grandmother's claim about tea being part of the solution to problems, tonight called for coffee. That was what Beth had served him his first night here.

Grandmother opened her mouth, then simply ducked her head and hummed to Elly in her arms.

"Dear," Grandmother said to Beth once they were all again seated at the table for their after-dinner routine of talking— and dessert if they had any, which they didn't tonight. "Was today a hard day for you?"

Beth closed her eyes and nodded. Timothy reached over

and covered one of her hands with his, and at that, her eyes flashed open. But he didn't let go. Nor did she pull her hand away from his.

She did, however, shudder before answering. "Judge Garrison stormed in this morning, and when Mrs. Martin told him his family wasn't getting Elly Rose, he was furious."

"Did he harm you?" He gripped her hand now, but instead of jerking away, she turned hers so their fingers entwined. "Threaten you?" If that man, no matter his position, had done anything to Beth—

"Not in words, no. But, oh, the glower he gave me. I've never seen anyone look so...so...vengeful." She shivered again, as though the man was standing in front of her once more. "And then Mrs. Martin said he's very influential in Boise and warned me that he might make things difficult for me."

"Oh, Beth." Grandmother adjusted Elly and reached for Beth's other hand.

"We'll watch out for you." Timothy squeezed her hand, in his heart sealing a pact. He wouldn't let anyone—judge or not—hurt Beth and her baby Elly. Not if he could help it. What a heel he was for being so prideful that he hadn't met Beth after work to escort her home.

He'd let Gideon Brighton's news at the candy store discourage him. The tinkling bell overhead as he'd exited had clanged out the last of the day's failures—from the library to the drugstore to the bookstore and others—as he stepped back onto the pavement and dragged himself home. Of course, no job was available at the moment, though Gideon promised if something opened up, he'd be in touch. But that hadn't been hope enough for Timothy to linger near the bus stop and wait for Beth's bus.

What if Judge Garrison had sent someone to follow Beth after work as she'd left alone, to see where she lived? Or to grab Elly on the way to the bus stop?

Tomorrow and Friday, her last day at the foundling home, he would be with her all the way up to the door and waiting on the doorstep when she got out of work.

"We'll do all we can to keep you and Elly Rose safe," Grandmother said.

"We will," Timothy agreed. "I promise."

And tomorrow he was going to find a picture of this Judge Garrison and be able to recognize him. To be prepared.

⁓

The day Beth had been dreading arrived. Friday, her last day at work after three years.

Timothy rode the bus to work with her, holding Elly as had become his habit, and walked them to the foundling home's door.

Beth eyed her surroundings from the steps but didn't see anyone lurking about. Nor did she feel eyes upon her. Had she missed her opportunity to meet the writer of that note altogether?

"I'll be back at five to escort you home," Timothy said, then waved as Beth stepped inside. "May God's grace walk with you. That's the prayer my mother used to send me off with."

With the door still open, Beth let his benediction settle around her. *Yes, Lord, please walk with us. Through this day and every day.* She'd cling to that prayer. "And with you also, Timothy," she called. "May you find the perfect job today."

He waved again, and Beth closed the door. After taking off her coat, she set Elly beside her desk and placed a piece of paper into the typewriter. Her last day.

"Beth." Mrs. Martin came up beside her. "We're so sorry to be losing you." She blinked hard, as though she might shed some tears. "I truly wish there was some way we could keep you. And Elly. But…"

She didn't have to say the words out loud. Beth knew from the fewer number of people coming to visit and even less letters to type that people weren't in a position to enlarge their families during the war. The Donaldsons and Garrisons seemed to be the exceptions. So no crib had opened up either.

"Thank you, Mrs. Martin. I've enjoyed working here. I know you don't have any other choice."

"Of course, I'll give you an excellent reference wherever you apply for a job."

"I very much appreciate that."

Throughout the day, a parade of workers made their way to Elly's basket, and Mrs. Martin didn't scold a single one or remind them to get back to work.

Pearl came out of the kitchen with a milk bottle in hand for Elly. "Let me hold this little one and feed her one last time. She needs to have a full tummy when she leaves here." She took Elly and settled onto a visitor's chair near Beth's desk.

"Thank you, Pearl. You've been so kind to us."

"It's my honor. I just wish there was more we could do."

Beth stuck one last sheet of paper into the typewriter and clicked away. "Everyone's done all they could, which has been wonderful."

"Once you get settled in a job, make sure you bring Elly back sometime so we can see her."

"I promise."

Beth proofread her last letter and addressed the envelope as Elly sucked down the final few swallows from the bottle.

Pearl patted Elly on the back. "I'll hold her while you pack up."

"Thank you." Beth placed her notebook and pen, her only belongings from nearly three years of working here, into her purse. And her employment was over.

Mrs. Martin entered the front office trailed by nurses with

some of the older babies in their arms. "We will all miss you, Beth. And little Elly." She held out an envelope. "Your pay."

"Thank you." Beth weighed it in her hand. "It feels heavy."

"Just a little extra I put in for you."

"Oh, no, Mrs. Martin. I couldn't take food from the babies."

"It's a small amount, but it's a gift from me to help until you get on your feet."

"I..." Surely, she'd need it, and it was a gift. "Thank you so very much."

"You're welcome. It's my pleasure. And although Elly wasn't a full-time ward of the baby home, since during the day she was under our administration and care, I've drawn up adoption papers for you. All you have to do is sign them. They'll be good for you to have—just in case *anyone* tries to make trouble for you." She gave Beth a knowing look.

Mitzi stepped forward and took Elly from Pearl while Beth signed the papers. With a final flourish of the pen, Elly was hers. Her heart swelled, part with awe and a bigger part with fear. Now that Elly was dependent on Beth for everything, what if Beth let her down? Or couldn't provide. Or—

"You are officially Elly Rose's mother." Mrs. Martin smiled as she placed one set of documents on her desk and stuck the other into an envelope and handed it to Beth. "May God bless your family."

The nurses cheered, and Mitzi placed Elly into Beth's arms. "Goodbye, little one. We'll miss you and your sweet smile."

"Times are hard for us all," Mrs. Martin said. "But if you ever need help or need milk for Elly, come here. I will not abide even one child who has been under this roof going hungry." She held out her arms toward Elly. "May I?"

"Of course." Beth transferred Elly to Mrs. Martin.

"May God bless you, dear child. Always live for Him. Remember that although you had a rough start in this world, the Lord has rescued you and placed you in loving arms.

Godspeed." She handed Elly back to Beth. "Now go. Be wise. And be careful."

And with Mrs. Martin's benediction, final tearful hugs and waves from the nurses, and one last kiss by Mitzi on Elly's cheek, Beth ventured outside.

On her own now.

Timothy was nowhere to be seen. Should she wait or head over to the bus stop? Maybe without him, the note-writer—surely, the lady in the brown coat—would come forward again.

But no one appeared. So Beth ventured off the landing, toward the bus stop.

Tomorrow she'd inquire for housekeeping positions. In a city this size, there must be some wealthy family who could afford a housekeeper—and had a heart for babies.

Check the Garrisons'.

No!

Where had that thought even come from? Judge Garrison would never hire her. And it'd be too hard on Mrs. Garrison to daily see the baby she would never have as her own. It was a foolhardy idea. Mrs. Martin had cautioned her to be wise—and careful. Seeking employment with the Garrisons was neither.

"We can give her everything money can buy. Even during wartime."

They had money.

And Beth now had legal adoption papers.

As if in synchronization with that thought, against the corner of the building, Beth spotted the lady with the scarf, this time staring right at her. The woman inched toward Beth, pulling the little boy along with her.

"Wait up, Beth! I'm here!" At Timothy's shout from down the sidewalk, the lady turned and fled around the building.

"Wait! Ma'am!" Beth started after her, but the woman was gone, and Timothy reached her.

"Who are you talking to?"

"There was a lady who I think was wanting to talk with me. But she ran off."

"Oh?" Something strange crossed Timothy's eyes. "Do you know her?"

"No, I don't. I've seen her before but have never met her." Until she did, she didn't know how much to tell Timothy of her suspicions as to who the lady was. "I was just hoping to find out who she is and what she wanted." She squashed the sudden resurfacing worry that she wanted Elly, after all. Surely, that wasn't true, but what did the woman want?

Timothy took Elly's basket from her with one hand and her elbow with his other. "We'd better hurry. I'm sorry I was a bit late."

"Yes. We don't want to miss this bus." She let him lead her down the street, but now how would she find the woman again? As tonight was her last time to sit and wait at this bus stop. Unless the woman showed up at Mrs. McPhearson's house again.

CHAPTER 9

Newspaper in hand, Timothy slipped out of the house early Saturday morning. The sky was clear, the air crisp, barely seeping through the old plaid scarf he'd found on the coat-tree and was now bundled tightly under his less-than-wintery coat. Not a soul was on the street other than him. But he had to get out and find a job. He would not mooch off of his grandmother. If he were to live with her, he would provide for her. Intentions did not bring in a paycheck, though, much less a job offer.

On Beth's side of the house, all was still in the pre-dawn. No light on yet, no shadows moving beyond the curtains. How was she? And Elly Rose? He missed them even though he'd just spent the whole evening with them over supper again. And escorting her home from work before that. He'd miss that, now that she wouldn't be taking the bus to the foundling home anymore. But whether in her side of the house or in Grandmother's, Beth and Elly Rose filled the rooms with their presence. Their love and brightness.

The last two days, he'd been too humiliated to let Beth know the details of what a failure he was. And he should be encouraging her in her new life as a mother to Elly and through her struggles and fears with her own job hunt.

Pride. That's what he was full of. But he longed for righteousness.

"'Oh that men would praise the Lord for his goodness, and for his wonderful works to the children of men! For he satisfieth the longing soul, and filleth the hungry soul with goodness.'" Stanley always knew how to encourage, how to speak truth. Usually using God's own Word to do it.

"Remember, Timothy, these Germans, the ones we call the enemy, are God's creation, too, just as we are. People He loves and longs for them to love Him."

Stanley's words the night before the attack snuck in. The verses, God's words—that's what Stanley would say. They were God's words to him.

Timothy stopped at the top of the steps and raised his head heavenward.

God? Would You fill my soul? Like You did Stanley's?

Only the stillness of the morning answered him. Maybe because, unlike Stanley who'd been so forgiving, Timothy still felt rage at the German soldier who had killed Stanley. The quick glimpse of the man's face, the scar running down his left cheek, the smoldering blue eyes were imprinted in Timothy's mind. The blond hair. The stubble on his chin. He'd seen him too many times in his nightmares to ever forget him.

Or forgive.

Grandmother was like Stanley—forgiving, accepting. She didn't care what country someone was from. To her, everyone was made in the image of God—therefore, someone to be loved.

But he could accept that in her. She'd never fought in the war, never been exposed to that kind of hatred. And if he could, he'd shelter her from ever finding out the depths of depravity man was capable of.

For the minutes between Grandmother's front door and the first shop he entered today on his job hunt, he didn't have to smile or pretend to be content and optimistic. Or hide the heaviness pressing down on him from the failures of yesterday's inquiries at another grocer and two department stores, even the bakery he'd bought the cinnamon rolls and cookie at.

Beth shouldn't have any problem finding a job—they were out there. The proprietors just didn't want him, it seemed. They were looking for hometown boys returning from the war or women, not a New Yorker with a questionable service record.

But this morning, the newspaper in hand offered a glimmer of hope. And that was all he needed to start again. Two ads of places looking for workers. One at a restaurant. The other at a hotel. So maybe…just maybe…today was the day.

If he could find places hiring, perhaps he'd hear of openings suitable for Beth to apply to as well, so she could provide for herself and Elly Rose. And then he'd be her—

"What do you think you are? A hero? You're no hero." Roland Johnston's words swirled in Timothy's heart, as spiteful-sounding today as that day in the hospital. The day Timothy had attacked Roland. The day he was discharged and his record stamped permanently.

No, not Beth's hero.

~

Beth knocked on Mrs. McPhearson's door. Nine o'clock should be a polite time to call on a neighbor—especially one she was about to ask a favor of. Dared she hope Timothy would answer?

Eyes peeked through the top of the glass in the door, and the door flew open. "Come in, come in." Mrs. McPhearson tugged Beth and Elly into the warmth of the kitchen. "I'll fix you breakfast. What would you like? Some eggs? Pancakes?"

"No, thank you. I already had a piece of toast."

"Pah, a piece of toast. That is not breakfast." She put a skillet on the stove. "Sit. I'll fix you breakfast. Eggs, yes? Just the way your father liked back when he was a boarder here." At Beth's hesitation, she added, "I have plenty. Much more than I need, seeing Timothy did not wait for me to get up and make him breakfast."

Beth sat. "Timothy has left already?"

Mrs. McPhearson pulled out eggs and cracked them into a bowl. "He must have been up before the birds. And already gone. Still searching for a job. That boy is diligent. But…work is hard for him to find these days for various reasons, but also he feels due to his limitation of vision."

"His vision?"

"Did he not tell you about his injury? And surgery?"

"No." But that explained why his left eye sometimes seemed to pain him or give him trouble seeing.

Mrs. McPhearson sighed. "I suppose I'm not surprised. He thinks of it as a weakness."

Timothy McPhearson was anything but weak. Especially not in character, where it counted.

"I'm rather in the same predicament now also. I need to go job hunting today too."

"Then you must eat something hearty." She whisked the eggs and poured them into the skillet. "Where will you start?"

"I thought I'd go to the north end today."

"Yes, yes. Start on Harrison Boulevard. Between lawyers and doctors and engineers, you should find someone to hire you. Try the mansions first. They're a good sign of wealth and children. Judge Garrison lives there. He likes to mention that when interviewed—Judge Garrison on Harrison. I guess he likes to use his little rhyme as a slogan—except I'm sure he wants people to know exactly what part of town he's able to afford."

She clapped a hand over her mouth. "Oh, forgive me—I should not speak of him like that."

Beth smoothed Elly's hair to keep from adding her opinion of the man, which would have been much worse. "Maybe that's a street to steer away from, then."

"No, that's the street most likely to have someone able to afford a housekeeper." Mrs. McPhearson dished up a plate of eggs and set them in front of Beth. "There you go."

"Thank you."

"Eat your fill. You'll need strength for the day." She pulled up a chair and held Elly while Beth ate. "But still, you should see his house. It's the most beautiful red-brick, white-columned house. Neoclassical revival style—that's what it's known for. You can't miss it. The two-story front porch is also white and enclosed on the bottom, and the top is railed in and open except where it's covered with a roof over the columns. And then on one side of the house is a bay window with another railed-in porch above it too. Beautiful. And right on a corner. You should at least see it."

Thank goodness her mouth was full so she didn't have to answer. But did she even want to see where Elly might have lived?

"Mrs. McPhearson," Beth said after she'd swallowed, "would you mind—"

"If I watch Elly Rose for you? Of course I will. I'd be delighted to."

"Oh, thank you."

"It's a blessing to me to watch her, you know. Timothy's parents—my son and his wife—died in a fire, and all I have left are Timothy and my sister. Elly reminds me that there is hope for the hopeless, that there's life and still something to live for. Like God is saying through her, 'I care.'"

Hope. Was that what Elly was giving Beth too?

Beth finished her eggs and scooted back. "I'll hurry as fast as I can. Pray that I can find a position."

"Indeed, I will, child. Indeed, I will."

Beth set out, assured of prayers behind her. And even though she hadn't seen Timothy this morning, his benediction from yesterday followed her every step. *"May God's grace walk with you."*

At the drugstore near the bus stop where she got off, she bought a newspaper and sat on a stool to look at the *Help Wanted* advertisements. She found three addresses seeking a woman to do housework, so perhaps she'd have her pick of them.

She stuck the paper in her coat pocket and headed up Harrison Boulevard. This end of Boise was so different from her modest neighborhood. Trees lined the snow-covered median dividing the street. In the spring, when the grass turned green and the trees bloomed, this would be lovely. Even strolls in the early-night hours would be enchanting, with street lamps at every intersection.

And there it was, up ahead on the corner, just as Mrs. McPhearson had described it—a large brick home with white columns, a white windowed porch, white railings, and white trim around the side bay windows. Undoubtedly, this was the Garrisons' home. Where Elly could have lived and grown up. Certainly, she never would have gone hungry here nor wanted for anything, at least anything of material value.

Again Beth questioned her decision, what she had denied Elly. But then she thought of her own father, of what the name Josiah Calloway stood for. Kind. Gentle. Loving. Understanding. Had Elly become a Garrison, that's not the type of father she would have had. Perhaps no father was better than a harsh one, like her own father had had. Her grandfather, Benton Calloway, a man she'd never met. Most of the time, he was in jail. And when he wasn't, he had no use for his son or family.

Beth quickly crossed the street and ducked her head. She didn't wish to be seen should anyone be outside or even looking out a window. Thankfully, the three addresses she had were for higher house numbers.

She shuddered. She couldn't imagine working next door to that family. Beth hurried past the house and onward four more blocks, where she came to the first address in the newspaper. The white Queen Anne was impressive in size, though inviting with its wide wraparound porch.

Beth took a deep breath and stepped up onto the porch and knocked. A kindly looking elderly man opened the door with a petite white-haired woman at his side.

"Good morning. I'm Beth Calloway, and I would like to apply for the job of housekeeper you advertised for in the newspaper."

"Carl, invite her in," the lady said with a smile.

"Yes, please do come in. We're the Millers, Carl and Lila. We're very anxious to hire someone. Won't you have a seat in the parlor? Lila, perhaps you could ask Cook to bring us some tea? With milk and sugar for our guest."

"Right away, darling." She smiled at Beth. "I'll be right back."

As they drank tea and ate scones, Beth felt at home with the couple.

Lila detailed the work expected, then stood. "Come. Let me show you around."

Beth followed her into the dining room but had no time to gawk at the table set for twelve or the upholstered chairs or the side garden enclosed by shrubs as Lila continued into the eat-in kitchen.

"As you can see, we have a back staircase for easy access to the upper story, but let me take you up the front stairs to the living quarters."

Upstairs, they walked into each of the five bedrooms and

two bathrooms. What a pleasure it'd be to help care for such a place.

"And that's the end of the tour, dear." Lila smiled. "Now let's go down the back staircase so you're familiar with the entire house." Lila took her back to the living room, where Carl sat reading a newspaper. "Please be seated." Lila sat across from her. "Now, what do you think? I hope it's not too much work for you. It is a big house, but we do pay well."

"Your home is beautiful, and I'd consider it a joy to keep it looking that way."

Carl lowered his paper. "Excellent. Do you have any questions for us?"

"Just one. I need to mention that I have a baby—"

"A...baby?" Lila's eyes widened while her husband's mouth opened.

"She was left on my doorstep during the snowstorm we had early last week, and I work—worked—at the foundling home. But they didn't have a bed for her, and I decided to keep her, but I need to bring her with me. She's—"

Both of them shook their heads.

"My dear." Lila reached out and patted her hand. "We're so sorry. Is there somewhere you could leave her during the day? We'd love to have you, but we can't possibly have a baby in the house at our age."

"She's very content, not fussy at all, if that's what you're concerned about." Beth sat forward on the chair. "She's very sweet and she naps, and I'd be able to get all the work done on time."

"No, dear. I'm so sorry. You're just what we're looking for. But we can't hire you if you need to bring her with you. If you find some other arrangement for her care during the day, please contact us again, as we'd love to employ you." Lila stood. "We wish you all the best."

Beth stood also. "Thank you, ma'am, sir, for your time. It was nice meeting you."

"We'll see you to the door," Lila said, and Carl joined her.

Beth held back her tears as she trudged to the next two addresses.

Two more very lovely families. One with young children themselves. But each family who had advertised turned her down. After the last house, she simply went up and down the block knocking on each door, shyly inquiring if they were in need of domestic help. But she avoided the entire block the Garrisons lived on.

Reasons varied as to why no one could hire her. She had no official experience. She had no references. She couldn't live in. But they all agreed on one objection—she had a baby she needed to bring along.

She crossed the street before she got to the Garrisons' block, ducked her chin into her scarf, and kept her eyes down as she scurried to the next block, her options for the day having run out.

CHAPTER 10

*H*opeless. That's what the day's quest had been. Timothy tramped along the sidewalk on the two-block walk from the bus stop back to Grandmother's house, his feet dragging more with each step.

"Oh, Lord..." While he whispered the words, his heart was crying them out. "Why can't someone hire me? I want to work."

Then they cried unto the L*ord* *in their trouble, and he delivered them out of their distresses.*

The verses Stanley made him memorize kept coming back. But he *was* crying out. So where was the deliverance from his distress? "Where is it, God?"

Oh that men would praise the Lord for his goodness, and for his wonderful works to the children of men! For he satisfieth the longing soul, and filleth the hungry soul with goodness.

"Remember those words, Timothy... Praise the Lord for His goodness. Hold on to that."

"I'm trying, Stanley. I'm really trying."

He climbed the porch steps back home, no better off than when he'd started out this morning. When he opened the door, the aroma of baked chicken, biscuits, and pie—blueberry?—

greeted him along with Grandmother. Was this the dinner Beth had planned to teach Grandmother to make? But this smelled exactly like one of his grandmother's meals.

"Mm, it smells like a feast." Timothy stamped his boots and unwound the wool scarf from his neck.

"It is. For my two hard workers."

Elly was on a pallet on the floor, but Beth hadn't come out to the door. Nor did he hear her in the kitchen. "Is Beth—"

"No, no, she's not back from job hunting yet. But she should be coming along soon to get Elly. And then of course, she'll stay for supper, since she'll be too tired to show me her recipe tonight. This way, she can just come in and eat. And enjoy the company." She winked at him.

"Oh."

"'Oh'? I thought you'd be pleased to have her join us. Well, she was coming over for supper tonight, anyway, and I intend to make sure she stays, even though she didn't do the cooking."

"It's just that..." Timothy hung up his coat and took off his boots, not meeting Grandmother's eyes.

"What, dear?"

Finally, he faced her. "I had no luck again today."

She waved her hand. "Is that all? Then this meal will fortify you after your hard day. And young man..." She pointed a finger at him. "Luck has nothing to do with it. The good Lord will find you the right job at the right time."

Timothy gave a small smile. "Now you sound like my friend Stanley."

"Good. The Lord gave you a friend of faith during the war. What more could you ask?"

A lot. Like Stanley's life. And that of the little German girl. No eye injury. No *Combat Fatigue* stamped on his medical records. A good job. A—

"Praise the Lord for what He has done, Timothy," Grandmother said, as if she'd been rehearsing the Bible verse too.

"I'm sure you can think of plenty." She eyed him, then walked over and picked up Elly Rose. "Here." She put the infant in his arms. "Hold her while I finish up supper."

"But—"

She walked away, and there he was left holding a baby. What if she cried? And why wouldn't she? He'd never held a baby in his life.

Should he talk to her? That's what Beth did. Or sing like Grandmother did? No, he'd stick with talking.

"Uh, would you like me to sit down with you?" How ridiculous was that, as if she'd answer?

Elly grasped his finger and smiled. Right into his eyes.

Oh, okay. He walked to a chair and sat. Repositioned her so she was sitting up on his lap.

Her blue eyes still followed him. And she still smiled.

She was a cute little thing. And happy. Content. Yet she had nothing. No family. No place at the orphanage. No—

But she did have something—she had Beth. Beth's love and care. Elly wouldn't lack for anything that Beth could provide, meager as it might be in material goods.

Oh that men would praise the Lord for his goodness...

"You're wealthy, Elly. Wealthy because God blessed you with Beth's love." In that, he was a bit envious of this little orphan girl.

And with his thoughts of Beth, a soft rap sounded on the door.

"I'll get it, I'll get it. You sit." Grandmother bustled out from the kitchen with a dish towel in hand. "It's probably Beth, not wanting to wake Elly in case she was sleeping."

It was Beth—but what had happened to her?

Her usually bright brown eyes were lackluster, even red looking and puffy, her cheeks streaked. Her hair was askew, sections sticking out from some kind of bun that she must have put it into. Her hat appeared to have fallen in muddied snow.

And she had no smile.

She walked into the house and fell straight into Grandmother's arms. Grandmother held her against her shoulder like Beth held Elly when she was upset. And that's when her eyes landed on him and her mouth dropped open. Aghast that he was holding her baby? Or to be seen in such disarray?

She pushed away from Grandmother and wiped her eyes with the sleeve of her coat. "I'm sorry."

No one said anything for a moment. Then Grandmother came to the rescue.

"Let me help you out of your coat. There. Now come into the kitchen, and I'll fix you some tea. That's my go-to for problems, you know. Plus, you need to warm up."

Beth headed the opposite direction, toward Timothy. It was Elly she wanted, not him, of course.

Grandmother took her arm. "No, no, dear. Elly's fine. Come." In her glance back at him was an order to stay put.

Fine with him. He didn't understand these female things, anyway. Elly Rose was enough for him to figure out for one day. Though Elly had snuggled right into his arms. As if...just as if she belonged there.

~

Beth warmed her hands on her cup and sipped chamomile tea, all cried out after unloading her woes of the day.

"Humph." Mrs. McPhearson planted her hands on her hips as she sat at the table. "Out of all those people you asked and who didn't hire you, it's their loss."

"It's because I can't bring Elly along. I know she'd be fine. Everyone at the foundling home loved her, and she was so good there. She didn't interrupt my work. I divided my lunch time up so I could take care of her during smaller breaks throughout the day. One family I asked today had children who would have even helped entertain her, I'm sure."

"The Lord will provide. Just like I told Timothy."

Timothy. Who, of all things, was sitting contentedly in the living room, cradling Elly like a father would. Thankfully, Mrs. McPhearson had wordlessly kept him in there. He was kind and honorable, gentle yet strong, the kind of man who'd make a good husband and father someday. Her heart twinged in jealousy at the thought of that lucky family.

Mrs. McPhearson rose and ran a towel under the faucet, wrung it out, and handed it to Beth. "Hold this over your eyes. I'll just heat some milk for Elly, and we'll be all set."

"Oh no! I was supposed to show you how to make my favorite recipe. I—"

"Dear, you can show me another time. I knew you'd be worn out when you returned after being gone all day, so I went ahead with tonight's meal. Oh. Just one more thing." She reached over, pulled the pins from what was left of Beth's bun, and fluffed her hair around her shoulders. "There. Now go get Timothy."

Beth stood and walked into the living room. "Supper is—"

"Shh." Timothy dipped his chin toward Elly sleeping in his arms. "She just fell asleep."

Beth's eyes teared up again, but this time from the scene right before her. "I can take her if you want," she whispered.

"I'm fine. But you've been gone all day, so you probably want to hold her. Here you go."

Beth bent close, and he transferred Elly to her arms, grazing Beth's hand in the process and giving Elly's cheek a lingering caress. Beth quickly straightened, burying her face against Elly's soft blanket to hide the blush that surely must be visible, what with her heating cheeks. Never had Lawrence's touch sent such a feeling of warmth through her, let alone right to her heart. And the tenderness Timothy had with Elly—

She really had to get this image of a family out of her head.

Timothy stood and took Beth's arm, creating yet more longing, as he escorted them into the kitchen.

Mrs. McPhearson turned from the stove, a potato masher in hand, as they entered. "Sit, sit." She beamed, her smile landing on Timothy's hand guiding Beth the short distance. She must love having her grandson here, someone to cook for. "Supper is ready."

Beth gently placed Elly in the basket near the table. "She's outgrowing this."

"She certainly is." Mrs. McPhearson filled their plates with mashed potatoes, golden chicken, biscuits, and carrots. "While Elly's sleeping, we'll enjoy our bounty together." She grasped Timothy's and Beth's hands, and Timothy reached for Beth's other hand. He held it in a strong, comforting way. Way too much like...family. "Timothy, would you ask the blessing?"

Timothy bowed his head. "Dear Lord, thank You for this food You've provided and Grandmother has prepared. And..." He cleared his throat. "Thank You for the blessings of the day."

Beth inhaled. So Timothy must have good news to report. She was glad for him—really, she was. But when he'd share his news and then ask about her day, she was afraid she'd burst into tears again.

Lord, please help me to rejoice with him that he found a job.

He must have said something more in his prayer, but all Beth caught was his ending "Amen." And she almost missed even that when he squeezed her hand before letting go.

In the silence of a few minutes of eating, Mrs. McPhearson turned to Timothy. "What is one of the blessings of the day that you had?"

He didn't answer immediately. He chewed. Then laid his fork and knife down. And simply stared at his plate.

Beth wanted to hurry him along. Why not just announce

his job? Or did he not want to make her feel bad over her obvious lack of one?

"Yes. A blessing of the day. My biggest blessing was..." The clock on the wall ticked off the seconds of his silence. "Coming home to this place. Where I'm loved. To family."

"Now, that's a mighty big blessing, indeed." His grandmother beamed at him, then turned to her. "Beth?"

"Um." What was Mrs. McPhearson thinking? She knew Beth had no blessings from the day. Hurt, hardships, and hunger had been her companions. But no blessings.

Timothy's and Mrs. McPhearson's eyes were on her as they waited.

"My...blessing..."

"Yes?" Mrs. McPhearson encouraged—or hounded.

"Is..." Beth swallowed. Her gaze landed on Elly, contentedly asleep, emitting sweet baby sounds. "My blessing is coming home to Elly."

"Such a sweet blessing she is." Mrs. McPhearson silently clapped her hands together.

And Beth smiled. God had blessed her, indeed. Through Elly, God had shown her His love. Given her hope. Reignited her dream of having a family someday. She did have a family, and Elly was the start of it. "She's a bundle of many blessings." How silly was that? She dipped her head over her plate, but when she peeked over her food, Timothy was smiling along with Mrs. McPhearson. So maybe it wasn't too corny. Beth met their eyes.

"Beth, dear..." Mrs. McPhearson seemed to be considering something. "Maybe I could watch Elly for you if your hours weren't too long."

"Oh! Would you really?"

"I don't see why not. I love this little girl, and it'd help you to get on your feet. And give me something useful to do during the day."

"Mrs. McPhearson—you're the biggest blessing of the day!"

"It's truly my pleasure. So you pick the family you most want to work for and go back there on Monday morning ready to start."

What an answer to her prayers. She could leap for joy. Maybe she would, once she put Elly to bed for the night.

They were in the middle of eating the still-warm blueberry pie when the telephone rang. Mrs. McPhearson rose to answer it in the living room, and snatches of her end of the conversation drifted into the kitchen.

A loud gasp.

"Oh dear!"

"...as soon as I can."

Beth caught Timothy's gaze, and he stood as his grandmother returned.

"What is it, Grandmother?"

"My sister. Cora. She fell and is bruised and banged up. I need to return to Sandpoint for a few days to help her." She turned to Beth and wrung her hands. "Just for a few days. If I can still leave tonight, I'll get started right away—and get back to help you sooner."

Beth stood too. "You need to be with your sister. Now go. I'll manage here." Beth gave her a gentle nudge in the direction of Mrs. McPhearson's downstairs bedroom. "Let me clean up the kitchen so you can pack and get ready."

"I'll see you to the bus station, Grandmother." Timothy gathered their plates and took them to the sink.

"Thank you, dears." Mrs. McPhearson gave each of them a quick kiss on the cheek and bustled to her room.

Within half an hour, Beth and Timothy had the kitchen cleaned up, the dishes washed and dried and put away. He grabbed Mrs. McPhearson's suitcase when she appeared and set it by the door.

"Please call when you arrive so we'll know you got there

safely." Beth got Elly and her reheated milk bottle and stepped out the door with the others and went into her side of the house. While she kept a smile on her face as she waved to Mrs. McPhearson and Timothy from her front window, she was glad the day was ending. From disappointment after disappointment, to Mrs. McPhearson challenging her to find a blessing. And what seemed like the biggest blessing she could have imagined with Mrs. McPhearson's offer to watch Elly Rose.

But now with Mrs. McPhearson on her way back to Sandpoint to help her sister...the day still had ended just as it'd started. With another disappointment.

CHAPTER 11

Timothy held Grandmother's suitcase in one hand and her elbow with the other as he guided her across the porch. Beth stood at her window, waving with Elly in her arms and a smile on her face. But at the devastation in her eyes, Timothy almost stumbled down the steps. He regained his balance, nodded to Beth, and helped his grandmother off the porch.

Of course, Beth was brave. He'd known that all along. But her kindness, her composure, struck him yet again. Not once had she given any inkling that the prospect of a job again being yanked away staggered her under its weight.

He'd see Grandmother to the station, then get back here and check on Beth. What was the right thing to do? Of course, Grandmother was torn between helping Great-aunt Cora and watching Elly. Beth, by urging Grandmother to go help her sister, ended up with no job prospect. And he was caught between his love for Grandmother and his—concern—just concern, for Beth. But if he could get to know her more, well, love wouldn't be too hard to imagine.

She was unlike any girl he'd ever met. And there had been

plenty overseas who wanted to get to know an American serviceman. But he and Stanley had always sat on the sidelines at get-togethers.

"Watch how they interact with others," Stanley had said. *"With their girlfriends, with individual men, and especially with the servers."* And what an eye-opener that had been. Flirtatious, giggling girls. Girls who ostracized those in not as pretty or new dresses. And the way they snipped at and ordered those serving food and showing hospitality to the guests. *"Look for a girl who loves others."* Stanley had nodded, like he knew something about love.

And from what Timothy observed, that described Beth. What she had already sacrificed to be able to take care of Elly. Her job, perhaps her very home—though he couldn't imagine Grandmother ever evicting her—and possibly a future family. All because she loved this little girl.

Already Beth was drawing his heart to hers. Not that she knew it. But what he wouldn't give to be the object of her affections.

"Easy down the stairs, Grandmother." He hefted her suitcase higher. As they reached the bottom step, Beth's porch light illuminated the tail of a brown overcoat flapping around the side of the house, and a muffled cough broke the silence of the evening air.

"Stop!" He helped his grandmother down onto level ground, dropped her suitcase, and ran around the side of the house. "Hey!" The lady's little boy slipped in the snow, and the woman—yes, the scarfed woman he'd seen before—grabbed him to his feet. Recognition flashed in the little boy's eyes when he saw Timothy.

"Mutter—" But his mother, again with muffled coughing, pulled him along, zigzagging through the neighbors' backyards. Faster than Timothy could keep up in his dress shoes.

Something bright on the path they'd tramped through the

McHenrys' yard caught his eye. Blood. Had the little boy cut himself on something buried in the snow when he'd fallen?

Should Timothy catch the local bus to get Grandmother to the station or find out who this woman was and discern the severity of the boy's injury? Another bus wouldn't come along in time to get to the station for the last northbound bus headed toward Sandpoint. He walked back to where he'd left Grandmother.

"Who was that?" she asked.

"I don't know. But I intend to find out." Not only who—but what this German's connection to Beth was.

He checked up and down the street. Was the woman waiting for them to leave so she could sneak back and talk to Beth? Was Beth even safe while he was gone?

"Come along, then, Timothy."

And really, he had no option but to pick up the suitcase and march forward.

He barely got Grandmother to the station on time and on the bus. After he extracted her promise to take a taxi from the Sandpoint station to Aunt Cora's and call when she got there, hired a Checker cab himself, and returned home, the house was dark on both sides.

He certainly couldn't peer in, so he raised his hand to knock. Then dropped it. He didn't want to scare her. Or awaken Elly. Or Beth, if she had gone to bed already. But wasn't it still early for Beth to retire for the night?

Was she even inside? She could have gone off somewhere with the German woman.

With the porch light off now, even in the moonlit night, he couldn't tell if there were extra footprints at her door, coming or going. He unlocked Grandmother's door and went in. There was no use switching on the porch light, as the illumination on Grandmother's side didn't quite fully reach over to Beth's door. The porch had been shoveled pretty good and tromped on so much through the days that he probably couldn't pick out extra prints even in broad daylight.

All he could do was go inside for the night. And pray.

~

Mama and Papa had been wrong.

Beth huddled in a corner of her bedroom in the dark, listening to faint sounds of steps out on the porch. Again. Vibrations rumbled through the old floorboards beneath her, even back here.

Her parents had agreed to her living in Boise only if she could reside here, renting this side of the house where Mrs. McPhearson lived. The home where Papa had lived when Mrs. McPhearson ran the entire house as a boardinghouse, back when Mama and Papa had met.

And they said this was a safe haven. Where she'd feel loved and protected. She did feel loved by Mrs. McPhearson, who was every bit as kind as in their stories about her. But she was scared like never before. How could she protect Elly when she was frozen with fear? What if Elly woke and cried? Needed to have her bottle warmed? Then whoever was out there would know she was home. Alone. With a baby.

Oh God, please help us. Please keep us safe.

Were these steps the same person who had been up on the porch after Timothy and Mrs. McPhearson had left? Maybe that had been the woman with her boy, wanting to talk. But whoever it was, they had neither knocked nor left anything earlier. But these seemed heavier. Like a man's. What if it was Judge Garrison? She drew her arms tighter around herself.

It was too early for Timothy to be back, as the local bus ran far and few between on Saturday nights.

The wind howled down the fireplace, and the house groaned. Maybe the creaks were the same familiar sounds she heard every night, but in the shadowy room, they were ominous. Unseen forces in the dark.

So she sat huddled with a blanket wrapped around her as tears slid down her cheeks.

"Elly," she whispered, if only to fill the room with a human sound, "would it really be so bad if I returned home? Just until I could figure out what to do?" Elly slept peacefully next to Beth, her protector from the world.

"I don't know if I could bear seeing the sadness in Mama's eyes every day as she looks at Susannah's scars. But Mama would love you, Elly. Like one of her own. She really would. And Papa—he'd carry you around, and at dinner, he'd bounce you on his knee." All things he'd done for each one of them. "And the boys—they'd all beg to hold you. All of them would watch you if I could find some kind of work in Caldwell. Maybe another typist job. There must be someone hiring a typist. Not too many people would likely be looking for a housecleaner there, though, with the war. But I could find something to do."

She reached over and patted Elly. "And we'd be safe."

Sometime during the night, Beth must have drifted off, as when she sat up, the sun was sneaking into the room, and Elly was stirring.

Oh, thank You, Lord. We're safe. And Elly slept through the night.

Beth scooped Elly up and changed her and put some milk on the stove to warm.

And then she remembered—Mrs. McPhearson hadn't called. But most likely, she would have called Timothy, since she would have gotten in quite late. But why hadn't Timothy called? Because it'd been too late?

Beth toasted a slice of bread and ate it quickly, making it more palatable with a cup of black tea. She missed the sugar and milk the Millers had served theirs with and the splash

Timothy had added the other night, but all the milk she had was saved for Elly.

"It's time to get dressed for church, little one. I want to go early and pray before people arrive. We need God's blessings." His guidance, wisdom, and so many things...

She bundled Elly and slipped out of the house. Softly she closed the door behind them, careful not to bang around and bother Timothy next door, as he must have returned very late. While she'd dozed off.

Head lowered against the wind blowing down the nearly empty street, she trekked the three blocks to church. Before the service started, maybe there'd be an opportunity to ask Reverend Farmer to pray for Mrs. McPhearson and her sister.

Inside, she didn't see anyone, so Beth proceeded to the front, set Elly on the first pew, and knelt, head bowed, eyes closed.

Lord, I know You see us. Please help Mrs. McPhearson and her sister. And please give me guidance. She swallowed. *You gave me Elly—so please help me to provide for her.*

Footsteps coming down the center aisle stopped at the front pew, and she opened her eyes. "Reverend Farmer. Good morning."

"Good morning, Beth." He nodded toward Elly on the pew. "And who do we have here?"

"This baby—Elly Rose—was left on my porch two weeks ago in the snowstorm. The foundling home had no bed for her, so I'm keeping her. But with doing that, I no longer have a job there."

He studied Elly a moment. "So you have need of prayer, I see. In being her mother and, I presume, in need of another job?"

"Yes. For both."

"Might I join you for prayer, then?"

Surely, God would hear the prayers of a reverend faster

than hers. She nodded, and he knelt beside her. "I also would like to ask if you could pray for Mrs. McPhearson's sister who fell and needs help. Mrs. McPhearson returned to Sandpoint to be with her. She was going to watch Elly while I worked"—she shrugged—"but she's no longer available."

"Hmm. So you need a job where you can take Elly Rose with you or to find someone to watch her?"

"Yes, Reverend."

"You're in the right place, then." He tipped his head to her position. "On your knees before God."

"I know."

He placed a hand on Elly. "Dear Lord, we come to You this morning. You see Your beloved Beth and Elly Rose and know their needs. Your eye is on the sparrow, so how much more we know You care for these dear ones of Yours. Please lead Beth in her pursuit of a job and the means to provide for her and Elly Rose. May her life continue to bring glory to You, wherever You lead her. And please also be with Mrs. McPhearson as she aids her sister in Sandpoint. In Christ's precious name, amen."

"Thank you, Reverend Farmer."

He sat on the pew and motioned for Beth to join him. "I'll continue to pray. What type of work are you looking for?"

"I was thinking I could do housecleaning."

"Ah. Not too many are still able to afford housecleaning. A few perhaps, but..."

"I already know. No one wants a baby along."

"I'm sure that's the case." He tapped his knee. "I wish Mrs. Farmer and I had the money to hire you ourselves. But this just makes it more of a miracle when God does provide."

"Yes." A miracle was what they needed for sure.

He sat quietly a moment. "You know, there is a member of our congregation who mentioned to my wife that her sister needs domestic help."

"Really?"

"I have the address in my Bible. I was going to announce it during the service this morning." He stepped up to the pulpit and flipped through the pages of his thick Bible.

"Here it is." He returned to Beth and handed her a scrap of paper with a Harrison Boulevard address written on it. "I believe they love children as well."

"Thank you so much, Reverend Farmer." *Oh Lord, thank You.* This just had to be their miracle.

CHAPTER 12

All Sunday morning, Timothy listened for Grandmother's telephone to ring. He didn't dare leave, not even for church, in fear he'd miss knowing Grandmother had safely reached Sandpoint. As the morning progressed, so did his worry.

Now would be a good time for those verses in Psalms Stanley had insisted he memorize. But even though Stanley had begged him to remember the chapter and verse numbers, Timothy hadn't bothered. Maybe one hundred something? One hundred seven? That sounded about right.

He reached for Grandmother's Bible on the lamp table and opened it midway to Psalms. He flipped pages until he found chapter 107. Forty-three verses? Eventually, he'd find them. With verse one, he started reading.

O give thanks unto the Lord, *for he is good: for his mercy endureth for ever.*

Stanley had loved to talk about God's goodness, His mercy.

Let the redeemed of the Lord *say so, whom he hath redeemed from the hand of the enemy.*

Stanley hadn't been redeemed from the hand of the enemy,

though. He'd been killed by the hand of the enemy, by that German soldier who'd shot him in cold blood. The scarred face clouded Timothy's view of the pages on his lap. He wiped the image away and kept reading.

And gathered them out of the lands, from the east, and from the west, from the north, and from the south.

And then there they were, right in front of him—the verses he and Stanley had memorized together.

> They wandered in the wilderness in a solitary
> way; they found no city to dwell in.
> Hungry and thirsty, their soul fainted in them.
> Then they cried unto the Lord in their trouble,
> and he delivered them out of their distresses.
> And he led them forth by the right way, that they
> might go to a city of habitation.
> Oh that men would praise the Lord for his
> goodness, and for his wonderful works to the
> children of men!
> For he satisfieth the longing soul, and filleth the
> hungry soul with goodness.

Timothy closed the Bible.

He was pretty sure he knew what God wanted him to do to turn from a hungry, thirsting soul to one filled with God's satisfying goodness. And what Timothy couldn't do.

Forgive.

The phone rang and he jumped up, the Bible toppling off his lap. He picked it up, slid it back on the lamp table, and reached for the receiver. "Hello?"

"Good morning, Timothy, dear."

"Grandmother—are you at Aunt Cora's? Are you safe? Are you—"

Grandmother laughed, pure and sweet, into the phone.

"Yes, Timothy. I'm at Cora's. I'm sorry I didn't call earlier, but all is well. And I can barely keep her from trying to hobble around and wait on *me*. My goodness, you'd think I was the guest or the invalid myself. She's tenacious." She laughed again. "I certainly don't know where my younger sister gets that."

Timothy could imagine her winking at Great-aunt Cora, who was most likely listening and chuckling.

"Now, Timothy, I want you to be sure to encourage Beth however you can until I get back. I have plenty of canned vegetables left from the Victory Garden last summer. If you can make another of your nice soups, you could take her supper occasionally. Or if need be, invite her over for supper to keep an eye out for her and Elly in light of Judge Garrison's threats. I'm sure under the circumstances, that'd be appropriate."

"Yes, ma'am. I'll watch out for them." Gladly.

"All right, then. Let Beth know I've arrived safely, and please tell her again how sorry I am that I can't help right away. But when I get back, my door is always open to her."

"Okay, Grandmother."

No sooner had they hung up than Timothy heard bouncing footsteps on the porch. Bouncing? He lifted a corner of the curtain and peeked out. Beth, with Elly's basket on her arm and a smile on her face. Apparently, coming from church.

Maybe he should have gone.

Beth took a step toward his door, then retreated back to her own and set the basket on the porch. While she dug in her purse, Timothy rapped on the front window, then ran to the door and flung it open.

"Hi, Beth."

"Hello, Timothy." She went back to digging in her purse.

"Grandmother called."

"Did she make it safely to Sandpoint? Did—"

Timothy chuckled. "She's there. Come in, and I'll make

some soup. And tell you all about her call. If you're okay with that?"

"Thank you." Beth blushed a pretty pink. "Elly and I would be delighted to." She stopped rummaging in her purse, picked up her basket, and walked across the porch to his door and stepped inside. Her brown eyes sparkled, and the pink in her cheeks faded a bit to what was probably left from the cold. Still very attractive.

"If you want to get Elly settled and warmed up, I'll get the soup going and heat some biscuits." He was rambling. "And I'll warm milk for Elly."

He poured some into a pot, then hunted down jars of Victory Garden produce Grandmother had canned. Carrots. Beans. Peas. Tomatoes. Onions. And two potatoes from the bin. He was depleting Grandmother's winter supply, but this was what she'd practically ordered him to do.

Beth followed him into the kitchen. After placing Elly in the basket on the floor, she stood by the warming milk. "So tell me what your grandmother said." She was polite to a fault, but the light in her eyes indicated she was bursting to tell him some news of her own.

"She arrived safely, but Aunt Cora is trying to still be the hostess and wait on Grandmother instead of the other way around. But by the end of the day, I'm sure Grandmother will be back in charge."

"I'd love to see the two sisters trying to out-serve each other. Your grandmother is so sweet."

"She is." He dumped the vegetables into another pot, added some water to the broth, and gave it all a stir. "Aunt Cora too. For the two-plus years since Farrragut—the naval training base—opened near her, she's been involved with serving one way or another. Especially reaching out to the women."

"The WAVES? Didn't she ever try to get you to join the navy

instead and go up there? Be a matchmaker?" Her eyes twinkled as she grinned at him.

"No!" Although, she'd hit on one good reason he hadn't been up yet to visit Aunt Cora in Sandpoint, as she opened her home to the WAVES for meals, Bible studies, whatever she could think of. And the ones who worked as nurses on base? No, thank you. A nurse or a woman officer who saw his eye problem as a detriment was not what he needed. Or wanted.

Surprise lit her eyes at his tone, so he added a forced smile to soften his vehemence. "No, it's so far north, farther away from Grandmother than I'd like to be."

"Of course. I understand the three of you are the only family each of you has now."

He nodded. "Yes, so I want to do what I can for them. Grandmother is trying to convince Aunt Cora to come live with us here so we can all be together."

"I hope she'll come." Beth turned the burner off under the heating milk.

"Well..." He cleared his throat. "If you'd like to feed Elly her bottle now, the soup will probably be ready by the time she's done."

She prepared the bottle and sat at the table with Elly in her arms.

"Did you enjoy church?" Without Grandmother here filling in the social niceties, Timothy muddled along with his best guess as to what to talk about. "I mean, I assume that's where you were coming back from?" He gestured to her navy polka-dot dress with a bow arranged like a smile under her face. Then moved his eyes back up from the belt around her small waist and her knees just covered and her lace-up boots.

"I did." The light was back in her eyes. "I went early to pray, and Reverend Farmer came and prayed with me. And the most amazing news—he gave me the address of a family someone told his wife about who is looking for a housecleaner—and who loves children. There's a possibility they'd let Elly come along. Isn't that wonderful?"

Hope. That's what sparked in her eyes. "Yes, it is."

"At least it's another place to try. So tomorrow morning, I plan to go apply and take Elly Rose with me. Right from the start, they'll know it's me and Elly together."

Beth with her love, loyalty, compassion, determination—and her shining brown eyes—smiling at the sweetest baby he'd ever seen... The two of them were a family.

Then she smiled at him. And whatever Beth's connection with that German woman, it didn't matter.

All he wanted was to someday be a part of Beth's little family too.

~

Timothy Calloway was so unlike Lawrence. Unlike any man Beth had ever met.

When she announced her grand news, he didn't laugh, not even in a teasing manner. He simply turned his caring hazel eyes first on her, then Elly. Like he wanted to say something but an unexpected emotion clogged his throat.

The image of him yesterday holding a sleeping Elly in his arms, shushing Beth when she'd come in so as not to awaken the baby... She wouldn't ever forget that picture. This man who claimed he didn't know what to do with a baby had the facets of a father's heart...for a little orphan girl. Oh, that he might also consider the orphan's new mother in the same light.

And she couldn't extinguish that longing of family she had around him. Every day, it embedded itself deeper into her soul.

But she wasn't experienced at anything. Not at being a mother. Not in providing for a child. Not in being appealing to a man. Nothing but being a typist. And she didn't have that option any longer, anyway.

"Timothy..." His eyes cleared as if he'd been shaken out of some thought. She nodded toward the stove. "I think the soup is ready."

"What? Oh, the soup!" He turned the burner off just before the boiling broth cascaded over the top of the pot.

Beth smiled, then laid Elly in the basket she was outgrowing. "I'll get the bowls if you can get the biscuits out of the oven."

"Um, yes. I can do that." He pulled them out of the oven and dumped them into a bowl while she ladled the soup.

When they sat, Timothy reached for both of her hands, as if it was the most natural thing to do, even without Mrs. McPhearson here. "Heavenly Father, thank You for our food. Thank You for Grandmother's safe arrival in Sandpoint. Please bless her and Aunt Cora. And Beth as she goes on her job pursuit tomorrow. May Your grace walk with her each step. Please open the eyes of this family she's to interview with and show them what a gem Beth is and help them to welcome Elly as well. Amen."

In the moment after he said *amen*, the moment he should have released her hands, he still clasped hers. "Beth?"

His eyes searched hers. "I'll be praying for you tomorrow, too, that you'll get this job."

"Thank you."

He squeezed her hands, then released them and raised his spoon to his mouth.

Oh, Lord—may it be. And she didn't mean only getting the job.

The afternoon turned into evening, and they moved into the living room in front of the fireplace. She surely needed to leave before darkness settled in, but the thought of going back to her empty side of the house brought fear. What if whoever was on the porch last night returned? Or Judge Garrison showed up?

"Beth, is something wrong?" He tucked Elly's blanket yet tighter around her, though it was toasty in the house already.

"I... You'll probably think me silly, but I was just thinking about last night." She wrung her hands together.

"Last night?"

"Yes. After you left to take your grandmother to the bus station, there were footsteps on the porch. No one knocked or anything. Just climbed the stairs, and, I guess, waited. Then after a little bit, left. Then later, I heard steps again and..." She sighed.

"And you were scared?"

So frightened she'd sat curled in a corner, petrified. "Yes."

Timothy took one of her hands. "Maybe the second time it was me you heard. I took a cab back, so I returned earlier than expected. But when I am here, I want you to call, no matter the time, and I'll come right over. We could also have a signal if you ever need help. I wonder if I'd hear you if you knocked on the wall between the living rooms?"

"Not if you're upstairs, certainly."

"True. How about three knocks? And if you don't get a response, run upstairs and knock on the inside wall."

"The upstairs of my side of the house is closed off. Your grandmother had a door installed at the top to block off the second floor, and she has the only key. The access to the rooms is from her side of the upstairs."

"Really? Then she has them closed off there also."

She shrugged. "I think she was hoping one day to rent her side to a large family and use my smaller side for herself. She doesn't seem to know what to do with such a big house."

"I guess not. Anyway, always call me anytime of the night. Promise?" He squeezed her hand and didn't release it until she nodded. "I don't want you to be afraid over there."

"I never was until last night. Yes, three knocks will be our secret signal." Though she hoped she'd never need to use it.

"I'll walk you and Elly home before it's dark, and I'll have a look around the outside of the house. How's that?"

She smiled at him. "That'd be nice. Thank you."

She'd breathe easier now with Timothy only three knocks on the wall away. And if the person from the porch didn't return in the night.

CHAPTER 13

As Beth walked down Harrison Boulevard on Monday morning, Elly in her arms, she wasn't quite as confident as she'd been at the table with Timothy the day before. But she and Elly were braving the world together, so together was how they'd show up on this family's doorstep.

If they were searching for household help, though, why hadn't this address been listed in the ads in the newspaper? Perhaps the family wanted only direct referrals? Or church attenders? That must be it, if the only place they were looking was through the church of a relative. Or maybe the position opened up too late to be included in the Saturday paper.

Or maybe God was saving the job just for her.

Beth's steps slowed as she got closer to the house number listed on the paper Reverend Farmer had given her.

Right ahead of her was the block she needed to hurry past. But it only had two houses on this side of the street—the large corner lot with the Garrisons' beautiful red-brick and white-columned mansion. And the next house, a slightly more modest gray Colonial with dark brick steps sweeping up to the front door. Beth checked the house number on her slip of paper again. No! No, it couldn't be. The gray house? How could she work next door to the Garrisons, especially with Elly? Surely, neighbors—or hired help—talked to each other on the street.

Beth took a deep breath. If God meant for this to be her job, He'd protect them. Of course he would. And she'd be working inside, hidden from their view. Thankfully, the yard between the two houses was lined with large trees and bushes on the boundary, like camouflage.

"It'll be all right, Elly. Don't worry." Elly smiled up at her as Beth scurried past the Garrisons' house and stood in front of the Colonial. "Dear Lord, please bless our mission here. Oh, please. Amen." She strode forward, up the set of steps from the street, across the paved walkway, and up the brick stairs of the house itself. "Smile like you usually do, Elly, so they see how sweet you are." She put the door knocker into motion.

Within moments, footsteps crossing a foyer sounded, then the door opened. A tall woman in a calf-length teal tea dress and heels and coiffed honey-blond hair opened the door.

"Yes? May I help you?"

"Yes, ma'am." Beth smiled. "I'm Beth Calloway and this is Elly Rose. Reverend Farmer at the South Boise Baptist Church gave me your address. He said your sister spoke with Mrs. Farmer about your need for help cleaning. I would like to apply for the position."

"Oh my, yes, I do need help. I didn't know someone would respond so quickly. Please come in, dear."

"Ma'am—I must say before you interview me that I am unmarried. Little Elly Rose was left on my porch one night, and I decided to give her a home. I do need a job and would love to work for you, but I have no one to leave Elly with—at least right now. She'd have to come with me. She's very sweet and almost always quiet. I'd make sure I get all of my work done—"

"Dear…" The woman laughed. "Please come in. First of all,

let me introduce myself." She held out a hand. "I'm Mrs. Connor."

Beth grasped her hand. "I'm glad to meet you."

"Now, come into the parlor, and we'll get to know one another a bit. Would you care for some coffee and muffins? I was just about to have some myself."

"Oh—yes, please."

"Excellent. Have a seat, and I'll let Hilda, our cook, know to add another setting. Hilda is the only other employee here," she added as an afterthought.

"Your house is beautiful, ma'am." Light poured in through windows behind the opened country garden toile curtains. Beth chose the plush sapphire-blue chair sitting atop the salmon-and-blue Persian rug.

"Thank you. We're a more modest home than"—she gave the slightest glance next door—"some of the larger houses on the boulevard. But we try to be quite neat, so you shouldn't find the work overwhelming." She smiled, her blue eyes welcoming. "Excuse me for a moment, and I'll be right back."

Beth settled Elly on her lap and surveyed the room. Very neat, indeed. Not an item was out of place, not a speck of dust on the lamp table nor a trace of dirt on the shiny wood floors.

Mrs. Connor returned and took a seat on the sofa across from Beth. "Do you think Elly Rose would let me hold her?"

Beth blinked. "Oh, yes. She loves to be held." She stood and transferred Elly to Mrs. Connor. "I worked as a typist at the foundling home the other side of town, and the nurses loved holding her and feeding her."

"And you no longer work there?"

"No." Beth repositioned Elly's pink blanket and took her seat again. "I kept her in a basket by my desk since they had no extra bed for her. The director said the arrangement was temporary, especially now that she's getting too big for her basket. Even though, uh...one family wanted her, I decided to keep her, so that's why I need to find another job. I'm a hard worker and keep a tidy home where I live."

"You chose keeping Elly Rose over your job?"

"Yes, ma'am."

"And now you're struggling to support yourself and her when another family would have taken her?"

Beth lowered her chin. How selfish did that sound, subjecting an innocent baby to being poor and raised by a single woman when she could have been raised in wealth? But she hardly was going to disparage Judge Garrison to his neighbor. "Yes, ma'am." She met Mrs. Connor's eyes, firm in her decision no matter what this potential employer thought.

"Then after our refreshments, I'd like to show you the house and explain your duties and hours. This is not a live-in position, however. Does that suit you?"

"My...duties?"

"Yes." Mrs. Connor smiled. "If you'd like to work here and are agreeable to the pay, which we'll discuss, you're hired."

"Yes—oh, yes! Thank you!"

The plump cook came in silently with a tray and set it down.

"Thank you, Hilda. Beth, this is our dear Hilda, who's been with us for years. Hilda, this is Beth, who will be our new housekeeper."

She and Beth nodded and smiled at each other.

"Will there be anything else, ma'am?" Hilda asked their employer.

"We're all set, thank you," Mrs. Connor said, and Hilda headed through the door that must lead to the kitchen. "Let's eat Hilda's wonderful blueberry muffins while they're still warm, then I'll give you the tour. I do entertain every so often, so if you're available some evenings, I could have extra work for you in helping Hilda, if you'd like. It would mean extra pay, of course."

"Oh, thank you." She couldn't wait to tell Timothy—and Mrs. McPhearson.

Thank You, Lord, Beth whispered in her heart as Mrs. Connor transferred Elly back to her and poured the coffee.

"Milk and sugar?"

"Yes, please."

"Coffee or tea and some treat will be served each morning, and you may eat your lunch, which will be provided, with Hilda in the kitchen." She smiled again. "And of course, milk, and eventually whatever else little Elly Rose will eat, will be kept stocked."

This was more than an abundant answer to her prayers.

"When would you like me to start?" Beth surveyed the room, anxious to get to work. "I can begin today if you'd like." Though she hadn't brought the basket, while she worked, she could set Elly on her blanket on the floor within easy reach.

Mrs. Connor laughed. "I see that you are quite an eager worker. If you truly would like to start today, you may. After the tour of the house, you can start with tidying downstairs."

"Thank you so much, Mrs. Connor. I'll do everything you assign me to the best of my ability."

"I have no doubt about that. And while you work, I'll enjoy sitting with Elly Rose."

∼

Timothy stood beside the mail slot in the post office, his Victory Mail letter in hand to post.

On nights when those nightmares occurred with that German soldier standing over him, ready to shoot, he was left exhausted by morning. And they were coming more frequently. If he could just find out what had happened in those last minutes of Stanley's life, how it was that Timothy was alive and Stanley gone, as the gun had been pointed straight at Timothy. And what had happened to the little girl? Surely, a German soldier wouldn't have shot a child—and a German one at that.

One person knew the answers. Roland Johnston, the first from the rest of the platoon to arrive on the scene. If Timothy could track him down and get him to write back—hopefully, without the details he needed being censored by the army—maybe one day he'd learn what happened and the nightmares would stop.

Johnston's reluctance to talk about it in the hospital was perhaps to be expected, after witnessing such an atrocity and being injured himself in the process. But maybe now that some time had passed, he'd be willing to share what happened.

Not only was Roland Johnston the key to the mystery, he was Timothy's last hope.

When Timothy had woken up in the hospital, Roland, a private from his own unit, had been in the next bed.

"You're one lucky guy, McPhearson. You should be dead," he'd said.

An odd greeting, but Timothy had nodded, moved his arms, his legs. Everything was working fine. Except his eye. He lifted a hand to it—bandaged and stabbing with pain. But just being alive meant he was extremely blessed.

"Were you part of the rescue?" Timothy managed to turn his head toward Roland enough to see that he seemed intact except for the sling cradling his arm.

Roland Johnston narrowed his eyes—eyes that turned cold, empty-looking—and curled his lip. Nodded.

"What happened? Where's Stanley? He's going to be okay, isn't he? Is he here?"

"Stanley didn't make it." He hadn't bothered with any preface, just the cold fact.

"No! Not Stanley." Timothy's patched eye throbbed, but the working one filled with tears. His chest ached—from the gun thrust at it or his heart breaking? The dead one should have been him. "The girl. There was a little girl there. Where is she?"

"McPhearson, you ask too many questions." Johnston rolled over, his back turned to Timothy. Like that was the end of the conversation.

And that's when Timothy jumped out of bed and grabbed Roland by his good arm. "You know! Tell me. Where's the little girl? What happened to her?"

"Private!" The doctor bustled over. "Stop this ruckus this minute." He pried Timothy's hand off Roland. "What's the meaning of this?"

"He knows!" If only Timothy hadn't jerked free from the doctor and grabbed Roland's collar with both hands. Maybe then *Combat Fatigue* wouldn't now be stamped on his discharge record. "Where is she? Where's the girl?"

The soldier's face was ashen. He shook his head.

"No!" Timothy tightened his grip, resisting, disobeying the doctor. "She was just a little girl!"

The doctor wrapped an arm around Timothy's neck and pulled him off Roland again. "Gather your belongings, soldier, and get out of here. Now. Before I have you thrown in the guardhouse." The doctor motioned to the nurse, and she stuffed his few possessions into his duffel bag and shoved it at him.

"Johnston! What'd they do? Tell me!" Only then could he accept it. He'd tried to protect the girl. And Stanley. Apparently, they were both gone. But he was alive. Why?

"Leave it be," Roland muttered, his back still to Timothy.

"No—please! Tell me what happened. You were there. You know."

"McPhearson! I said you are to leave." The doctor glared at him.

Timothy hefted his duffel bag over his shoulder and shuffled toward the door, feeling the doctor's anger following him.

And just like that, Timothy was done in the army and with no place to go. Except Idaho.

But Roland Johnston knew. He'd been with Stanley the night before. Even on the night before his death, after drilling Timothy on their weekly memorized Bible verses, Stanley had been talking with Roland, reading to him from his Bible, still open on his lap. *"If we confess our sins, he is faithful and just to forgive us our sins, and to cleanse us from all unrighteousness."* Timothy had seen a flash of something—hunger for God's truth, perhaps?—in Roland's eyes. Though Timothy hadn't stuck around to listen to what had sounded like a private conversation.

Now, Timothy still clutched the Victory envelope in his hand. What if he could not only find out about the ambush from Roland but also carry on Stanley's legacy of ministering to people with the Bible? Correspond with Roland, write out a Bible verse for him on each one-sheeted V-mail letter? That would make Stanley's death not completely in vain.

"Move it, buddy." A man with an envelope came up alongside him at the mail slot and snickered. "If it's to your gal, just mail it. She'll be glad to hear from you, I'm sure—unless she's found herself a nice recruit overseas."

Timothy glared at him. "Sorry." He dropped his letter—using the same Army Post Office address in New York City he'd used as his overseas address—into the postal slot and turned, ready to set out for another day of job hunting. And that's when he saw the sign.

Mail Sorter Wanted.

He could do that. And he'd seen workers beyond the clerk's counter. Some women, yes, but also men. Men not in the armed service. Though they did all seem somewhat older than he was. But still, the post office was hiring men.

He got in line at the counter.

"How can I help you?" The clerk barely looked up.

"I'd like to apply for the mail sorter position advertised." Timothy nodded toward the posting.

The man slid a form to him. "Fill this out and get back in line. Next."

By the end of the day, Timothy finally had a job.

As he walked the last half block from the bus stop, lights in Beth's windows were a welcome beacon in the darkness. Almost like coming home.

He shook that thought from his head. Except...maybe now that he had a job, he could really pursue her. Should he ask how to go about courting her? Write to her parents?

When he spoke with Grandmother again, he'd ask her, as she claimed a part in bringing Beth's parents together years ago. But for now, the light in the window, the satisfaction of having a job, and the prospect of hope quickened his step. He hit the porch steps, and Beth's curtain pulled up on one side. She peeked out the window and smiled and held up Elly to see him. And it was exactly like coming home.

Beth. Never had he met anyone like her who brought such joy to his life. To Elly's. To Grandmother's.

He waved, and the curtain dropped. So did his heart. But before he crossed to his door, Beth flung hers open.

"Welcome home! Won't you come for supper? I don't have much to offer, but I have so much to tell you."

"I'd love to."

"Did you see Elly smile? She recognizes you. Maybe after you take off your coat—" She clapped her hand over her mouth.

"What, Beth?"

She shrugged. "I was going to say...maybe you'd like to hold Elly while I put supper on the table."

"I would. Thank you for letting me."

Her eyes widened in what he'd call amazement. Was she surprised that he'd cherish Elly? Yes, probably she was, given his first introduction to Beth with a baby in her care. He fully intended to make that up to her.

He took off his coat, draped it on the sofa, and sat. When he reached for Elly, Beth placed her in his arms.

"See her smile at you?"

Between Beth's smile and Elly's, yes, this was where he wanted to call home for the rest of his life.

Once Beth retreated to the kitchen, he whispered to Elly Rose. "Listen, I'm going to tell you a secret. Hopefully, it won't be much longer before I tell Beth. But I wanted you to know too. I want you and Beth to be my family. I'm going to talk with Grandmother about how to go about courting Beth. And then soon—very soon, I hope—we'll be a real family. You, me, and Beth. You'll have not only a mother who loves you but a father. And a great-grandmother. What do you think of that?"

Elly smiled her beautiful baby smile.

"So that's your vote of approval?"

"What are you two talking about?" Beth asked as she practically danced her way into the living room.

"Just a little something between the two of us. For now." He winked—winked! He, Timothy McPhearson, was not one to wink. Or flirt. But somehow he was doing both. He stood. "May I help in the kitchen?"

"Okay. Let me take Elly, and I'll have you take the meat pie out of the oven."

"Mm." He handed Elly Rose to Beth. "Meat pie sounds delicious."

Beth laughed. "Maybe 'meat' is a little too extravagant sounding for what it is. It's vegetable pie with a little bit of hamburger."

"It still sounds good. And smells so good." He strode into the kitchen, inhaling the aroma of Beth's dinner. It smelled like a stew—carrots, potatoes, maybe beans? And beef. And oh, the glorious scent of a flaky, golden crust.

"I'm celebrating," she said from behind him.

"Oh? What?"

She laughed out loud and twirled around in a circle, holding Elly high. "A job."

Timothy grabbed her arms mid-twirl and danced around the room with his two girls. "That's wonderful. Tell me all about it."

She stopped and grinned. "I'll tell you over supper. But it's beyond anything I could have even dreamed of. A glorious blessing. And, Timothy—"

Oh, he was mesmerized with her beautiful brown eyes.

"Timothy!"

He blinked. "Uh, what?"

"Could you take the pie out before it burns?"

Her full, bubbly laughter followed behind him to the oven as he opened it and pulled out her celebratory supper.

And now that he had a job and hope, maybe they really could be a family one day.

CHAPTER 14

Three wonderful weeks at the Connors' home, and Beth felt the Lord's blessing—His grace—walking with her each day. And each evening, she and Timothy spent suppertime with Elly, sharing their happenings at work.

And now it was Monday morning again and Beth would be starting her fourth week in her job in minutes. The bus rolled up to her work stop, and she stood, shifted Elly onto her hip, and debarked.

Mrs. Connor was such a delight to work for, always thankful and gracious and welcoming Elly. Beth had even persuaded Mrs. McPhearson to stay and help her sister as long as needed, that there was no hurry to return. And break time was wonderful, getting to savor Hilda's baked goods and tea served with milk and sugar. Hilda must have stockpiled their rations, for somehow they seemed to never have a shortage of sugar, generous as they were with it. Today Beth brought something to share as well. Though certainly not as sweet as Hilda's, her last jar of strawberry jam was a gift of love.

Every day of the prior weeks, Beth had passed the imposing, silent Garrison house in trepidation, head down, scurrying past the corner until she felt safely hidden by the bordering trees and bushes between their property and the Connors'.

Today, though, as Beth crossed to the corner where their house took up most of the block, a car pulled up in front of the house. A man exited the enclosed front porch—Judge Garrison. And there was nowhere to hide.

Beth clutched Elly tightly against herself and ducked her head into the folds of the blanket to hide her face. He marched down the steps and stopped at the bottom, then looked behind him. She took this chance to scoot past the house but couldn't avoid hearing his loud words.

"When I return home tonight for dinner with the mayor, I expect this house to be spotless. Hire someone or do it yourself. I don't care. But it'd better be done!"

Beth dared a peek back to the columned porch to see who he spoke so harshly to. Mrs. Garrison stood in the doorway with Lionel clinging to her hand. Beth buried her face again next to Elly's just as Judge Garrison turned and resumed his march toward the car.

Had he seen her?

She quickened her steps, and once to the Connors' property, almost ran up the stairs.

"Beth, you're out of breath." Mrs. Connor held the door open. "You're not late."

Beth shook her head. She had no idea whether the Connors and Garrisons were close, so she dared not say anything against them. "I...I just..."

Mrs. Connor reached for Elly. "Hilda?" She nodded to the cook peering at them from the hallway. "Could you set the teakettle on now? Let's get Beth warmed up and calmed before work."

"No, ma'am, I'm fine." Beth took off her coat. "I can get right to work."

"Nonsense. You'll not be docked or considered a slacker for

sitting at my request, if that's what you're worried about. Mr. Connor just left for work, and I'd love a bit of company with my ladies." She included Hilda, Beth, and Elly in her smile.

"Thank you, ma'am."

"Let's sit in the kitchen. It's homier in there."

Hilda beamed and led the ladies into her domain and bustled about setting out tea service.

"May I help?" Beth needed to remember her place, that she was a servant, not one of Mrs. Connor's friends.

"Sit, dear. In fact, Hilda, you sit too," Mrs. Connor said. "I'll pour the tea—and heat milk for our little Elly."

And how was Beth to remember her place when Mrs. Connor treated her like one of the family? The three of them sat and enjoyed tea and scones with Beth's jam and light-hearted chatter while Beth fed Elly her bottle.

A soft rap sounded on the kitchen door, and Hilda jumped up to answer. She cracked the door open and spoke to the visitor in a hushed voice, then drew a lady with tears on her cheeks inside and closed the door.

"Mrs. Connor—" Hilda motioned her over. "We have a problem."

The pale, frightened-looking lady wiped her eyes and shook her head. "No, I cannot bother you, Mrs. Connor."

"Nonsense, Irene. Take your coat off and join us for tea." Mrs. Connor pulled out another place setting as the lady obeyed, and underneath the coat was a maid's black uniform.

"Irene, this is our new housekeeper, Beth, and her little Elly Rose. Beth, this is Irene, who works for our neighbors next door, the Garrisons."

Beth gasped, then coughed to cover it. What if Irene mentioned her and Elly to the Garrisons? If the judge knew Elly was right next door, would he concoct a plan to get her? Or threaten Beth? But she nodded a greeting, which Irene returned.

"Now, Irene," Mrs. Connor said, "what's wrong, and how may we help?"

The maid sniffed and wiped her arm across her eyes. "It's Mrs. Garrison. She doesn't know what to do as this morning Jud—" She glanced at Beth.

"Go ahead, Irene. It's fine for you to talk in front of Beth and myself." Mrs. Connor turned to Beth. "Everything you hear within my home is to be kept in strictest confidence always."

"Yes, ma'am, of course." Beth wrapped her arms tighter around Elly, sure this had to do with what she'd already overheard this morning.

Irene wiped her eyes again. "As you know, Charlotte quit on Friday. And the mayor is coming tonight for supper. Judge Garrison has decreed to Mrs. Garrison that the entire house must be perfectly clean for tonight, or—" She let the image of whatever that might be hang in the silence. "Our cook is busy with the food preparation, and Judge Garrison does not tolerate any regular household duty undone. Plus, with watching over Lionel... We don't know what to do, as the house will not be spotless by tonight."

Mrs. Connor rose. "It will be, Irene. Hilda and Beth, you may be excused from your duties here today and go over and help Mrs. Garrison. I'll watch Elly Rose for you, Beth."

Beth wrapped Elly yet closer against herself, fear pounding through her heart. "But—"

"This is what neighbors do for each other. What Christ has commanded us to do. To serve others and to love them. We show our love by our service."

Beth couldn't refuse her employer. But neither could she step foot inside the Garrisons' house—with or without Elly.

Hilda got to her feet also. "I'm ready."

Beth should pack up Elly Rose and run. Run back to Mrs. McPhearson's safe haven. Or even back home to the pig farm if she had to. Anywhere but next door.

127

"Beth?"

Slowly, she scraped her chair back. "Yes, ma'am."

∽

*B*eth had never been in a mansion in her life. How she now wished she had told Hilda or Mrs. Connor about how she already had met the Garrisons. Even what she'd overheard this morning outside their house. And that she was already petrified that Judge Garrison had spotted her on the sidewalk. He was a judge, with power. And if he wanted Elly, what would Mrs. Martin's signature on a piece of paper giving Elly to Beth mean to him?

With dust cloths, buckets, brooms, and mops, Beth and Hilda followed Irene across the yard and through the back entrance of the Garrisons' house. Beth stopped inside the doorway. Even the back staircase sweeping up from the gleaming dark-wood floor of the magnificent kitchen spelled opulence.

"We'll start at the front of the house and work our way back and then up," Irene said. "Follow me."

Down the hallway they went, past a formal dining room already set for dinner. French doors opened into a room with several velvet sofas and cushioned chairs. Mirrors reflected paintings and art objects. A bay window seemed a gathering place for an intimate conversation with two wingback chairs and a small round table between them.

Onward Irene led them toward the enclosed front porch.

When Beth slowed or stopped to gawk, Hilda prodded her on. "You'll see it all soon enough."

Beth nodded, still drinking in the lavishness, the luxury they passed. This could have been Elly's. But the verses Reverend Farmer had spoken on in his sermon yesterday quieted her heart. *Take no thought, saying, What shall we eat? or, What shall we drink? or, Wherewithal shall we be clothed?...for your heavenly Father knoweth that ye have need of all these things.*

God had been taking care of her and Elly right along. Never had they gone without food, and even now, God had provided this wonderful position with the Connors.

Yet with all the opulence in the Garrison house, a heaviness of fear reigned even in the judge's absence. Irene, Hilda, Mrs. Connor with babysitting, and Beth were all working together to help Mrs. Garrison fulfill Judge Garrison's demands. In a small way, this felt like something she could offer as a thank-you to God for His blessings.

Beth quickened her steps behind Irene and Hilda. They stopped in the enclosed porch in front of Mrs. Garrison with her head bowed, shoulders heaving, Lionel curled in her lap.

"Ma'am," Irene said softly. "I have brought help."

Mrs. Garrison lifted her head, her eyes glittery and unfocused on who was standing with Irene. She clasped Irene's hand, then slumped in her chair. "Thank you."

No, Elly did not belong here. Elly who already had a rough start in life but who now had a sweet joy about her. How long until it would have been snuffed out had she lived under this roof? Beth wanted to gather this poor woman in her arms and comfort her.

Mrs. Garrison, indeed, was far from wealthy in the things that mattered to one's heart.

Irene patted Lionel on the shoulder. "Lionel, you be a good lad and stay with your mother."

He bobbed his head, but the fear and sadness in his eyes broke Beth's heart.

"Hilda, Beth, come with me." Irene was already heading back through the house. "We'll start with the hall and front rooms. Hilda, could you do the floors? And Beth, could you do the dusting?"

They got their supplies and set to work. By the time they

finished those tasks, the Garrisons' cook insisted they stop for soup and crusty bread. After taking only minutes to eat, the women moved upstairs to continue the job. The downstairs had been quiet all afternoon, and late in the day, Mrs. Garrison climbed the stairs and went into her bedroom—now tidy and spotless—and closed the door. She was so frail and pallid. Was she even well? What if Beth were to go in to her to—

"Beth, Hilda." Irene hissed from behind them. "Hurry down the back stairs. Judge Garrison is arriving. Quickly! And without a sound."

Beth stumbled down the hall to the back set of stairs, Hilda close behind her. She mustn't get caught within his house.

The front door slammed just as they hit the landing at the bottom of the stairs off the kitchen.

"Louisa! Where are you? Lionel! Out of the way, boy." The judge was headed toward the kitchen by the nearness of his voice.

"Go, go!" Hilda grabbed Beth's arm and pushed her toward the back door.

"What about our coats?"

"We leave them!"

They slipped out the door, and Hilda clicked it gently closed behind them. "Stay alongside the house until we get to the tallest oak. Then we'll cross into the Connors' yard."

Never had Beth had to sneak around like this. She'd never return to Judge Garrison's house, but if he found out she'd been there, would she and Elly even be safe next door at Mrs. Connor's?

CHAPTER 15

~~~

What was keeping Beth?

Timothy checked the clock again. She should have gotten off work and been home an hour ago. Not that he needed to worry—yet, anyway. Maybe Mrs. Connor had some overtime work for her. But he had news.

He turned down the oven. The added wait should make the small pot roast he'd splurged on extra tender.

With a grin, he tried out what he wanted to say, what he'd just discussed with Grandmother on the phone. Though staying a few more days with Aunt Cora, she'd given her wholehearted blessing.

"Beth, I want to court you if you'd be willing. Should I ask your parents?"

No, he should greet her as if nothing was different and then ask her during supper. No, during dessert. But he needed, as Grandmother advised, to lay his heart bare to Beth—boldly and clearly.

And this evening—if Beth ever got home—was the time to do it. While he still had the courage.

She did feel something for him, didn't she? Surely, he hadn't imagined the sparkle in her eyes around him, the glow on her cheeks, her ease in sharing her thoughts. And her expression when he held her Elly girl.

And then he heard it—footsteps on the porch stairs. But they weren't the sound of the past weeks' light, energetic tread. They were too quick. Almost like someone was being chased, running for safety. Timothy pulled back a corner of the front window curtain. It was Beth. But now she stood outside her door, head down, trying to adjust Elly in her arms as she dug deep into her purse and peered over her shoulder every few moments.

He strode to his door and flung it open. "Beth!" Her face jerked up, pale and wild-eyed. "Come in over here."

She staggered across the few steps to his door and plowed inside. He closed the door and grasped her shoulders, careful of Elly.

"Beth, what's wrong? Let me take Elly, and you get out of your coat. Come to the kitchen, and I'll put the teakettle on." That would help, right? That's what Grandmother did in times of distress.

She released her grip on Elly, and he cradled the baby against his chest. But Beth still didn't say a word. Whatever happened? It couldn't be a problem at work, as she loved her job at the Conners'.

She took off her coat and followed him into the kitchen. He put on the kettle. What else could he do? Milk. He pulled out a small pot to heat milk for Elly.

Beth sat and reached for Elly. "Something smells good."

Timothy retrieved milk from the refrigerator. "It's a roast with potatoes, carrots, and onions. I was waiting for you to get home so I could invite you to supper."

"Thank you."

He poured Elly's milk into the pot, then took a chair next to

Beth and clasped her hands, snugged against Elly, with his own.

"Beth, sweet—" Oh how the word wanted to escape, for he thought of her as his sweetheart. "Something frightened you."

She nodded, her eyes still glazed-looking. "It was awful. Just...awful."

He stroked a finger across one of her hands. "Tell me what happened."

And with each word of Beth's story, anger grew deep in his chest. Not unlike what he felt toward that German soldier. But this was an American and a man in an official position treating his own family in such a callous manner. A man who had wanted Elly. A man whom, by the grace of God, Beth through her courage had thwarted.

"Judge or not, that man is undeserving of a family." He bit his tongue to keep from spewing what was in his heart at the moment. "And—"

"Timothy." Beth nodded toward the teakettle and milk, and he got up and tended to them. "There is nothing we can do. I just hope Mrs. Garrison doesn't realize that I was there and saw glimpses of her existence in that house. I can't bear to think what if Elly—"

"Shh." He knelt next to her. "God protected her. Through you. Beth, you are so courageous, and I—" He swallowed. "I care so much for you, both you and Elly." He laid a hand on Elly's head and covered Beth's hand with his other. "Beth, this dinner—I wanted to tell you tonight how much you mean to me and that—that I would like with all my heart to court you. Please tell me what to do, if you're willing. Should I write your parents? Make a trip to meet them? I'd do anything for you and Elly if we could one day be a family."

Beth's eyes teared up as he spoke, and her mouth opened. "Timothy, I feel the same way. I can't believe it—you want me *and* Elly?" Her eyes were wide with something like disbelief mixed with hope.

"Yes. Both of you. I love both of you."

Beth swiped at her eyes and laughed. "I don't know what to say. I can't believe it. I never dreamed—"

Timothy wiped away the last of her tears. "Believe it, dear Beth. Please believe it."

"I love you, too, Timothy. Both of us do."

He drew her and Elly—his whole little almost-family—into his arms and did what he'd been longing to do for weeks now —kissed her. Sweet and explosive. And the way she leaned into him, as if she'd also found her heart's home... He put a hand on the back of her head and drew her yet closer, savoring the electric moment. When they pulled apart, he met her eyes, eyes alight with the same pulsing joy in his heart.

"Timothy. That was..." Maybe she was too proper to supply the only word befitting such a moment.

"Wonderful." He grinned, and her smile was all the agreement he needed. Yes, Beth Calloway was his heart's home. And little Elly Rose made both of their lives complete.

"What do we do next to make this official? Should I call your father? Or would you like to take a trip out to see them, and I'll ask your parents' blessing in person? Or—"

Beth put a finger to his lips. "I know they'll love you and give their blessing. But let's wait a little bit. At least until your grandmother returns. And in the meantime, hold our news close to our hearts."

"Okay, if that's what you want, then we'll wait to tell them. But know this, Beth Calloway. I want the world to know how much I love you, and I want to do right by your family by including them."

"I know you do. Thank you. And we will. But tonight, let's enjoy the meal you made and celebrate, just the three of us."

She drew his head down close to hers, and he kissed her

again. Slow and gentle, sealing all his promises to her without a single word.

He couldn't wait until he could share their news with the world.

~

*B*eing loved and in love changed Beth's world. As each day progressed into another, she put aside her fear of Judge Garrison little by little. By the end of the week, Hilda had reported no repercussions from next door—at least none that she shared during their tea times.

But how much longer could Beth put Timothy off about asking her parents' blessings? He was so honorable, wanting to do things properly. While she would take the easy path—writing them of Timothy—he wanted to meet them and ask their blessing in person.

Of course, they'd like him. But she couldn't bear the shock she'd see in their eyes that someone wanted her. Had chosen her. And to tell them of Elly Rose—that someone had entrusted Beth with their baby.

No, she was content with her life the way it was, just the two of them knowing for now. After work each evening, they spent time together, eating, sharing happenings of the day.

And Timothy added a new daily event—reading Bible verses and praying together before going their separate ways at the end of the day. A practice, he said, that his friend Stanley had intended to implement once he made it home and found a sweetheart. Though Stanley would never be able to do that, Timothy could. And that's how he wanted to start building their lives together.

Sunday morning, she got Elly ready and met Timothy on the porch to be escorted to church.

They strolled down the street, Elly in Timothy's arms, just like the family Beth had never dreamed possible.

"I have some news for you, Beth." He tugged at his tie. "Grandmother is returning today by bus. I plan to meet her at the station after church and escort her home."

"That's wonderful." She clapped her mittened hands. "I've missed her and her wisdom."

"Me too. I'm sure you and she will have womanly things to catch up on and advice to seek as well." He winked at her and laughed when she blushed. "And then, how about we plan a trip to Caldwell?"

Her feet stumbled at the word. "Caldwell?"

"Yes. You wanted to wait until Grandmother was back and we told her together before going to see your parents. I can't wait to meet them. And your brothers and little Susannah. And"—he grabbed her hand—"to finally ask their blessing."

"Um, yes. We'll have to figure out when we can go." And the worry came right back to suffocate her. Of course her family needed to meet Timothy. She swallowed. "Yes, we'll make a plan."

Definitely, she should have mentioned Timothy before this. They hadn't even known about Lawrence. She shuddered. God had blessed her so beyond measure—not only in bringing Timothy to her but in protecting her from Lawrence. Would he have turned into a Judge Garrison one day?

They reached the clapboard church building, and Reverend Farmer greeted them as they entered—apparently, the first worshippers of the day.

"It's wonderful to see two—no, three—early birds today." He shook hands with Beth and Timothy and smiled at Elly. "Is your job still going well with the Connors, Beth?"

"Oh yes. It's so wonderful working for them—a true blessing. Thank you yet again for sending me there."

"Well, I'm not sure I can take the credit for sending you their way. It seems that was all the Lord's doing."

"It was. I give Him thanks too."

"Well, find your seats, and we'll start soon. As soon as everyone else shows up, that is." He grinned and then welcomed another couple entering.

Once the service began, Beth took extra pleasure in singing as Timothy's hand met hers under the shared hymnal. During the sermon, Beth had to concentrate on the pastor more than Timothy leaning forward, intent on the pastor's words. He was a godly man, the kind she wanted for a husband and a father to Elly. But to get to that point, he needed to meet her parents.

"Let's go back to review these verses I spoke on a few Sundays ago to finish up in Matthew chapter six," Reverend Farmer said, "before we continue on to the next chapter. 'Take no thought, saying, What shall we eat? or, What shall we drink? or, Wherewithal shall we be clothed? (For after all these things do the Gentiles seek:) for your heavenly Father knoweth that ye have need of all these things.' We spent some time on those verses learning how God always provides for His own. And the next verses also. 'But seek ye first the kingdom of God, and his righteousness; and all these things shall be added unto you. Take therefore no thought for the morrow: for the morrow shall take thought for the things of itself. Sufficient unto the day is the evil thereof.'"

Though his eyes encompassed the entire congregation, Beth felt he was looking right into her heart. "Each day has plenty to take care of without—shall we say—borrowing trouble from the next day. If we follow God, rely on Him day by day, He will provide not only for our physical needs but our every need, including spiritual needs. Live for Him. Rely on Him. Trust Him."

The morrow shall take thought for the things of itself. She'd just have to trust that somehow God would work out Timothy meeting her family.

Timothy reached over and folded her hand into his, as if in a silent *amen*.

After the sermon, a final hymn, and the benediction, Beth bundled up Elly for the cold outside.

"Beth." Timothy reached for Elly and ushered Beth into the aisle. "Would you accompany me to the bus station to pick up Grandmother? She should be arriving shortly, and it'll be my treat to take all my ladies out to a restaurant. There's a nice café not far from the station."

"That'd be lovely." They'd share their news over lunch—though Beth had a suspicion Mrs. McPhearson already knew. But it'd be so good to have a woman friend to ask advice of. And just to have her dear landlady back home again.

"And then we can make plans to go to Caldwell to ask your father's permission now that Grandmother will be back."

No. No. "I think we should wait." The words barreled out before any thought of trusting God had a chance to form.

"Wait for what? Why?" He stopped right in the aisle, a frown marring his face.

The church was not where she'd wanted to tell him, if ever. But he should know everything about her. "In case you change your mind."

"About what? Marrying you? Why ever would I do that?"

She edged him back into the now-empty pew. "I suppose I should tell you. We can't go to Caldwell because I can't go home."

He stared at her, his mouth opening, then closing. "Can you tell me why, sweet Beth?"

She checked that no one was close enough to hear, yet still lowered her voice. "You asked me why I didn't like working with the children at the foundling home."

He nodded.

"It's because I'm not responsible enough."

"Not responsible? You're very responsible. Taking in a baby and making sure she's cared for, working at the orphanage."

"I try to be now. I wasn't always."

"Oh, Beth. What happened?"

She ran a hand over Elly, snuggled in Timothy's arms. Swallowed. "I told you I have four younger brothers and a little sister."

Timothy nodded. "Susannah."

"Three years ago, I was still living at home. We live on a farm—my father raises pigs on a piece of the family horse ranch. My mother was helping my father with a sow giving birth and asked me to watch the children. Alfie was thirteen, so he went out to help in the barn. I watched them a lot—Susannah, who was six months old, and the other boys—three, six, and ten. I put an apple pie in the oven, and Susannah was in a basket on the floor in the kitchen, right where I could see her. That's when the boys started roughhousing."

Timothy kept quiet as Beth shared her story, but from the pained look on his face, he fully expected it to not have a good ending.

"They were out in the yard playing, and Cal came in tattling that Abe and Peter were fooling around with a rake. I stepped out on the porch and told them to come in, but they didn't listen. So I marched out into the yard to corner them. Then Cal came out on the porch and was yelling that my pie was burning. I grabbed Abe and Peter by their collars and ran back in. The kitchen was filled with smoke and Susannah was crying and coughing."

Beth stopped, and Timothy guided her onto the pew and sat beside her. "It's okay, Beth. If it's too hard to talk about, you don't have to."

She took a deep breath. No, she needed him to know no matter his reaction. And before he picked up his grandmother.

"I took pot holders and opened the oven, and the smoke just swooshed through the room. I grabbed the pie. Susannah was howling. The boys were running around the room flapping kitchen towels through the air. Our dog was barking and chasing them. And in the smoke, the chaos..." She leaned over and buried her head on her knees, and Timothy rubbed her back.

"The dog pushed one of the boys into me, and I dropped the pie."

"Oh, Beth."

Tears slid down her cheeks, and she couldn't meet Timothy's eyes. "It landed..."

"Shh. It's okay. You don't have to tell me."

She raised her head, fortifying herself for the reproach she'd see in his eyes once she got the words out. "The whole thing...went flying...right toward Susannah."

"Oh, sweet Beth." Timothy wrapped an arm around her.

"Susannah was screaming." Beth wiped her eyes. "The smoke was clearing, but everyone was yelling, and our dog was still running back and forth barking. I picked up Susannah and...and it was horrible. One side of her face and her ear were burned. She must have turned her head just in time to miss any more harm." She shuddered, and Timothy tightened his hold. "Mama came in and screamed when she saw Susannah. But she knew what to do. She told one boy to get Papa immediately and another to wet towels and another to get bandages. And me—me—" Beth's heart still ached from the loss of her relationship with Mama. "She said nothing to me. Didn't give me a task to help with. Didn't let me tell her what had happened. She just took Susannah from me."

"Ah, Beth." Timothy's sigh echoed her own of grief.

"Someone called the doctor, and he took over from Mama once he got there."

"But Susannah is fine?" Timothy asked.

Beth swiped her eyes again. "Susannah is three-and-a-half now. She's fine except for the blotches on the side of her head. Though with time, some of the angry-looking red has faded."

"Thank the Lord for that."

Beth shrugged. "Yes. But I try to be very careful with Elly when I cook or heat her milk."

"Of course. But you're brave and responsible, Beth. Elly's blessed to have you. And so is your family." He pulled her head against his shoulder. "We'll work it out."

With his eyes filled with compassion, Beth believed him. She wiped her eyes one last time and reached for Elly. "Should we go meet your grandmother now, then?"

He took her elbow and helped her stand, then led the way to the door, giving folks a nod of greeting but not stopping to talk with anyone.

They arrived at the station right as the bus was pulling in.

"Welcome home, Grandmother," Timothy called as Mrs. McPhearson stepped off, wrapping her in a big hug when she reached them.

"Indeed, it is very good to be home. Now let me give my girls both a hug too." She embraced Beth and then took Elly Rose into her arms and cooed over her. "Look how you've grown while I've been away. Do you remember me? Thank the Lord we're all back together again." She winked at Timothy. "My little family."

Beth grinned, her spirits revived, ready to burst waiting for the day when she and Elly would truly be a part of the welcoming McPhearson family.

CHAPTER 16

The next day after work, Timothy bounced up the steps when he arrived home. On the porch, he glanced at Beth's front window. No lights were on and no movement visible inside, so she must not be home yet. Or maybe she was already over at Grandmother's.

He opened Grandmother's door. "Hello. Grandmother? Anyone home?"

Grandmother hurried out from the kitchen, drying her hands on her apron, then digging into its pocket. "Here. This arrived for you today. It looks quite official, so I wanted to be sure to give it to you the moment you arrived."

She handed Timothy a V-Mail letter. His heart thumped at the return address—an APO New York address, which was expected, but with *PFC Roland Johnston* scrawled in the corner.

Perhaps this letter held the answers to his questions. His nightmares. But between the army's censorship of any location information and Roland's usual reluctance to talk, Timothy shouldn't expect much. While a letter could wind its way from Boise, across the ocean, onto the battlefield, and into the hands of a specific soldier, the sender would have no idea where the recipient was. What had he even been thinking, that somehow he could track down Roland's whereabouts? And then do what? Try to strangle the information out of him again?

At least Roland had responded.

"Thank you, Grandmother." He walked to the couch and sat, turning the letter in his hands. Was he prepared to deal with whatever was in it? Answers? The lack of information?

Sufficient unto the day is the evil thereof.

The contents were the same whether he ever opened it or not.

Lord, please prepare me. My heart.

Grandmother stood in front of him, wringing her hands. "I'll put some tea on."

Yes, maybe this time he really did need it. "Thank you."

As she headed to the kitchen, he carefully opened the sealed letter.

> To Timothy McPhearson:
> I don't know why you wrote.

Timothy could still hear the mocking in Roland's voice from the hospital bed next to his when Timothy had asked Roland what had happened. *"I don't know why you're asking me. You should be thanking me I showed up to save your sorry hide."* Timothy pushed his anger down and continued.

> I can tell you nothing about what you are asking. Just let it be. Stanley is gone and that is that. Many men from our company have died since then. I am being discharged and am returning to the States. Maybe I will be a radio operator one day. That is what I wanted to be before the war.
> Roland Johnston

Timothy stared at the letter. That was it. Nothing even

blacked out since it said nothing. But who else had died? *Please not Herb*—he was getting married when he returned home. And Gil. His girl had written him every day. She'd been wanting to marry him since elementary school. And Clarence. He was all his mother had left.

And even Roland. Had he healed and been wounded again, maybe more severely this time? Timothy hoped Roland received a medal of honor for leading the rescue of Timothy, even though he hadn't been able to save Stanley. Something horrible must have happened for Roland to close up, not wanting to talk about it. And he got that—he really did. But because Stanley had died when it should have been him—

Timothy crumpled the letter. No, he couldn't let it go. Somehow he was going to track down Roland and find out what had happened, even if it took years.

Maybe then he'd be free from the nightmares. And he'd thank Roland for trying.

"Timothy?"

"Yes, Grandmother."

"The tea is ready." Her gaze landed on the letter balled up in his hand. "Come. Beth should be here soon, and she'll appreciate warming up with the tea too."

"Didn't you watch Elly today?"

"No, not today. Beth insisted I rest up today first. Though…"

"What?"

Grandmother shrugged. "Maybe she changed her mind about me caring for Elly. It seemed like she didn't want Elly away from her."

"I'm sure she wants you to watch Elly. She knows how much you love her."

"I do. I know Elly couldn't have remembered me, but she came to me right away yesterday. We would have been fine."

"Of course you would. Probably tomorrow you'll have her all day, once she lets Mrs. Connor know you're back."

"I do hope so."

At a knock on the door, Timothy jumped up and jammed Roland's letter into his pocket. "That's probably her now. I'll let her in." He needed her arms around him, her joyous spirit to calm his pounding heart.

As soon he opened the door, she snuggled herself and Elly right into his arms, head under his chin, right where they fit perfectly together.

"What a glorious day." She tilted her head up. "And to be here with you is like the frosting on a cake—with no sugar rations."

He laughed along with her and pulled her tighter against himself, careful of Elly, who was smiling and reaching for his hair.

"Our girls are here at last." Grandmother came from behind him and clapped her hands. "Tea is brewed and ready to be poured. You and Timothy drink that while you warm up, and I'll put supper on the table. In fact, why don't the two of you drink it in here, and then I can set the table and work without getting in your way?"

Grandmother quickly brought two cups on saucers in to them. "I'll take the little one." She held out her arms, and Beth transferred Elly, who gave one of her heart-tugging smiles too. Grandmother winked, and Timothy was grateful for some time alone with Beth.

But should he tell Beth about Stanley now? About Roland and his letter? He knew the answer to both. Yet not today. This evening, he'd just enjoy his little soon-to-be family. And tomorrow he'd devise a plan to find Roland Johnston now that he'd be stateside.

But she'd shared the depths of her heart with him yesterday, even though she'd seemed reluctant, maybe even fearful in trusting him. Shouldn't he be equally trusting with her?

"Beth?"

"Yes?"

And oh the light in her eyes, filled with trust. Maybe she'd understand, help him sort things out. "Let's sit." They moved to the sofa as he felt Roland's crumpled letter in his pocket. "I received a letter from a fella in my unit in the army today."

"From a buddy?"

Not a buddy in any sense. "No. I, um, was on a mission in Germany with my friend Stanley as an advance scout. In what we thought was an abandoned apartment..."

"But it wasn't?"

"No. When Stanley and I got in there, there was a little German girl hiding under a table. She was calling for her parents, then a German soldier came in, and Stanley tried to shield the girl." Telling Beth how the man had been standing over Timothy with a rifle pointed into his chest he could skip. "A shot went off, and the doorframe splintered, so I didn't see exactly what happened, as I was injured."

"Is that what happened to your eye—a piece of the wood hit you?"

Timothy gritted his teeth, refusing to relive those days of pain, of lying in that hospital bed. "Yes. I couldn't open it at all, and there was so much pain, I could only keep my good eye open long enough for short glimpses. I had surgery, and the doctor said it'll heal. But in the meantime, mostly it's smoke that irritates it."

"And Stanley?"

Timothy was silent until he was sure his voice wouldn't wobble. "Stanley didn't make it back. That German—" He stopped himself before he said any more. But maybe sharing even this much with Beth was enough, as her eyes filled with compassion. "I'd written Roland asking about it."

"Did he tell you?" Creases wrinkled her forehead.

"No. But he's the key to my questions. He said he was coming stateside, so I hope to one day find where he is and"—

he shrugged—"maybe talk with him in person. That's what I'd really like to do."

"Did he say where he'll be living? It might be a long ways away."

"No, but if he'd talk to me, I'd travel wherever."

Beth leaned forward for her teacup and took a sip. "This is very important to you."

"It is."

"So many terrible things happen in a war. I know my papa saw plenty in the Great War. And with something that affected you so deeply... I pray you find answers. And peace."

Peace was exactly what he needed. "Thank you." So maybe that was all he needed to share for now and to hear—the fact that she did know something about the horrors of war from her father and would support his search to find his answers and pray. For without prayer, he didn't know what he'd become.

∽

Supper last night with Mrs. McPhearson and Timothy had been delightful as usual. Except for the worry or sadness that had shrouded him when he spoke of his letter from the soldier Roland. But the fact that he'd shared bits of that part of his life just endeared him yet more to Beth.

With each stroke of the cloth as Beth polished the oak furniture in Mr. and Mrs. Connor's bedroom upstairs this morning, her heart sang with joy. Every day with Timothy she grew to love him more. When the doorbell chimed downstairs, it just added a counterpoint to her song.

Now that Mrs. McPhearson was back, her presence and love filled her home. And though Timothy's eyes had seemed shadowed when Beth arrived, Mrs. McPhearson had her teakettle whistling. By the time Beth and Elly left, his usual spark was back. So maybe Mrs. McPhearson's claim to tea being the remedy to calm stressful situations was true. And starting tomorrow, Elly would stay with her all day.

A couple minutes later, footsteps scurried along the hallway, and Hilda stepped into the bedroom.

"Beth." She gasped in a breath, as though she'd run up the flight of steps. "Come downstairs. Mrs. Connor needs to see you."

Beth dropped her duster. "Is it Elly?" Already she was headed toward the door.

"No, no. She's fine. It's—just come. Quickly."

With her heart pounding, Beth followed the cook down the back staircase, practically tromping on Hilda's heels. At the bottom, Hilda pulled up short. "Catch your breath and now walk sedately."

"Yes, of course." But what if it was Elly? She needed to get to her.

Hilda escorted Beth into the sitting room where Mrs. Connor sat on the sofa with Elly on her lap. And in a chair across from her—Mrs. Garrison.

Beth contained her gasp before it echoed throughout the room. Had her feet not felt nailed to the floor, she would have run over to Mrs. Connor, scooped up Elly, and bolted down the boulevard.

"Ma'am?"

Mrs. Connor patted the cushion beside her and handed Elly to Beth once she was seated. "Louisa—Mrs. Garrison—would like to speak to you."

Beth tightened her arms around Elly. She would not give her up. "Hello, Mrs. Garrison."

"Oh, Beth." Mrs. Garrison's voice came out as stiff as her posture, and she put a hand over her mouth. "Woodrow saw you that day last week. He sent me over to verify it is you and the baby we wanted." Her shoulders shook, and she dabbed her eyes with a lacy handkerchief. "You must flee, Beth. Today."

Beth bounded to her feet with Elly, ready to do exactly that.

Mrs. Connor put a hand on her arm and gently tugged her back. "Listen to Mrs. Garrison first, Beth. Then together we'll plan what to do. Keeping Elly Rose safe is our priority."

Mrs. Garrison nodded.

"Hilda—could you please prepare coffee for us?"

Beth shook her head. There was no time for that—even Mrs. Garrison had indicated time was of the essence.

Mrs. Connor nodded to Hilda to proceed with her request. "It'll do us all good. I think we need something to warm us up and give us a moment to think the situation through. Now, Louisa, please tell Beth what you told me."

"Of course. But may I—please—hold baby Elly Rose? Just one more time?" Her voice cracked as she focused longingly on Elly.

Beth tightened her hold on the baby, but Mrs. Connor opened her arms toward Beth as if requesting permission to take Elly and lay her in Mrs. Garrison's arms. And in that moment, Beth understood. Mrs. Garrison wasn't going to grab Elly and run out the door with her and hand her over to Judge Garrison. She would protect Elly just as Beth would. This was her goodbye—not only to Elly Rose but perhaps to her dreams of ever having another baby in the house.

Beth stood, crossed the few steps to Mrs. Garrison, and laid Elly into what must be arms aching for love. "I know you wanted to love her, Mrs. Garrison. So, yes, please hold her. No one can be loved too much." Her words ended on a whisper as she witnessed another mother's breaking heart.

Mrs. Garrison's eyes filled with tears. She nodded to Beth and buried her head atop the bundle in her arms.

When Beth returned to her seat, Mrs. Connor clasped Beth's hand in her own.

Hilda brought in a tray of coffee and some kind of pastry,

which Beth wouldn't be able to take a bite of, but she accepted a cup and plate as Hilda served them.

Mrs. Connor took a sip of her coffee, then spoke to Mrs. Garrison. "Louisa, whenever you're ready."

"Yes." Mrs. Garrison lifted her gaze to Beth. "Woodrow left the house angry last Monday morning shortly before you and Hilda came over to help. I cannot thank the two of you enough for what you did for me that day. Truly. Woodrow said nothing about the ordeal that evening when he returned, nor the next day, nor the next. Not for a week. Then he announced last night after supper that he knew where he would find the child we had been denied by 'that snippet of a girl.'" Her grimace at Beth held an apology. "He told me he'd seen you walking down the street that day as he came out of the house on his way to the car picking him up. He saw that you came to this house, and he threatened my staff to reveal enough information to confirm his suspicion. He's just been biding his time, but this morning, he told me we would have our baby girl in our home within days." She burst into tears. "Beth, for the sake of Elly Rose, please run. I don't know where you can go, though. He will find you."

Beth turned to Mrs. Connor, who squeezed her hand tight.

"I believe we need to take his threat seriously. I am releasing you from your duties, as it seems best for you to leave to be safe. It's been a pleasure having you and Elly Rose in our home, and we'll miss you terribly. But as Louisa said, we will all do what we can for the sake of this precious baby."

And just like that, Beth was again jobless and possibly very soon, also homeless. But her worst nightmare had just come true. Judge Garrison would pursue her until he had what he wanted—Elly Rose.

CHAPTER 17

Timothy reached home well before dark after his day at the post office, but something wasn't right. Beth's inside lights were already on. Was she sick? Or Elly? Her side was always dark when she trekked home from the bus stop.

He hesitated at the top of the steps. Should he go on over to his side of the house—or check on her first? He wouldn't be able to do anything else until he knew they were safe, so he knocked.

Tentatively at first. After no answer, he knocked louder. Then he heard footsteps, and the door opened. Beth stood in her stocking feet, eyes red, cheeks wet, hair hanging in straggles out of her bobby pins.

"Beth, sweetheart!" He stepped inside. "What's wrong? Are you all right?" He checked around until his gaze landed on Elly on a blanket near the fireplace.

"I—I—oh, Timothy." And she was in his arms.

He guided her to the sofa and sat next to her, took her hands in his. "Tell me what happened."

"It was awful, and I don't know what to do—"

He clamped a hand over his left eye that blurred and

stabbed so he couldn't even keep it open. Only one thing still bothered it like that—smoke. He jumped up and, sure enough, smoke billowed from the kitchen with flashes of flames by the stove.

"I forgot the milk!" Beth took two steps toward the kitchen, and Timothy yanked her back.

Maybe it was small now, but small fires turned into raging ones that killed. For all he knew, it could've been milk on a stove that flamed into a building fire that took the lives of a whole floor of apartment occupants, along with his parents.

"Grab Elly and get out. I'll take care of it." If he could even get in there.

"But you can't see!"

"Never mind." He gave Beth a push toward Elly. "Go!"

Beth grabbed Elly, who was now crying with all the commotion, and Timothy mostly felt his way into the kitchen. He turned off the stove flame and wadded a towel to shove the boiled-over milk pot off the burner. But a potholder near the burner was on fire, and there was nothing nearby to use to get it to the floor or over to the sink. And every moment, the smoke and flames grew.

He ran to the front door and barely made it out, coughing and doubled over, holding his eye that felt like it, too, was on fire. "I'll get Grandmother out. Go to a neighbor's and call the fire department."

"Elly's locket! I have to save it for her—it's all she has left of her heritage!"

"No—don't go back in there."

"I have to!" She held Elly toward him.

"I'll get it. Where is it?" If only he could get a wet towel over his eye. He grabbed her arm to break the hysteria clouding her own eyes, forcing her to focus. "Where, Beth?"

"In my top bureau drawer in a box. Wrapped in the baby gown she arrived in. Please save that too."

"Get Grandmother out and away from the house, and have someone call the fire department." Timothy reentered the house. He had to do this for Beth, for Elly.

Please, Lord, help.

He felt his way to Beth's room down the hall, shoving aside the awkwardness of entering her bedroom. Thankfully, the bureau was near the door. He edged in, opened the top drawer, and half saw, half felt a rolled-up baby gown and withdrew it. A box fell from the folds onto the floor, and a locket tumbled out. He picked up the heart shape and staggered out of the house with the items clutched in his hand. Once on the porch, he bent over the rail, taking deep breaths of the less-smoky air.

In the sunlight, he squinted open his good eye enough to see Beth, Elly, and Grandmother safely on the McHenrys' porch next door. With intermittent peeks down at Grandmother's own porch when he could open his one eye, Timothy found some clean-looking snow under the railing. He scooped a handful into Elly's gown, and the locket fell onto the porch boards. Once he plastered the snowpack against his left eye and got some relief, he bent and picked up Elly's necklace. On the front was an inscription he could make out now. *Psalm 107:2–3.* Verses he knew, the verses right before the ones Stanley had made him memorize. The ones he'd been reading recently to add to his memorized portion. *Let the redeemed of the* Lord *say so, whom he hath redeemed from the hand of the enemy, and gathered them out of the lands, from the east, and from the west, from the north, and from the south.*

He turned the locket over. And stared at the word on the back. A German word he recognized.

Liebe.

Love.

He shut his eyes, and the face of that German with the scar jamming the rifle into his chest filled his vision, even with his eyes closed tight. The injustices of war. The anguish over Stanley. The rage in his heart.

No. No, God, no. Sweet little Elly—the baby girl he loved, the daughter of the woman he wanted to marry—was German? Was that why the German woman with the little boy had been watching Beth and sneaking around? Was she Elly's mother?

He sank onto the snow-covered porch, the locket sliding through his fingers. Pain sliced through him, stabbing his heart much worse than his eye.

"Timothy!"

"Timothy!"

He couldn't separate the voices. Beth? Grandmother? A man's voice?

Someone tugged him so he was half sitting, half leaning against the railing. A hand removed the ice-cold gown from his eye and pressed something warm against it. Finally, he was able to crack his good eye open a bit, as it was irritated from the heavy smoke almost as much as his other one. Grandmother stood over him as firemen going in and out of the house tried to shoo her away.

"Are you all right, Timothy?" Grandmother bent beside him. "You gave us quite a scare."

"Indeed, you did." Beth was now kneeling next to him.

Where was Elly? He squinted around but didn't see her.

"I'm so sorry, Timothy." Beth's voice caught. "I never should have placed so much value on Elly's belongings. But thank you. It'll mean a lot to her someday when I tell her her story." She opened her hand and exposed the silver heart she must have picked up.

That condemning locket he'd forged through the smoke for —only to salvage the confirmation that Elly was German.

∼

Where was Elly? Had Judge Garrison snatched her in the commotion?

Beth took her eyes off Timothy to look around. Mrs. McPhearson was here on the porch. Mr. and Mrs. McHenry from next door, where they'd waited, were now standing by the fence separating their properties. But no Elly. In the yard, a crowd had gathered, and Beth searched the congregants one by one. Elly wasn't among them either.

"Mrs. McPhearson." Beth tried to keep her voice down so as not to alarm her, but her pitch was too high, too panicked. "Where's Elly Rose?"

Mrs. McPhearson's eyes widened. "Elly? I handed her to Mrs. McHenry."

"Mrs. McHenry!" Beth stumbled over to her standing near her fence. The lady's arms were empty. "Who has Elly?"

"Your friend asked if she could help by holding her. I was sure you wouldn't mind."

"My friend?" Beth grabbed the fence to support her legs before they gave out.

"Yes. I've seen her come over several times. The lady with a little boy. She wears a black head scarf and a long brown overcoat."

No! Oh, no, no, no! But at least not Judge Garrison.

Tears scalded her eyes. "I don't see her now. Do you know where she went?" How far away had the lady gotten with Elly? How much of a head start?

"I'm so sorry if I shouldn't have let her hold Elly. I'm sure she's fine, though."

"I don't even know the lady!"

"She said she'd wait for you around the house and watch Elly until you came."

Beth ran around the corner—and there was Elly, cradled in the scarfed lady's arms. The woman huddled on the ground with her back against the house. She hugged Elly as she swayed side to side, talking softly to her. Elly Rose was smiling up at her. The little boy stood over them, cooing to the baby, imitating his mother.

At Beth's appearance, the woman stilled. She turned her head away from Elly and coughed into her coat sleeve, leaving a splotch of wetness on the fabric. Her eyes were dark and hollow, yet they held a gentleness.

"We meet finally. I am Anneliese." The words were spoken with a heavy German accent. She attempted to stand, but her legs seemed to buckle under her midway up.

Beth sat down next to her in the snow. Her heart wanted to snatch Elly away from the lady, but the longing—love?—in Anneliese's eyes as she hugged Elly and then the little boy stopped her. "Are you her mother?"

Anneliese squeezed her eyes closed. When she opened them, she shook her head. "You are."

"Why me?" Beth asked softly.

Anneliese again turned her head and coughed. "I can keep little ones no longer. They need good home. You are good. I watch you at the orphanage. I trust you."

Beth cast her gaze down as she fumbled for words. And that's when she saw the bright red drops staining the snow. And knew what the wetness on Anneliese's coat from the coughing was. Blood. "You're ill."

Tears filled Anneliese's eyes, and she nodded. "The *kinder* need a home. And liebe. Love. You do that."

"I named her Elizabeth Rose. I call her Elly."

Anneliese's eyes brightened. "I name her Lisbet. Elizabeth. Same name."

"Yes, the same in both languages." Beth touched Anneliese's arm, her gauntness apparent even through the worn wool sleeve. "You must come with me. Stay with me while you get well."

"*Nein*. I will...not get better. Please. You must take my Nicholas too." She pulled the boy close to her side.

"What?"

"I am dying. Please care for both my children. I must know they are safe." She coughed again into her coat sleeve. The hacking seemed to have drained her energy by the time she quieted. She clasped Beth's hand and tightened her grip. "Please. Care for Nicholas. He is good boy. I will miss *meine kinder*. But to know they are safe with you will give me comfort."

Nicholas clung to his mother as if he'd never let go. But Beth had no means now to support even herself and Elly.

"Where is your husband?"

The tears now slid down Anneliese's cheeks. "Dead. My husband was American. When Wesley was sent to war, he moved us in with his parents. They were ashamed of me because my parents are from Germany. They think I am enemy. I stayed because Wesley wanted us there. He said we were safe. When he was killed in Germany, his parents sent us away. They do not want Germans in their home. They say we are German and Germans killed their son."

"But they would want to help raise your children—their own son's children—wouldn't they?"

A quick jerk of her head was her answer. "They wish no part of us. We are buried to them as is their son."

Beth couldn't take on another child. Neither could she abandon Elly's brother. Or leave a little boy an orphan when Anneliese died. For if she had what Beth thought the blood and coughing must be—tuberculosis—then surely, she would die without care. Timothy would agree, wouldn't he? He'd love Nicholas the way he did Elly.

She squeezed Anneliese's hand. "I promise. I will care for and love both of your children."

"Thank you. You are good woman." Anneliese pulled her

hand away and kissed Elly—her Lisbet—on the head, then ran her hand over the baby's fine blond hair. The pain in her eyes radiated that this was her last touch of her precious girl. "*Auf wiedersehen,* meine liebe. Goodbye, my love." She passed Elly into Beth's arms and with a hand on the house for balance, she stood. "Nicholas." She drew the boy into a tight embrace. "My Nicholas. I will miss you so. I love you."

"Mama!"

Beth stood up with Elly, ready in case Anneliese toppled over.

Anneliese put her hands on either side of Nicholas's face. "Be strong and brave for your new mama, ja?"

"Ja, Mama." He wrapped his arms around her and held on. "Please, Mama, do not go! Please!"

"I must, little one. I need you to take good care of Lisbet for me. Understand?"

Tears trickled down his face. "Ja."

"She won't remember me, and Papa did not get to see her, but you must tell her how much we loved both of you. Will you do that?"

"Ja, Mama."

"Oh, Nicholas. My sweet, sweet boy." She hugged him tight. "Now you will be American and must speak English in your new home, like Papa did. Yes?"

He leaned his head against her as his shoulders shook.

"Oh, how can I let you go?" But she did, and placed his hand into Beth's. Anneliese handed a tattered black suitcase lying on the ground to him. "Goodbye, my sweet kinder. Goodbye." With her hacking cough returning and doubling her over, she turned and fled around the corner of the house.

"Mama!"

Beth tightened her hold on the little boy's hand.

"Mama! Mama! Come back!" He stared in the direction she had run.

"Oh, Nicholas." Beth's own eyes burned as tears and confusion filled his. "Come. We will go back to my house. Our house. You'll live with your sister, Elly, and me. Just like your mama wanted you to do."

"Yes."

"Can you carry your suitcase by yourself?"

In answer, he hefted it higher against his side. All of what was left of his life as he'd known it fit inside. Were there any letters from his father? Toys? If he even owned any.

"Mama?"

"She loves you, Nicholas, but she had to go away. She wants me to care for you and Elly. We will help her by doing so, yes?"

He stared in the direction his mother had gone, and Beth's heart broke for these little ones. The two children God had given her.

Beth had been gone no more than a few minutes, but the crowd in the front yard had already dispersed when she reached it. Mrs. McHenry ran to Beth. "You found Elly! Thank the good Lord!" She pointed at Nicholas carrying the suitcase, still holding Beth's hand. "Who's that?"

"Elly was fine, just like you said. Excuse me, though, as I need to get the children out of the cold."

"But who is he?"

"We can talk later. I need to get them warm." She headed up her porch with her two little ones.

A fireman blocked Beth's door. "Ma'am, you can't go in there. There is some fire damage in the kitchen and too much smoke still—especially for a baby and the little boy to be breathing it."

"But—"

"I could perhaps allow you to go in to pack a bag, but not the children."

Where were Mrs. McPhearson and Timothy? She'd leave Elly and Nicholas with no one else at the moment. But she didn't see either one of them. She turned to the fireman. "The man who was on the porch—"

"The one with some eye problem?"

"Yes. Do you know what happened to him? And the older woman who was here?"

"They went into the other side of the house."

"Thank you." Beth walked over to the other door and knocked. She rocked from one foot to the other, bracing herself. She was being silly—there was nothing to fear. When Timothy saw Nicholas and she explained the story, of course, he'd open his arms and heart to him since he already loved Elly.

Mrs. McPhearson opened the door, questions gathering in her eyes at the sight of Nicholas. "And who do we have here, little man?"

"This is Nicholas."

"Welcome, Nicholas." She stepped aside and waved them in. "Come in, come in. Timothy is in the kitchen."

They went to the kitchen, where Timothy sat at the table holding a folded kitchen towel over his left eye and a cup of tea in the other hand.

"Timothy"—Beth urged the little boy forward—"this is Nicholas, and—"

Nicholas dropped his suitcase and ran straight to Timothy.

Timothy stopped mid-sip and set his cup down, his uncovered eye wide.

"My, my." Mrs. McPhearson beamed. "He's certainly taken with you already, Timothy. Or maybe he just knows a good man when he sees one."

Nicholas's eyes shone—with recognition?—as he smiled at Timothy. "Cookie Man!"

CHAPTER 18

What was the little German boy doing here? Timothy set the damp towel down. He didn't spot the mother behind Beth and Grandmother, so apparently, he was with Beth. With a suitcase, which meant what—that he was staying?

Why, oh why?

Except, even without the details, deep inside he knew. Beth had taken the boy in too. Because that was Beth—caring, loving, compassionate.

Timothy made no move to embrace the boy. "Grandmother, do we have something for him to eat?" That was the most he could muster.

"Yes, yes, of course." Grandmother hastened to the counter and pulled out a plate for something—probably the still-warm blueberry pie they were going to have after supper. "Nicholas, eat this pie for now with a glass of milk. I'll have supper on the table in a bit. This should hold you over until then. We'll get you filled up."

His eyes, a lighter blue than Elly's, lit up. Timothy pulled a chair out with his foot for the boy.

"Danke."

"English, Nicholas," Beth prompted him.

"Thank you."

Though his mind was full of questions, Timothy couldn't look at Beth. The story of how she came to have both children now didn't matter. She was good and kind. And he wasn't. It was as simple as that.

He wouldn't even give her an ultimatum like Lawrence had. How could he? He already knew what her choice would be. He was just as callous as Lawrence. Except worse. For Timothy had made promises to her, both in words and in his kisses. He'd promised that he'd care for and love both her and Elly. And if Elly, then, of course, Nicholas too.

But now he couldn't. Of course he knew the children were not to blame in any way. But the face of that soldier standing over him would not go away. What if he always saw that man whenever he looked at these innocent little ones? Always remembered?

It was best if he just left, for he could not keep any of his promises, all because of his hardened, wretched heart.

"Timothy." Maybe Grandmother had already called his name, for he felt her and Beth's eyes on him.

"Yes?"

"Please take their coats if you're able. They'll swelter in here all bundled up like that."

That at least he could do. He stood and helped Beth and the boy out of their coats and hung them on the coat-tree.

Beth was shaking her head when he returned. "No, thank you. I'll wait for supper."

As expected, Grandmother had extended an invitation to them. If he left the table and packed his duffel bag now, that'd be downright rude. At least he owed Beth the chance to explain.

"Timothy." Beth turned to him. "Is your eye feeling better now?"

"It'll be fine. The doctor said smoke would irritate it for a while." She'd probably been terrified seeing him helpless like that with not being able to see. Shouldn't his eye be better by now, though? Or maybe the surgery hadn't been as successful as the doctor had hoped, and he'd always have this weakness.

She wouldn't want him, anyway. Not once she figured out his vengeful heart toward Germans. She'd manage just fine with two children, and some man truly worthy of her heart would come along someday. That thought alone—her in the arms of another man, Elly and Nicholas having someone else as their father—almost took the breath from him.

"You're so brave, so sweet, Timothy. I know the locket and gown are just things, but they're all Elly has left of her life before...before..." She broke off in a sob. And though he yearned to wrap her in his arms, it was Grandmother who did so when he didn't budge.

Beth wiped her eyes. "When I couldn't find Elly, Mrs. McHenry told me a lady had asked to hold her in the commotion and would wait for me around the corner of the house. When I got there, there she was with Elly and Nicholas."

"Elly's—mother?" Grandmother asked.

"Yes."

"Do you think..." His grandmother nodded at Nicholas.

"That she wants them back? Of course, she does. But she cannot. She's—" Beth also glanced at Nicholas, as if choosing her words carefully in front of him. "She's ill, coughing up blood."

A sure sign of tuberculosis. Had the blood he'd seen in the snow been hers, not Nicholas's? Timothy exchanged a nod with Grandmother. A death warrant, surely.

"She begged me to take Nicholas." Beth wrapped an arm around his small shoulders. "Her parents were from Germany, but her husband was an American. A soldier, killed by Germans. Anneliese—that's her name—and the children lived with her husband's parents while he was overseas. But when he was killed, they no longer wanted them living there. His own family was now the enemy in his parents' eyes."

Her gaze landed on Timothy. Did she already see his hardened heart? Already know he'd seen the German word on Elly's necklace? Or know he was just as guilty as Elly and Nicholas's grandparents? Maybe not yet, for she continued.

"Do you know what Anneliese had named Elly? Lisbet. And she begged me to take Nicholas too. Everything he owns is in his tattered suitcase." Beth pointed to it, still on the floor where Nicholas had dropped it. "How could I refuse her last wish? To give her comfort that her children were taken care of? Loved?"

Oh, the word stabbed Timothy's heart.

"You could do nothing less, dear." Grandmother stroked Nicholas's hair. While still chewing his pie, he gave a small smile. "Beth, your side of the house is too smoky for you and the children. You will stay here."

A flash of longing, then panic flitted through her eyes. "I can't. There's something I need to—"

"Nonsense. There's plenty of room in the section over your half of the house. It's been in disuse for years, ever since I converted the house back from the boardinghouse. I do think I can find you enough items here so you needn't go back there today."

"But—"

"No arguments."

Beth opened her mouth with apparently another one, then seemed to accept Grandmother's edict. After all, where else would she go?

Timothy still didn't say anything, just watched Nicholas. He seemed like a nice kid, a good big brother to Elly. A good son to Beth. If Anneliese lived with her husband's parents while he was alive, she must have been welcomed into the family at some point. And given them two lovely grandchildren. None of this made sense. If they'd already been in the grandparents' hearts, what were they doing now on the streets? Rage—and grief—showed itself in ugly ways, as he well knew.

If not for the fact of them being part German, Timothy would have loved this boy too.

But the children would be safe here with Beth and Grandmother.

～

*M*aybe Beth hadn't tried hard enough to tell Timothy and Mrs. McPhearson about Judge Garrison. But was it wrong to enjoy one more night with the people she loved? If the judge hadn't shown up yet and her side of the house was dark, surely they'd all be safe until the morning. Where could she even go tonight with two children in the cold?

Beth's heart filled with love for each cherished one around the table whom God had placed in her life. Elly, Nicholas, Mrs. McPhearson. Her gaze lingered last on Timothy. He was so courageous and loving, so much like her own father, the way he'd sacrificed for Elly to have something meaningful of her history.

Then there was the way Nicholas had run to him, calling him Cookie Man. Had Timothy met or even fed the poor boy at some point? With a rare treat, no less—and most likely his mother, too, as the two were always together. Kindness was embedded in his heart. Yes, Timothy could act no other way. Even the way he studied Nicholas now—head tilted, eyes clouding, clearing, clouding again—as if the boy were a puzzle.

He pushed his chair back and stood. "Grandmother, let me help dish up supper."

Beth's heart thumped quicker at his sweet offer. See? Kindness.

Yet his movements were quick, mechanical, as if he were in a hurry. But a small roast and carrots and potatoes and hot rolls were on the table within minutes. After a prayer of blessing, even Nicholas, after his generous slice of pie, dug in. The poor boy was probably half starved.

When his plate was as bare as if he'd licked it clean, Nicholas cocked his head at Timothy. "Are you my new papa?"

Timothy's mouth opened, and his eyes filled with—

Not tears. What had flickered in his eyes? Something cold.

A shudder lightninged through her. Had she imagined it? No—for Mrs. McPhearson was staring at him now, too, her brow puckered.

His answer came out as a croak. "No."

No? That was true for now, but his tone sounded like *never.*

Nicholas blinked.

Timothy cleared his throat. "I'm not married to Beth—your new mama—so...so... No." He stood and grabbed plates off the table and ran water for the dishes. All the while, Beth and his grandmother stared at his back, then each other.

Beth stood and walked to the sink. "I'll help."

"No. I mean, that's all right—I'll do this. You and Grandmother take the children into the other room. Maybe...you could read to Nicholas."

"Are there any children's books here he might like?"

"No."

He turned to her, and now tears filmed his eyes. Or maybe she was looking through her own tears. Because something was wrong.

Very wrong.

Mrs. McPhearson took Elly and held out her hand for Nicholas. She nodded for Beth to stay and left the room quietly with the children.

Timothy took Beth's hands, and now that she was this close, those were definitely tears in his eyes. "Beth."

"Timothy, what's wrong? Please tell me."

He moved his hands up her arms, gripping them, yet not pulling her closer. "I love you, Beth. And—"

"I love you, too, Timothy."

"But—"

And there it was. *But*. Beth pulled out of his grasp and stepped back. "But?"

He reached for her again, and she backed up more.

"What is it? Just say it. Apparently, you don't think your love is enough to cover whatever problems we'll encounter." And he didn't even yet know what she was facing.

He dipped his head as if he couldn't bear to meet her eyes. "I have to leave."

She gasped. Tried to comprehend what he was saying. "Leave? Where? Why?" Was he moving and thinking she wouldn't follow, that her heart was tied to this house in Boise? She was the one who needed to leave. If she told him now, would that even change anything?

But he didn't volunteer any more, and she wouldn't beseech his help if his mind was made up and he didn't trust her with his plans. Or worse, with his heart.

Now she had two children to care for, no income, no one to share her burdens with. And after tomorrow, nowhere to hide.

CHAPTER 19

An early-March snow floated down the next morning when Beth descended the stairs.

Mrs. McPhearson stood at the front window with the curtain pulled back. "He left."

The words were nails into Beth's heart. "Already?" He must have snuck out in the early dawn, as his boot imprints across the porch were nearly covered. Beth put an arm around Mrs. McPhearson. "I need to tell you what happened at Mrs. Connor's house yesterday. Judge Garrison discovered I'd been working right next door, and he's determined to get Elly. I need to take the children and leave."

"Where will you go?"

"I'll find a place. But we can't stay here."

"Oh, Beth." Mrs. McPhearson sagged against her. "When?"

"This morning."

"Let me fix a good breakfast first. You and Nicholas will need your strength."

"I'll get them up and ready."

Mrs. McPhearson dragged around, her smile lacking, her eggs burned by the time she served them. Nicholas didn't seem to mind, wolfing down whatever food was set in front of him.

If Beth didn't have Elly's and Nicholas's needs to tend to, she'd be curled in a ball upstairs sobbing.

She'd trusted Timothy. Loved him. Let herself believe him and his words of love. The promises he'd imparted through his kisses. But she'd learned about real love from Papa's story in pursuing Mama while trying to make the Calloway name stand for something good.

Love didn't abandon.

Love pursued.

"Beth." Mrs. McPhearson broke the silence. "I'm going to the market to send you off with a packed basket before you leave."

She'd decline, except it'd be foolish to leave with no food for the children. "I can go. It'll be slippery out."

"No." She searched Beth's eyes. "I need to go out. To see the snow covering the muddied steps of the past and creating a clean slate for a new path gives me hope."

Yes, Beth understood that. "Please be careful. If something happened to you—"

"Shh, dear. We'll make it through. We will, once our hearts mend."

Beth wasn't sure about that, but she gave a respectful nod. "Hurry, though. We need to be on our way as soon as we can."

After Mrs. McPhearson left, Beth heated milk for Elly and fed her. Elly quickly fell asleep in her arms, and Nicholas curled up next to Beth on the couch. Their bags were packed and ready to be brought down as soon as Mrs. McPhearson returned.

Outside, the rumbling of a car broke the silence. It motored along, then slowed, as if the driver was unsure where to stop. Beth reached over and pulled back a corner of the curtain and peeked out. The car was stopping in front of the house. Maybe

Timothy had returned in a cab? The driver came around to one of the back passenger doors and opened it. Some dignitary arriving to visit someone or to ask directions, perhaps? Then the occupant got out. A man.

Beth's heart thudded. No—Judge Garrison! And he was motioning to this house. It was no wonder he'd tracked her down, but she'd never seen him leave his house this early.

"Shh." She held a finger to her mouth as she spoke to Nicholas. "We're going outside. Get your coat." She grabbed her coat, purse, and Elly's bottle. Quickly, she bundled Elly in her blanket and grabbed a heavier one draping a chair. "Very quietly so we don't wake Elly."

Nicholas nodded, alarm settling in his eyes, as if he already knew about running and hiding and staying quiet.

"Out the back door." She led the way out the door and shut it behind them just as the doorbell rang. Maybe she could cut through the McHenrys' yard and wait there until Mrs. McPhearson returned and Judge Garrison left. But if he saw them, would he take Nicholas too? Or separate them since he didn't want an older child? Beth wasn't going to let him have either one. She'd promised Anneliese.

She peeked around the corner of Mrs. McHenry's house. Mrs. McPhearson was coming up the sidewalk with her shopping basket on her arm. But from the porch, Judge Garrison had also seen Mrs. McPhearson and descended the steps to meet her, a big grin on his face, arm extended to take her load.

Beth grabbed Nicholas's hand and tugged him back close against the house. "Shh." Now she couldn't warn Mrs. McPhearson. Couldn't go back and write a note or even tell her where they'd be—for she had no idea where they could go.

"Good day, ma'am." The judge tipped his hat to Mrs. McPhearson, his voice carrying around the corner of the McHenrys' house.

Beth put her finger to her lips to remind Nicholas to stay still and quiet. *Please let Elly keep sleeping.*

She pointed to the yard behind the McHenrys'. "Come," she whispered. Ducking her head against Elly's blanket, Nicholas in tow, she ran through yards, alongside houses, until she reached a cleared side street where their footprints wouldn't leave a glaring trail in the snow.

Once they reached the back of the market, Beth crouched in the snow, tears brewing. She had nothing for the children. No clothes. No food. Elly was wide awake and crying from the jostling. Nicholas's lips trembled, though he made no sound, probably from being trained to be silent while hiding. She opened her purse and counted her coins. She only had enough for bus fare, which would take her only as far as—the orphanage!

"If you ever need help or need milk for Elly, come here. I will not abide even one child who has been under this roof going hungry."

Mrs. Martin would help her.

"Hold on, little ones," Beth whispered to Elly and Nicholas. "I know where to go for food."

Whether Nicholas understood her words or not, he clasped her hand tighter. *Oh Lord, may it be true.*

Surely, the bus driver would let Nicholas on for free. She had no idea if children paid or not—only that the driver had never required anything for Elly.

The bus finally lumbered up the street and pulled to a stop.

Lord, please. This is all I know to do. Our only chance—unless You intervene.

"Miss." The regular driver tipped his head in recognition of her and a puzzled look at Nicholas, as if wondering where this second child had come from.

And—*oh, thank You, Lord*—not one word about extra fare.

Beth and the children got off at the stop near the foundling home. Nicholas headed right down the street, leading the way to the orphanage. Of course, he knew where they were going, as he'd been here with Anneliese.

But as he headed for the front door, Beth pulled him back. "Wait." Who was working there now at her old desk? What if—would Judge Garrison be so devious as to pay someone here to inform him if Beth ever returned with Elly? "Let's go to the back door. By the kitchen."

They rounded the side of the building and headed to the kitchen. Nicholas stayed close alongside the walls, without being told. Sticking her head up just far enough to see in, Beth peeked into a kitchen window. Pearl was at the stove, stirring a wooden spoon in the tall soup pot. A cleaning lady came in with her mop and bucket and set to work.

"Come on, please hurry," Beth whispered. Nicholas stood silently beside her, a question in his blue eyes. "No, sweetie, not you. We need to wait for the cook to be alone before I knock on the door."

He nodded.

Before the lady was finished, two nurses came in, tiptoeing across the wet floor, and smiled at Pearl as they held out bowls. They finally left, then came a nurse with one of the babies. The little one that came the same day she'd first brought Elly?

They left, and finally, Pearl was alone. Beth raised her hand to rap on the window when in walked another nurse.

Mitzi?

Beth checked again. Yes. She knocked on the glass, and Mitzi and the cook both jumped and turned toward the window. Recognition hit them at the same time, and Mitzi hurried over to the door and opened it.

"Beth! Whatever are you doing out here? Elly—and—" Her gaze landed on Nicholas, and she pulled them all in as Pearl bustled over.

"Shh," Beth said. "I need help."

"What—"

"Can you get Mrs. Martin? We need food and—"

"That I can take care of." Pearl took Nicholas's hand. "I'll feed him. Mitzi, you take Elly like you're just carrying one of the babies here and go get Mrs. Martin."

Mitzi reached for Elly, humming to her as she hurried out of the kitchen.

"Mercy, girl," Pearl said. "We sure miss you and little Elly around here. That new girl can't type a lick. And she never visits back here. She brings her own lunch." She sniffed. "And now you have yourself another sweet little one? The Lord bless you, dear." She ladled two bowls of thin soup and held them out to Beth and Nicholas, then cut two larger-than-normal chunks of bread and put a dab of butter on them. "Fill yourself up, little man."

Nicholas sought Beth's approval with a lift of his brows. She nodded, and he smiled and dug in.

The kitchen door swung open, and Mrs. Martin entered, Mitzi and Elly right behind her.

"I'll hold Elly Rose." Mrs. Martin took Elly from Mitzi. "You stand at the door and don't let *anyone* come through."

"Yes, ma'am." Mitzi set up her guard position the other side of the door.

"Now, Beth," Mrs. Martin said, "tell me what you need and what's going on. I will help however I can."

As Beth told her story, Mrs. Martin's face paled. "My. Oh my. This is beyond what I feared. Now, how can we help? Food, of course. What else? Where will you go?"

Beth had thought and thought about that. She had no money with her, nowhere to go—except—

"My family's farm in Caldwell."

"Splendid. Wait here, and I'll get you some money for train fare. You must leave immediately." She slipped out of the room, and Mitzi peeked in quickly.

"All's well out here," she whispered.

Pearl busied herself with packing bread and cheese and apples—probably her own lunch or some for the nurses—and pouring soup into a jar and milk into Elly's bottle. "There." She handed a bulging flour sack to Beth.

"Psst." Mitzi motioned from the door. "Mrs. Martin found these for you to take for Elly." She handed Beth a baby gown and some clean rags that could be used for diapers. "And for the little boy." She held up a shirt and pants that Nicholas, being small, might fit into. "She found these in a closet."

Beth added them to her bag as Mrs. Martin returned. "Take this." She handed Beth several dollar bills—certainly not money from the orphanage, as they barely managed.

"Mrs. Martin—"

"Take it for the children. They need it more than I need a new dress. Mitzi will escort you to the train station and make sure you're all onboard. What else can I do?"

"Please get word to Mrs. McPhearson that we're safe—but don't tell her where we are. She'll be safer from Judge Garrison if she doesn't know."

"Yes, yes, of course. We'll be the only ones who know. Godspeed, Beth. May He watch over you and your children." With an unexpected hug, Mrs. Martin pushed them through the back door.

~

Beth clustered her children—yes, her very own children—to her outside the Caldwell train depot. At last, they were safe. Papa would have come to pick them up if he'd known, but there'd been no time to call before the train pulled in at the Boise station and Mitzi pushed them onboard. No phone call or wire also meant no trail of where they were going, not even through the purchase of the tickets, which Mitzi had handled.

Beth gulped a deep breath. Yes, she, the prodigal, would be returning along with two children.

"Mama?"

Oh, sweet Nicholas. Already he'd accepted that she was now his mother. She bent to look him in the eye on his level. "Yes, sweet boy?"

"I am hungry again."

"Of course, you are." The food in the flour sack was dwindling fast, Elly's milk completely gone. She calculated the remaining money in her purse. Maybe enough for a taxi or definitely enough for extra food. But not for both. If she could get home, Mama would welcome and feed the children. But if she was not welcomed back, she had no money for a return trip to—anywhere, really. "Would you like a bit of cheese?"

"Yes, Mama."

She reached into the flour sack and pulled out the last piece. "When we get to the ranch, my mama will feed you a feast."

He smiled as he took the cheese.

"Need a taxi, ma'am?" A scraggly-bearded driver leaning against a cab parked along the curb called over to Beth.

She stepped closer. "What is the fare to the Calloway Ranch—part of the Double E—on the outskirts of town?"

"For how many?" He straightened, maybe trying to look more professional.

"The three of us."

"Hmm. You related to the Calloways?"

"Yes, I'm the oldest of their children."

He scrunched up his face, as if trying to place her and the children. "Do you have luggage?"

"No."

"Well, get in."

"How much is the fare?" Beth asked again, as she would not be taken advantage of.

"Lizzie and Josiah are good people. Your grandparents, Eliza and Caleb, too. Just get in. I'll take you to them. If these are their grandchildren, I would've thought they'd be here with the whole swarm of kids to meet you." He shrugged. "Hope they're okay. Let's get going."

If he knew her parents and grandparents, he must be okay. And a free ride? "Okay. Thank you." She climbed in with Elly and Nicholas.

After the drive out of town, the taxi driver pulled into the pig farm and all that was familiar to Beth. Her family now lived in the original Double E white farmhouse with the wide front porch, and Grandma Eliza and Grandpa Caleb had moved to the smaller house that was the Calloway Ranch homestead when Mama and Papa had married. The red barn gleamed of fresh paint, and Bitterbrush, Mama's horse, stood by the paddock fence. "Thank you."

"My pleasure. Tell Lizzie and Josiah that Fred says hello. Eliza and Caleb too."

"I will." She got out with the children and closed the door, and the driver headed back down the driveway.

And there she stood in the yard with two children. No one came running out to greet her. Not even Kep the Fourth, the ranch dog. All was strangely quiet.

"Let's go inside, shall we? I promised you a feast of my mama's cooking."

His eyes grew wide at the pigs snorting and grunting in a pen and chickens strolling around the yard—sights and sounds he'd most likely never known before. His gaze lingered on Bitterbrush, who tossed his thick brown mane. He would love Kep the Fourth, whose name was passed down through generations of the family's original herding dog. Maybe one day she could buy Nicholas a dog all his own.

Beth led the way up the porch steps to the kitchen door. Locked. Why? Someone was almost always home except for church days. And with so many people coming and going and Kep here to guard the ranch, anyway, the door was never locked.

"Let's check out the barn, shall we?"

The door was closed, and the few horses inside whinnied and jostled in their stalls as Beth and the children entered. "Hello? Anyone here?" Where was everybody? She turned to Nicholas. "Would you like to see the bunkhouse?"

His eyes brightened, as if they were on an adventure.

Once they traipsed to the building, she knocked on the door and creaked it open when there was no answer. "Hello?" She waited a moment in the silence. "Huh. Grandma Eliza and Grandpa Caleb—maybe they're at their house." Though Grandpa should be in the barn working on crafting his saddles and Grandma in the paddock training horses. But they weren't inside their house either.

"Mama, where is the feast?"

"Oh, Nicholas." Beth drew him close. "I don't know where everyone is. Let's wait for them on the porch, shall we? Then we'll see them coming down the driveway. And when they do, my mama will find you plenty to eat."

She led him back to the porch and swiped snow off the two rocking chairs. "One for you, Nicholas, and one for me and Elly."

Elly cried, as of course she was hungry, wet, and cold. Nicholas didn't mention food again, but he no longer showed interest in watching the animals. Hunger surely gnawed his stomach now, as it did hers. She handed him the last of the food Pearl had packed.

After another ten minutes, Beth stood. "Nicholas, let's wait with the horses in the barn." She needed to get the children where it was warmer. Her family wasn't here, and that was that. She had to figure out how to care for these two in the meantime.

"Mama, I am—"

"I know, sweet boy." Whatever it was—hungry, scared, sad—she was too. "I know." And pigs and chickens and horses couldn't take any of that away. "Maybe we'll find a carrot in the barn that the horses will share."

Beth took them back inside the barn and found an empty stall filled with fresh hay. She huddled in the corner and settled Elly in her lap and pulled Nicholas close next to her. Body heat and the heavy extra blanket would help to keep them warm, but there was no food here. Not even the hoped-for carrot.

After a while, Elly and Nicholas dozed off, and all was quiet in the barn, even the horses. Until a bark came from outside. Kep? She sat up. Yes—he was barking at the barn door. The door squeaked and grated as someone slid it open, then walked across the floor. Papa? If so, his limp was barely discernible. With barks of excitement, not ones of warning, Kep ran ahead down the wide aisle, and Nicholas roused, clinging tightly to her arm.

Then Kep burst into the stall, with Papa right behind him.

"Bethy!" Papa's brown eyes and arms both opened wide, welcoming her home. She scrambled up—Elly against her, Nicholas behind her—right into his embrace. "You're home! Our sweet Bethy."

"Papa!"

He finally pulled apart and took in Elly. "And who is this?"

"Elizabeth Rose—Elly Rose. Her mother left her on my porch during a winter storm a few weeks ago."

He blinked but said nothing.

"And she asked me to raise her."

He showed no surprise at that part either. Then, "Welcome, Elly Rose. Welcome to the family." He grinned, and his gaze settled on Nicholas.

"Papa, this is Nicholas. Elly's brother."

In a moment, understanding flashed through her father's

eyes, and he bent and pulled Nicholas into a hug. "We welcome you to the family, too, Nicholas. We're glad to have you and your sister with us. Say, you look like a growing boy. Would you like to come inside for something to eat?"

Nicholas's blue eyes grew wide, and he nodded.

"And where it's warm." Papa turned to Beth. "What you are doing out here instead of in the house? You know you can go inside even when we're not here."

"It was locked."

"Locked? I don't know how that happened. We all went to visit a sick neighbor on the next ranch over. Your mama and grandma cooked them up plenty of food, and all of us menfolk went to help with the chores and livestock. We just got back, but with the way Kep was barking, I sent everyone else inside until I figured out what was going on in the barn. And what a nice surprise I found. But come in now and get warmed and fed. And properly welcomed home."

Papa offered a hand to Nicholas and hooked his other arm through Beth's. With Kep circling them and barking, they headed to the house.

As they crossed the yard, four boys followed by Susannah ran out of the house, with Grandma Eliza and Grandpa Caleb right behind them at a more sedate pace.

"Beth!" Alphie, the oldest of the boys, was the first through the door.

"Beth! Beth! Beth!" Cal, Abe, and Peter were close behind and ran down the stairs like a runaway herd of horses.

"Bethy!" Susannah bounded down the steps, ran to Beth, and threw her arms around Beth's waist. "I missed you!"

"You didn't have much of a welcome," Alfie said. "We went visiting and someone"—he narrowed his eyes at the youngest boy, Peter—"went and locked the door."

"I didn't mean to," Peter piped up.

Amid all the excitement and chatter, the one person whose reaction maybe mattered the most was missing. Mama.

And just like that, she stepped through the door. Stopped on the porch. Cupped her hands to her cheeks. "Oh, my Bethy!" Then Mama, who never rushed about unladylike, ran down the stairs and embraced Beth. She wiped at tears coursing down her face. "I've missed you so. But now you're home. Home. And who's this sweet little baby?"

"This," Beth said, "is Elizabeth Rose. I call her Elly. And her brother, Nicholas. My children."

With two words, quiet filled the yard.

"Bethy"—Susannah spun around in a circle—"where is Mr. Bethy?"

The entire family laughed, but Beth's heart sank. "There is none, Susannah. Nicholas and Elly were gifts to me straight from God."

The little girl beamed. "Perfect gifts?"

"Yes, sweetie. They're perfect gifts."

Grandma Eliza stepped up close and held out her arms. "May I hold this little perfect gift, my first great-grandchild?"

"Of course." Beth transferred Elly to her own grandmother's arms. Then Grandpa Caleb came up beside Grandma Eliza and, with a wink, wrapped an arm around her shoulders.

"Mama, Papa." Beth kept her voice low while the others clustered around the children. "I lost my job at the foundling home because I couldn't bring Elly to work with me any longer. I found a housekeeping job for a wonderful lady who let me bring Elly there, but her neighbor—a judge—had wanted to adopt Elly. When I kept her, he was furious. We're here now because he's threatened to get her back and showed up at Mrs. McPhearson's house this morning looking for her."

"Oh, Beth, how frightening." Mama gripped her hand. "We'll talk more later."

"We'll make sure you're safe here," Papa said. "I'm glad you came home."

Mama clapped her hands. "Everyone, inside now. I'll put food on the table and fix hot chocolate and warm milk for these little ones—and anyone else who wants some." She laughed at the chorus of chiming voices. "I believe that's everyone. Come on inside, then. After we get you warmed up and fed—and Elly changed—we'll all talk."

Beth had so many questions to ask and to answer, but none of those mattered in light of that moment of embrace by Mama. Of being welcomed. Did that mean she'd been forgiven?

Before Beth could move, Susannah grabbed her hand and tugged her down. "Can I see the baby?"

"Of course, you may." Beth picked her up and walked over to Grandma Eliza so Susannah could peer right into Elly's face. The two little girls smiled at each other. "Is she my sister?"

"You're really her Aunt Susannah. But since you'll probably play together, you'll be more like her cousin."

"What about him?" Susannah whispered, pointing to Nicholas.

"He's more like a cousin too. He's baby Elly's big brother just like Alfie, Cal, Abe, and Peter are your big brothers."

"Okay. Bethy, can we go inside now? My belly's hungry."

Beth laughed. "Nicholas and Elly are hungry too. Let's go fill all these bellies."

When the hot chocolate was ready and stew was heating on the stove, with Elly sucking on her bottle, Beth's family gathered around the table. She was right where she'd never imagined she'd be tonight—happily home.

It was almost enough to make her forget for a few hours that her little family would never be complete. Not without Timothy.

CHAPTER 20

After supper and things had quieted down in the house, Mama took a seat beside Beth at the table.

"Beth, dear, now that we have a moment to ourselves, I wanted to tell you how happy we are to have you home. How much we've all missed you." She squeezed Beth's hand. "Especially me."

"You—you did?"

"Of course. You're my firstborn, and though I knew one day you'd spread your wings, I so miss your company, our discussions, seeing how good you are with the children."

"Mama…" Maybe now she could say the words she'd never said before running away. "I let you down."

"How is that, Bethy? You always were quick to obey and show respect, a wonderful example to the littler ones. You were so mature, always helping, growing into a responsible young woman. That's the only thing that made it easier when you left for Boise—that I knew you were capable to handle whatever was out there for you. You're an adventurer like I was at your age. And Grandma Eliza as well."

"But, Mama—I wasn't careful. It's my fault Susannah got burned." Beth bravely held her mother's gaze.

"My goodness, Bethy." Mama vehemently shook her head. "Surely, you didn't think it was your fault." She studied Beth. "Dear girl, I guess you did. Oh, Beth." She grasped Beth's hands. "It was an accident. If anyone should be blamed, it is I for being too busy out in the barn. But it was an accident. Of course you'd never purposefully hurt Susannah. And when you look at her, do you only see her scars? Or a happy, bubbly, beautiful girl who loves life?"

"I guess...a happy girl."

"Of course. We've worked hard for her to be content. God protected her from something more tragic. She's alive and completely healthy. She's a joy to our family. And you're a blessing. While I'm sorry for the circumstances that brought you back to us, I am not sorry in the least that you're here." She stood and engulfed Beth in her arms. "We love you and your children so much, Beth. All of you are always welcome here."

"I love you, Mama." This was where Beth had longed to be, cocooned in her mother's arms. And maybe God had used the fire and even Judge Garrison to bring her home for this moment.

The next day brought yet more hope—a typist job at the College of Idaho and plenty of people to watch Elly while Beth worked. And a week later, Beth sat at the kitchen table and counted out two ten-dollar bills from her pay and slid them into an envelope. Even if she could never return to Mrs. McPhearson's, she owed her for repairs from the fire damage so new renters could move in. She'd mail the money to Mrs. Martin at the orphanage, who'd give it to Mitzi to mail to Mrs. McPhearson. No return name or address would be listed on either of the envelopes.

Beth licked this envelope, listening to the giggles coming from the other room. Supper was eaten, the dishes put away, and the boys and Susannah were entertaining Elly and Nicholas. Her brothers and sister seemed to never tire of playing with her little ones, including them like they were their own brother and sister. Nicholas and Elly were well loved and cared for here.

Mama came back into the kitchen. "Mind if I join you for a bit?"

"Please do."

Mama pulled out a chair and sat. "You don't know how much we enjoy having you and your children with us."

"I sure missed all of you and even life on the ranch."

"I sense something else is bothering you besides worrying about Judge Garrison. You know both your father and I are here for you should you want to talk."

"I've missed our talks so much."

"As have I." Mama laid a hand over Beth's. "Would this by any chance involve—as Susannah called him—a Mr. Bethy?"

Beth sighed, "Yes, actually, it does. His name is Timothy McPhearson."

"McPhearson—would that be Bea McPhearson's grandson, perchance?"

"He is."

Mama's face lit up. "If he's anything like dear Mrs. McPhearson, then we already like him."

"Mama, that's just because she helped you and Papa get together."

"Indeed, she did. Perhaps she has a special gift." Her mother's wink held a hint of mischief.

"Oh, Mama." But her heart gave a little flutter at the thought. "Let me go back and start with Lawrence."

"Lawrence, hmm?"

"Yes. I met him at the library, and he was charming and..." She shrugged. What else was he? She couldn't think what she had even seen in him, other than the fact a man had finally noticed her.

"Go on, dear."

"I thought he wanted to even marry me. Until he discovered I had taken Elly Rose in. Then he made it very clear what his intentions were. He made me choose between him and Elly. And even if I did choose him, he wasn't interested in children. Or getting married anytime soon."

"I'm glad you chose Elly over him, Beth."

"Me too. And then Timothy came along. He was medically discharged from the army due to an eye problem and came to visit his grandmother. But she was up in Sandpoint when he arrived unexpectedly. Oh, Mama, he was the kindest, gentlest man. And he loved Elly and wanted the three of us to be a family."

"So what happened?"

"I don't know." Beth wrung her hands. "I just don't know. Everything was fine until the fire, and then I met Anneliese and she begged me to take Nicholas too."

"Are you my new papa?"

"No."

"I knew Timothy would be surprised, of course, but I thought he'd be thrilled. He loved Elly. Wanted to court and marry me and be Elly's papa. Several times, he asked when we could come here so he could meet my whole family and ask Papa's permission. So why wouldn't he want to be Nicholas's father too?"

Her mother steepled her hands. "Did he say he didn't want to be?"

"Oh yes. He made that very clear. But apparently, he had already met Nicholas somehow. Nicholas went running to him and called him Cookie Man and was so happy to see him. He even asked Timothy if he was his new papa."

"What did Timothy say?"

"'No.' Not a *not yet* or *I hope to be soon*, but no with a tone of finality. I wonder...could it be from telling him and Mrs. McPhearson about Anneliese and her German heritage? He did fight in Germany. His best friend had been killed by a German. Nicholas is German. But so is Elly."

"It's possible." Mama's sweet face scrunched up with the same puzzlement Beth had in her heart.

"Except, he was acting strange even before I told them Anneliese's story. Had he already known? And now that I think about it, it was after he returned from rescuing Elly's locket and baby gown from the fire. The locket...with the German word on the back. Oh, Mama—did he not want Elly either?"

"Beth"—Mama gripped her hand—"don't think like that. Surely, that's not the case."

"No, it can't be. I cannot believe that would be true. How could such a kind-hearted man be so heartless and cold?"

"Beth, dear, you must talk to him. Find out the truth of what's going on."

"But facts are facts."

"They are, but things are not always as they seem. At least hear him out. And let the Lord work in his life."

Beth buried her head in her arms on the table. "What should I do, Mama? I'm not giving up my children. No matter what. I promised Anneliese."

"Of course you did. But do you truly love him?"

"Yes. I do."

"Then go after him. Find him. And ask him. Maybe you can have both."

~

Timothy's bus pulled in front of the station in Sandpoint. Marching band members clustered around the station door, and their instrument cases and a bass drum clogged the sidewalk. He stood to disembark...if he could even get through the crowd and inside the station for a soda.

The passenger behind him caught up with him on the pavement. Recruitment age, duffel bag slung over his shoulder, probably headed on to Farragut. "Last stop for you?"

"Yeah, guess so." For two weeks, Timothy had been wandering from one military base to another, anywhere he could easily get to by bus. Seeking information on the whereabouts of Roland Johnston was fruitless. Checking with personnel, asking about new radio operators—all information no one was willing to give out. As a civilian—if Roland had already been discharged and was stateside—he could be anywhere, and the army wasn't aiding in his search. So Timothy meandered, too ashamed to return to Grandmother's. "For now, anyway."

"Yeah, me too. Heading out to Farragut."

Of course. Wasn't everyone Timothy's age in the vicinity of Sandpoint heading over to the naval training center either as a recruit in the navy or to work as a civilian? Even the women.

"Maybe I'll see you around." The man saluted and walked on ahead, weaving a path between band members and the drum up to the station.

Shame had been Timothy's cloak for these last two weeks, ever since the morning he'd fled like a child—or a coward—running away from home. From the dearest people in his life. Grandmother, Beth, Elly Rose. Most of all, Beth. She deserved someone faithful, loving, and loyal. None of which his rage and prejudice proved him to be.

He hated giving up his search, but if he couldn't return to Boise, his only other family was Great-aunt Cora here in Sandpoint. It was as good as any place to start over. And though the Farragut Naval Training Station nearby wasn't army, they did hire civilians. Maybe one day he'd get a lead as to what happened to Roland Johnston. Farragut offered radio operator training. All he needed was one good contact. If he had the right connections, someone there might help him find who had access to discharge records across the armed forces.

But he'd also heard the rumors—no, the fact—that since February, German POWs who'd been captured by US troops in Europe and Africa were being brought over to Camp Farragut. And word had it that they worked throughout the various Farragut camps right alongside navy men. They could be one of the gardeners or groundskeepers, one of the volunteer forest fire fighters. Or out on the soccer field or at a pool table. Surely, they'd be wearing POW shirts. Otherwise, how would anyone tell a prisoner from a civilian or a recruit?

The burning in his heart came to life again. Getting out of Germany, even being discharged from the army, hadn't erased Germans from his path. They were here in America too. Like Anneliese. Elly. Nicholas.

No. He didn't want to think of Beth's children. Of Beth. Of the family he almost had.

He didn't want to imagine Anneliese's husband, an American soldier marrying a girl right here in America, only to have his family turn on her the moment their son was killed by the Germans.

Or the deserted apartment building he and Stanley had hid in before running to the one across the alley where they were ambushed, the smashed framed photo of a family. A German family. The total building abandoned, destroyed, by whom? Americans. Did the Germans in that village hate the Americans like he hated those unseen people? But really, there was no reason to hate the civilians. They'd had no part in whatever had happened there. No part other than to lose their possessions, their homes. Their families.

Germans... Americans... He was tired of the killing. The rage. Why hadn't Roland just told him that day in the hospital what had happened from the time Timothy was injured to when he was rescued? A matter of seconds, perhaps? If only he could remember details.

He quickened his pace, trying to outrun the images. The girl under the table. Stanley protecting her. Timothy trying to protect them both. The scar-faced German soldier thrusting his rifle into Timothy's chest. The soldier jabbering in German.

If only he had learned more German words while overseas. And then, yes, that evil laugh. But...that hadn't come from the same German soldier, had it? He wasn't laughing. He'd lifted his rifle off Timothy's chest.

Timothy found an empty seat at the end of the soda fountain counter of the bus station, needing to sit down. He clasped his head in his hands, closed his eyes. He couldn't remember. Couldn't think. Couldn't forgive. The war inside him was worse than the war he'd fought. The truth was, both sides needed God.

"What can I get you?"

Timothy opened his eyes. A waitress in a red-and-white striped apron pulled a pencil from her upswept hair and stood waiting, order pad in hand. "I'll have a Coca Cola, please. And a grilled cheese sandwich."

"Got it. Be right back with the drink."

Oh, God. Please. Please. He didn't know what to pray. Only that he needed help. God's help. And the words Stanley had made him memorize wound their way again into his heart. He could almost hear Stanley.

"*Say it with me. 'Then they cried unto the* Lord *in their trouble, and he delivered them out of their distresses... For he satisfieth the longing soul, and filleth the hungry soul with goodness.' Always praise God for His goodness, Timothy. Always.*"

Stanley had lived those verses, among the men, even in battle.

The waitress returned and slid his Coca Cola across the

counter to him. "Here you go. Be right back with your grilled cheese."

But what goodness was there? Stanley and how many thousands of others were dead. Timothy tapped his fingers on the counter. Just one thing to praise God for...

Stanley's friendship.

And Beth's. And how she loved children and cared for them with everything in her.

Grandmother with her deep love for him.

That he was alive. Though he wished Stanley were alive, too, should he not praise God for his own life? And that the only injury he had was healing?

Here, sitting on a stool in a bus station soda fountain, he whispered the words growing in his heart. "Oh, Lord, please satisfy my soul with Your goodness. Like You did for Stanley."

"Mister—here's your sandwich."

Timothy blinked up at the waitress.

"Your grilled cheese. Are you all right? Or are you praying?"

"Uh, yes. Praying."

"Listen." She leaned an elbow on the marble countertop, resting her chin on her knuckles. "If you're headed over to Farragut for training, you're not alone. There's thousands of boys there. Probably all praying. But enjoy your sandwich. Who knows what you'll get there. Though, I hear those new German POWs are quite the cooks."

And there again, a reminder of Germans around him.

The waitress reached under the counter for a cloth, ran it under the faucet, wrung it out, and wiped the surface around him. Then leaned toward him again, saying something, the white cloth in hand, now inches from his face. The cloth—

Bits of that day in Germany came to him. The German soldier had removed his rifle from Timothy's chest, and the feet that'd been straddling him moved away. Then the man returned, crouched beside him, and placed a cold, damp cloth over Timothy's burning eye.

Why would he do that when he'd been ready moments earlier to shoot?

"Mister, are you listening?" The waitress stood with her arms crossed, one brow lifted.

"Huh? Could you repeat that, please?"

"I said, is something wrong with your sandwich? You haven't touched it."

Timothy pulled the plate closer. "It looks great." He took a bite of the crisped, buttery grilled cheese but swallowed without chewing it. "Yeah, it's real good."

"Okay, then." She moved down a few spaces and continued wiping the counter.

But Timothy stared at the cloth moving back and forth. That German had helped Timothy, had shown compassion in the midst of war. So would he have then shot Stanley in cold blood? But if not him, this soldier he'd hated, then who? Now more than ever, he needed to find Roland Johnston to learn the truth.

Oh Lord. I'm no better than the Germans. I'm a man filled with hate. Oh please set me free from it. Forgive me.

If only the bass drum out front would thunder out a roll, letting him know God had heard him, had forgiven him. But all was quiet. Even his heart. As if a peace had settled there instead of the rage. Was that possible?

He crammed down the rest of the grilled cheese and gulped his Coca Cola. Maybe Aunt Cora would have some wisdom for him. Or at least a peaceful place to think, if no WAVES were visiting. He handed his money to the waitress.

"Thanks, mister." She opened the cash register and deposited the bills, then winked at him. "Keep praying."

That was something he intended to do.

Once outside—thankfully, the band must have gotten on

their bus—Timothy hailed a taxi and arrived shortly at Aunt Cora's.

"Welcome, Timothy. What a wonderful surprise." Aunt Cora enveloped him with a hug as warm as Grandmother's. "Just look at you all grown up. I got your picture you sent"—she pointed to it on the mantel—"but you're more handsome in person. You look so much like your father." She led him to her kitchen. "I'll get you something to eat, and you get settled in."

"I just ate a sandwich at the bus station."

She eyed him up and down. "You look like you could eat more. How about some cookies now and then I'll make a nice welcome supper for you?"

"I can hardly refuse that."

With that, she bussed him on the cheek and set about pulling out much more than just cookies. "Now, if you want to use my phone, go ahead and call your grandmother. Bea will want to know you're here."

Yes, she probably would. "Okay." He put the call through but never had a chance to let her know anything other than his whereabouts.

When he hung up, he sat dazed.

Aunt Cora set a plate of cookies and snacks down next to him. "What's wrong? Is Bea all right?"

"She's fine."

"And your Beth?"

His Beth. He swallowed the lump in his throat, but the one in his chest grew heavier. "She's gone."

"Gone? Where?"

"Grandmother doesn't know. The day I left"—oh, he never should have—"Grandmother came back from the market, and Judge Garrison was waiting. She saw Beth and the children hiding alongside the neighbors' house, so she led Garrison inside her house to give Beth a chance to get away. But she never came back."

Silence lapsed between them for a moment. "Then go after her."

"If Grandmother doesn't know where she is, I sure don't. And it's been two weeks. Maybe she's safer wherever she is."

"Then she would've gone somewhere she knew was safe. To her parents?"

"No. That I'm sure of. There was an accident a few years back, and she said they don't want her around, that she can't go home. So...no. She wouldn't go there. But with no job and two children to care for, I don't know what she'd do." Or where she could hide from Judge Garrison's reach.

"Well, then, we'll pray about that."

Yes. And he'd pray daily until he had a clue where to look... and until he found her.

CHAPTER 21

In the morning, Timothy went over to Farragut to see what civilian jobs he could apply for. Something to keep earning money while he figured out how to find Beth, to support his family once he found them. Because, in spite of his wrongs—and if Beth would still have him—he was going to make them his family.

He took the first position offered—cleaning in the hospital. But every day, the prayer was in his heart—*Lord, please be with Beth and the children.*

In the evenings, he'd tiptoe into Aunt Cora's house, always wary of whether she was alone or if she was entertaining WAVES on their off-hours. They soon learned he wasn't interested in them. And like tonight, a week after his arrival in Sandpoint, the ones sitting in the living room ignored him.

He entered, nodded stiffly, then went into the kitchen. Their voices drifted in, but he could rattle around enough to mostly cover up their incessant chatter.

"Timothy," Aunt Cora said as she came in to refill a pitcher of water for them, "why don't you join us out there? The girls won't bite."

There she was wrong. They just might. "I'm not interested in them."

"Of course not, not while you're pining for Beth. But it might do you some good to just be a bit social."

He waved her off. "No thanks. I'd rather stay in here and eat."

"Very well. But they are a nice bunch of gals." And she left to rejoin them.

Two of the WAVES—nurses still in their uniforms—came into the kitchen. One he recognized from the hospital as she often worked on the floor he cleaned. She smiled and nodded. "Hello, Timothy."

"Bernice." The other didn't even bother with a nod.

"So, Bernice"—her companion grabbed her arm and pulled her toward the sink—"tell me, what's he like?"

"He's only been here a few weeks, but we've been out almost every night already. He's tall, suave, and so very handsome."

"He sounds like such a dream."

"Oh, he is. Except..." Bernice was frowning. "There's something wild about him. Every time he passes those German POWs, particularly one, there's a burning rage in his eyes. If I were a German around here, I'd stay clear of him." She shrugged. "But otherwise, he's the most charming man I've ever met."

Blah, blah, blah. Timothy tuned them out, but the words he'd already heard stuck. Was that what Beth would say about him? Not the handsome and suave part—but had she seen the rage in his heart? Embers still burned, although he'd confessed it to the Lord. Maybe not being able to rush back to her was for the better. At least until he could get the last flickers out.

The nurses finally exited the kitchen, again with Bernice nodding to him and the other not acknowledging his existence. Which was fine with him.

195

The next day, he was back to work. Routine work where he could spend his days praying while doing his job. Seven-and-a-half miles of corridors. Timothy could believe that figure after a week of pushing a broom up and down hospital halls, around and around patient wards. And he wasn't even doing all the hallways or rooms. Twenty-three hundred beds. And twenty-three hundred hurting people when fully occupied.

In the early-morning shift, he swept his broom slower as he passed a window overlooking the hospital grounds. Now at the end of March, spring was here to stay. A few of the German POWs—thankfully, identified by the *PW* on their shirts—were working in the yard, trimming hedges and mowing the lawn. Did whoever was in charge of the POWs really think it was a good idea to arm them with hedge clippers? But even so, the grounds were beautiful in their budding glory.

A dog ran onto the lawn, and all the workers—except the one who was off to the far side working alone on a hedge—and even the guards stopped their tasks and chased after him. The POWs took turns throwing a stick for the golden-haired canine to retrieve. They must be allowed a break now and then—as long as they finished their jobs to earn their eighty cents a day. The lone POW kept working on the hedge while the group continued to play.

A movement at the end of the hedge caught Timothy's eye. Was it a civilian or a naval recruit stepping around the corner? He couldn't tell from up here. And then a couple of the WAVES from Great-aunt Cora's get-togethers strolled down the hallway —Bernice and her aloof friend.

The friend pulled Bernice over to the window next to Timothy.

"Hi, Timothy." Bernice smiled at him.

"Hi, Bernice." At least she was polite enough to acknowledge him.

The friend rolled her eyes and turned her back to him. "Maybe we can see your beau from here."

"Maybe. He said he had to go to the gardens to track down somebody's dog. Isn't he sweet? Oh, look at the dog playing with those POWs. I bet that's the one. They found him, but I don't see—"

"Bernice, look, there he is." The other WAVE grabbed Bernice's sleeve and pointed. "Isn't that him over there?"

"It is." The man in question stepped up to the German POW and grabbed the clippers. "But whatever is he doing?"

Timothy's same question as the man raised the hedge clippers over the German's head.

Bernice clutched Timothy's arm. "Timothy, do something—he hates Germans! What if he—"

Killed him? That's exactly what the man's intention seemed to be.

Timothy took off down the stairs and out the side door.

Was this American taking his own revenge on any German he could single out for the killing overseas? But this wasn't war—it was cold-blooded revenge and hate.

By the time Timothy got to the hedge, he no longer saw the POW or the other man. The POWs had gone back to work, the mowers now filling the air with their noise. Should he have called someone to help? Maybe Bernice and her friend had. Hopefully, someone would be coming.

Where could the two have gone in those couple of minutes it took him to run down the stairs? Without the other POWs noticing anything. Maybe the other side of the hedge, out of sight?

Timothy rounded the corner. And stopped.

The man with the hedge clippers stood bent over the POW now on the ground. "I told you I'd track you down. And today's my lucky day. Now I'll finish what I started with no witnesses."

He raised his arm with the clippers and started the downward thrust.

"Stop!" Timothy sprang forward, and the man jerked. The POW rolled away in that split second, and the clippers gashed open only his arm.

The attacker turned, a snarl emerging out of him.

"Roland?" Timothy stared at him, then at the POW on the ground. Blond hair, dark-blue eyes, a scar across his left cheek. He'd seen the face too many times in his nightmares.

He'd found both his enemy and Roland. The two men who, combined, held the answers he needed.

"I—I—" The German stared at Timothy. Then he smiled through gritted teeth. Smiled? "Want say...*vielen dank*. Thank you."

Thank you? For what? Keeping him from getting killed instead of just gashed? Timothy hadn't known who he was until now, but still, he wasn't going to watch him be murdered in cold blood.

"It is you. You not know me?" The man cocked his head.

"Shut up." Roland spat the words.

"Yes, I know who you are." Timothy clenched his hands, fists that could so easily swing into the German's face.

"You help my *kleines mädchen*—little girl—in our apartment building in war. In German town."

"I said shut up!" Roland waved the hedge clippers over the man. "If you say one more word..." He ended with a laugh filled with evil promises.

And that laugh...

The POW kept talking to Timothy. "I say thank you."

"The other American soldier with me—did you kill him?"

"Nein. Not I."

Timothy turned to Roland for the truth.

But Roland's eyes were cold. Dead. "I told you," he ground out to the POW, "you should have left him there to die too."

And that's when Timothy knew.

"You killed Stanley!" Timothy lunged for Roland, going right for his throat. "You'll pay!" And all thoughts of the forgiveness he'd had earlier vanished.

~

"*Go after him.*" Mama's advice still rang in her heart days after Beth had told her about Timothy and what she suspected. She cracked a dozen eggs into a bowl and whisked them in time to Mama's words.

Mama thought there must be more to this. But Mama was a romantic with her own love story with Papa. And anyway, Papa had come to the ranch seeking out Mama, not the other way around.

Timothy certainly wasn't here, looking for her. Though that didn't count since she was hiding and even Mrs. McPhearson didn't know where she was, even if Timothy had asked her.

Go after him.

This time, it wasn't Mama's voice she heard so much as an urging in her heart. But she couldn't just up and leave. She had two children to care for. A job she needed to help support them and to pay off her debt to Mrs. McPhearson. And a man who didn't want her with her two German children.

"...go after work?" Mama stood in the doorway looking at her.

"Oh—what did you say?"

"I asked if you could pick up some supplies at the market after work."

"Of course." She gave the eggs a final stir and added oil to the skillet.

Mama walked to the stove and gently pushed Beth aside and lit a burner. "I think today at work, you should make arrangements to be gone a while, starting tomorrow. We'll take care of Nicholas and Elly for however long it takes. If you travel alone, you'll be able to slip in and out of Boise easier to avoid drawing attention to yourself in case Judge Garrison is still watching."

"But, Mama—"

Her mother winked. "I know when a woman loves a man. Now get going to work. And never mind about the supplies. I'll pick them all up myself after seeing you off on the train tomorrow."

"Oh Mama!" Beth hugged her tightly. She'd been so foolish, thinking she wouldn't be welcomed home. But had she not left, she wouldn't have Elly and Nicholas now—or have met the man she still wanted to marry. "Thank you."

CHAPTER 22

Twenty-three hundred beds.

Timothy had barely escaped landing in one of them this morning. But the German POW was in one with his arm bandaged, and Roland was—Timothy didn't know where for sure, just that he'd been hauled off by guards. And Timothy would have landed right beside him, too, had it not been for the German who had pulled him off of Roland before... Well, all he could do was say *thank You, Lord* for the German soldier who had saved him. Again, apparently.

Maybe he needed an interpreter to get the details, but for now, he sat next to the POW's bed, trying to figure out what had happened.

"I walk in to save my girl," the POW said. "Not know you protect her. Other man—American soldier—come in and shoot your friend also protecting girl. Americans take me prisoner, think I kill soldier. I did not. But American soldier say he kill my family, my girl if I tell he did it. He say he track me down to make sure I do not tell. He found me here."

Timothy leaned forward, elbows on his knees, head cradled

in his hands. "Why would Roland kill Stanley? Stanley was the best man I knew."

"He good man. Also protect my girl. Your friend, he beg soldier Roland not to kill. To turn himself in for stealing. Bible say no steal and no kill. Soldier Roland afraid your friend turn him in. Would be discharged. No honor. Soldier Roland say, 'Never. Only you in my way.'"

The night Timothy had seen Stanley talking to Roland—had Roland not been wanting to hear what Stanley had to say from the Bible but already plotting how to kill him?

And yet, how was Timothy any better? He'd attacked Roland to—to what? He'd been so filled with rage that he hadn't been thinking.

And even now, his thoughts were all jumbled. The only good man in all of this had been Stanley. And...this German POW. What had he done wrong? Nothing. He'd been protecting his little girl. He'd placed that damp cloth over Timothy's eye to try to relieve the pain. He had protected his own family by not reporting Roland but by suffering being separated from them and imprisoned in America as a POW.

"I try to save soldier Stanley, but am sorry. I could not."

"I just don't understand." Timothy lifted his head. "Why? What was Roland stealing?"

"I do not know. Something important."

"How could he kill another soldier and our unit not know?"

"Soldier Roland come first. Alone. After he shoot, other Americans come. Soldier Roland tell them I shoot their soldier."

"No one checked what gun shot Stanley?"

"No. No one. Soldier Roland tell them lie."

Timothy bowed his head again. As much as he hated to believe it, this POW had to be telling the truth. Roland had been about to kill this man out behind the hedge. And the cold hatred in his eyes... Yes, Roland Johnston was capable of murder.

Of course, Timothy would be questioned. About this morning's events...and that day in Germany. He needed to talk with Roland. Find out how he could kill Stanley in cold blood.

But he also had to do what was right and stand up for this German soldier lying in the hospital bed. The man he'd hated for months.

All because he'd never searched hard for the truth.

When had he become a man who let hate take over above finding the truth? Over seeking mercy?

Dear God, please forgive me. I'm guilty of all the things I held against this German man. Even against Roland. Please forgive me. Make me a righteous servant of You.

Timothy studied the man who just lay there quietly. Peacefully. Where was his anger toward Americans for landing him in another country as a prisoner? Separated from his family? "What is your name?"

"Kristian."

Timothy nodded. Smiled. How appropriate. "That's a good name." He reached out his hand, and Kristian grasped it with no hesitation. "I'm Timothy. I thank you, Kristian. You saved me twice." Maybe three times. Because now, with his hand clasped with that of this German soldier, Timothy was perfectly free. And oh, the possibilities that brought with it. He was free to truly love Beth along with her whole little family. Now more than ever, he was ready to wholeheartedly be both Elly and Nicholas's father. If Beth would still have him.

"Kristian, again, thank you." Timothy released his hand. "I hope to see you again, but if you'll excuse me now, I need to find who to tell that you were innocent in the death of Stanley. Then I have a bus to catch."

~

The next morning as soon as Beth was packed, the rest of the household was up to see her off. Of course, everyone wanted to ride along to tell her goodbye, but Papa said only Mama and Cal would go, leaving him and Alfie to look after all the little ones and the chores.

After hugs all around, Beth knelt before Nicholas, with Elly in her arms. "Sweet boy, I'll be back as soon as I can. I'm going to go find Timothy—Cookie Man—to bring him home." Hopefully, to be the little boy's new papa. But she didn't dare voice that promise. "And, Elly, sweet girl, I shall miss you also." She gave both a tight hug and a kiss. "I'll miss you both. I love you so much."

Nicholas clung to her, tears pooling in his eyes. He didn't have to understand perfectly in English to know the tighter-than-usual hug and the suitcase beside her feet meant she was leaving. Signs to him that she'd never come back for him, just like his other mama.

"I'll be back, Nicholas. I promise."

"I love you, Mama."

With a final hug and handing Elly to Papa, Beth picked up her suitcase and walked with Mama and Cal out the door.

"Wait right here," Mama said once they were on the porch. She disappeared around back and returned with a branch of bitterbrush still in its dormant stage.

"What's this for?" Beth fingered a gray-brown twig. "It's not in bloom yet."

"No, and even that's part of Elizabeth Rose Roberts's legacy to our family."

Of course, Beth had grown up with the story of Great-great-grandmother Elizabeth Roberts planting the bush out back months after she'd arrived in the wilds of Caldwell from New York City sixty-some years ago. Offshoots of that bush were still there, and every year, the story got retold when it bloomed.

"Mama—your Grandma Eliza—often said the beauty of the blossoms offered a promise of hope, of God's provision. Of His goodness and faithfulness. When I left home for Boise years ago, I stuck one in my hat for the journey. Just as something to remind me that God would go with me. God is with you, too, Beth, on this pursuit. So though the beauty isn't yet seen of the flowers themselves, even in this stage the bitterbrush stands for the promise of God's faithfulness. That He will provide in His time and make something beautiful even when we can't see it yet."

"Thank you, Mama." Beth tucked the branch through the handle of her suitcase. "I love you."

Mama stroked Beth's cheek. "I love you too."

"Me too." Cal wrapped his arms around Beth.

Beth wiped her eyes. "All right. Now I'm ready to go."

As much as Beth was torn, hating to leave her whole family and Caldwell behind, she had a plan by the time she debarked from the train in Boise. She'd wait at Mrs. McPhearson's for Timothy to get home from work at the post office, seeking encouragement and wisdom from her. Then after Timothy had eaten, she'd tell him how much she loved him and that her family wanted to meet him. He could come back to Caldwell with her, and they'd be a family.

Surely, he'd had time to get over the fact of Elly and Nicholas being German—and only part German at that. They were born in America, their father had been an American, so they were Americans. Not that it mattered, but maybe he'd forgotten that fact. And if they could possibly find Anneliese, she'd let her know the children were doing fine and doted upon.

Beth stayed on the fringes of any group of people she could walk beside nonchalantly, hoping to not draw attention to herself. Surely by now, Judge Garrison had given up trying to find her. She rode the bus to her old familiar stop, got off with a group, and skirted behind the houses on her short walk to Mrs. McPhearson's house. When she got there, she went around to the back, the very place she'd left from just weeks ago.

Beth fingered the bitterbrush branch still around her suitcase handle, hope and joy in God's faithfulness blooming, just like the flowers that were yet to come. She was here safely and would be reunited with Timothy.

A few soft raps on the back door brought Mrs. McPhearson, all aflutter.

"My dear! Come in, come in." She all but yanked Beth inside, grabbing her suitcase and lugging it through the door too. "I can't believe you're here. But—the children! Where are the children?"

"They're safe. I can't tell you where, though, just in case Judge Gar—"

Mrs. McPhearson nodded. "I haven't seen him, but I do not trust him either." She took a whistling kettle of water off the stove. "Sit."

Beth took a seat. "We have much to catch up on. And by the time we're done, Timothy should be home for supper."

"Timothy." Mrs. McPhearson poured tea into two cups that rattled as she set them on the table. "He won't be here for supper."

Did he somehow already know she was here and refused to see her? "I don't understand."

"He never returned home from when he left after the fire."

"He didn't?" The words barely came out. "Where'd he go?"

"He ended up in Sandpoint with my sister. He's working at the hospital at Farragut Naval Station."

"The naval station? But he's army."

"Was, my dear. Now he's a civilian. And they hire civilians, and he needed a job."

"So he plans to stay there?"

Mrs. McPhearson shrugged. "It appears so. When he called,

I told him about Judge Garrison and you running, but I didn't know where you were. Whatever happened—between you two or why ever he left—we need to let the Lord speak to his heart, to lead Timothy back to us."

But—Go after him. Was that still the call now?

Did she follow the urging in her heart? Could it be from God? Or should she follow Mrs. McPhearson's wise advice?

She was anxious to go to the bus station and buy a ticket to Farragut. Anxious to persuade Timothy to return from the north. But the inner urging that had told her *go after him* no longer pressed into her heart. Was she meant to wait, like Mrs. McPhearson advised? But what good would waiting do? The children needed him now. She needed him now.

Lord, what should I do? Go?

Silence filled her heart as she took a sip of plain, weak tea. It seemed that even Mrs. McPhearson was getting low on her rations.

"Oh Beth." Mrs. McPhearson stopped mid-sip. "I forgot. Nicholas's suitcase is here. Perhaps you could take it with you this trip when you return to him."

Of course. His suitcase. Filled with—what? She'd never had a chance to open it. Clothes, hopefully, as Peter's pants and shirts, even rolled up, engulfed Nicholas.

"Yes, I'll take it with me. I should look through it now even."

"It's still upstairs in the room you stayed in overnight. You're welcome to go on up."

"Thank you." Beth went up the stairs, imagining the house as it must have been back when Mrs. McPhearson ran it as a boardinghouse. People coming and going throughout the day, gathering together for meals in the morning and again in the evening. Perhaps games played in the old parlor. Mrs. McPhearson bustling about in the kitchen, preparing food for her boarders with Mama's help serving it. Providing hospitality to strangers, some of whom became like family. Such as Papa.

Which room had he rented and forfeited so Mama would have a place to stay?

All these upstairs rooms now stood empty, with the lower level divided and Mrs. McPhearson only using the first floor of her half. She hadn't even rented out Beth's side of the house yet. Not that Beth could imagine Mrs. McPhearson moving from here, but what a shame for the house to be so silent now.

In the bedroom she had shared that one night with the children, Beth placed the tattered suitcase on the bed. The suitcase Anneliese had packed, knowing she was dying and sending her son to join his sister.

She opened the suitcase. Yes, some clothes. Not many and not in good shape—and probably already too small for Nicholas. Beth pulled out two pairs of pants and two small shirts missing buttons. There were some cloths she could use as diapers. And a dress for Elly. Brand new, like a gift that had been given for when the baby grew a bit. From her grandparents before her father had been killed? And underneath the garments—

Beth picked up the framed picture, a wedding photograph of Anneliese and her husband. Elly and Nicholas's parents. Anneliese with her blond hair in curls touching her shoulders, ringlets framing her face. Small earrings dangled from her ears, and what were no doubt real pearls graced her throat in a choker necklace. And she was wearing not a church dress or suit but a white wedding dress. The cut was simple but elegant with lace trim. Anneliese was beautiful with the smile that lit up her face and the joy that the camera had caught.

Tears brimmed in Beth's eyes. Anneliese had gone from riches to poverty, not able to seek medical help or to raise her children.

On the bottom of the suitcase was an envelope. She stared at the return address—*McLaughlin & McLaughlin, Attorneys.*

She knew the name. Had typed correspondence from the orphanage to them. And they had a reputation of being tough.

What if Judge Garrison had hired them to get Elly back?

Her heart pounded. Whatever was in here, she should have seen it weeks ago. Maybe they weren't even safe anymore at the ranch. She needed to get back to the children immediately, pack them up—and run.

Beth sat on the bedspread and ran her finger under the flap. Pulled out an official-looking typewritten document.

Last Will and Testament

I, Anneliese Kruger Torrington...

Beth stopped reading, her hands trembling. This was a legal document. What if Anneliese had decreed that the children be returned to their grandparents...grandparents who didn't want them? What if Beth had been granted only temporary guardianship of the children?

Maybe she should take it downstairs and read it together with Mrs. McPhearson. But if the children were being taken away, Mrs. McPhearson would obey the law.

Beth took a deep breath, stilled her hands. She'd force herself to read it first. Then decide what to do.

She read the rest of the document, ran downstairs, grabbed her coat and pocketbook, and fled the house via the back door again.

CHAPTER 23

By late afternoon, Timothy stood on Grandmother's porch. Finally, back in Boise, where he never should have left.

Should he walk right in? Or knock, since he'd left and technically it was no longer where he lived?

Maybe his steps had been too heavy and given his presence away, as Grandmother peeked out from behind the front room curtain. Her mouth fell open, the curtain dropped, and within seconds, the door was swung wide open.

"Timothy! Oh, Timothy!" She pulled him inside, embraced him, kissed him. A real prodigal homecoming. "Oh my!" She wrung her hands. "Oh dear."

"Grandmother, what's wrong?"

She just shook her head. "Come sit in the kitchen. I'd better put coffee on."

Coffee? This was serious.

"Beth, Beth," Grandmother murmured as she filled the coffeepot and put it on the stove. She pulled down two cups, yet two cups already sat on the table, both with tea still in them.

"Did something happen to Beth?" He about fell into a chair as his legs shook.

"She's gone."

"What do you mean? She was here?"

Grandmother nodded. "Yes, yes, maybe an hour ago, two hours. I don't know. We were sitting here…" Her gaze landed on the used cups as if she was surprised to see them there. "I told her that Nicholas's suitcase was upstairs, and she went up to look at it. Then she came running downstairs and out the back door before I could even get out here from my bedroom."

"Were—were the children with her?" He didn't hear them. "Are they here now? Upstairs?"

"No. She was alone. I don't know where she'd been or where the children are. She must have run back to them."

"Did she take the suitcase with her?"

"I don't know. I think maybe not. I didn't think to check."

"Okay." He had to stay calm so he could think, like he'd been trained. The trait that had made him a good advance scout. "May I go upstairs and see?"

"Yes. The last room on the left."

He ran up the stairs and found the room. The suitcase was there, open on the bed. Some clothes were strewn on the quilt —little pants, shirts, a baby's dress—and a framed picture. He picked it up and examined it. Anneliese? He barely recognized the vibrant, beautiful, glowing woman in the photo. Her wedding picture. He studied her husband, the children's father. Tall. He had a kind face, an adoring expression in his eyes as he'd locked gazes with his wife. Nicholas took after him with his dark hair, his straight nose.

Timothy turned the picture over. Hand printed on the back were names—*Anneliese and Wesley Torrington*. And a date. *January 22, 1940*. During better times, as evidenced by their clothes. Before the US had entered the war, before Wesley was a soldier and their dreams had been shattered. Anneliese could be any happy American bride. Someone he could see many a man turning his head at.

Now Wesley was dead, and quite likely, so was Anneliese. How generous, how loving she had been to bestow her most precious gifts to Beth. And once he found Beth, he wanted to share those gifts with her.

But where to find her? His training stopped short of that.

He had no clue where to look. Why was she here, even? And why had she fled all of a sudden? What could have frightened her that badly?

He sat on the bed and ran his hands through his hair.

Think. Think.

Lord, where'd she go? Please help me to find her. All of them. Please keep Beth—and the children, wherever they all are—safe.

The Lord was kind and gracious. Forgiving. Even able to redeem the mess Timothy had made by walking away from the precious family God had led him to.

Oh Lord, may it be so.

He jumped up and ran back downstairs. "Grandmother!"

"Do you have an idea where to find her?"

"No. But in the meantime, I'll visit the places she loved, starting with her job with the Connors."

"But what if she returns while you're gone?"

Doubtful. "Then tell her to please wait for me. Don't let her leave." He kissed his grandmother on the cheek. "I have to go." And the urgency in his soul pushed him out the door and down to the bus stop.

Finding the Connors' house wasn't hard, as Judge Garrison apparently made no secret of where he lived. Judge Garrison on Harrison. After asking around a bit, he found the Garrisons' house. And there was only one house next door to it on the entire block.

He walked up the brick steps to the gray Colonial and rang the doorbell.

A woman answered. "Yes?" There was a smile in her tone and eyes as well as on her face.

"Mrs. Connor?" She fit Beth's description of an efficient and friendly demeanor.

She nodded. "I am."

"Hello. I'm Timothy McPhearson, I'm a...friend of Beth Calloway."

The smile vanished completely. "How may I help you?" The polite words were clipped with suspicion.

Hadn't Beth said how charming Mrs. Connor was? "I—Well, I was wondering if you'd heard from Beth."

"I'm sorry. She is no longer in my employ and left no way to contact her." She edged the door closed a few inches, then apparently, her manners stopped her. "Was there anything else?"

"No, ma'am. Just if you do hear from her to please let her know I was looking for her. Timothy McPhearson." He barely got his name out before the door closed firmly this time. Had Beth left her in the lurch when she'd fled? He ran the conversation over again in his head. And he wasn't imagining it—that at the mention of Beth's name, Mrs. Connor's manner had changed.

He got back on a bus and rode to the familiar stop near the foundling home. He'd loved riding the bus with Beth and holding Elly, as if he actually belonged with them, then escorting them up to the foundling home steps. This time, he didn't stop at the steps but went inside.

So this was where Beth had worked. A large window with the street view and a smaller one on the side of the building gave plenty of light to the utilitarian room. There was only one desk in the space, so it must have been Beth's station.

A woman, maybe a bit younger than Beth, now sat at the desk, chewing gum and pecking at the keys on the typewriter.

213

"Who're ya here to see?" The typist didn't bother raising her head.

"Um—" He couldn't very well ask to just stand here and take in the surroundings of where Beth had spent the last three years working at this desk. Where she had set Elly beside her in the market basket. Were the babies' cries coming from down the hallway the same children she'd heard each day or new ones?

"Well? Do you have an appointment or not?"

"No. I don't. I guess I'm not here to see anyone. I was just wanting to...look around."

"This ain't a place to come in and just look around. If you want a baby, you have to make an appointment. No one's allowed beyond here without one. So ya'd best be gone, mister."

"Yes, ma'am. I'm sorry to have bothered you." He took one last glance around to memorize this room, then headed to the door.

"Timothy?"

He turned and was looking at a matronly woman who must be Mrs. Martin, whom Beth had spoken of.

"Are you Timothy McPhearson?"

"Yes, ma'am. I am."

"I thought so. I'm glad to meet you. I'm Mrs. Martin, the director of the foundling home. I'd seen you escorting Beth to work a few times back when she was working here and bringing Elly Rose."

"You did?" He'd never noticed anyone watching them.

"My window has a pretty good view of the comings and goings. And I saw you pass by just now." She gave a quick smile, then motioned him forward. "Come with me."

He didn't have time to socialize. What he needed was to keep moving, to somehow find Beth. Or get back home to Grandmother and figure out what they should do.

"Mrs. Martin, it was nice meeting you, but I really need to be going. I—"

"I need to speak with you. So please, come." That must be the no-nonsense voice she used in running the foundling home. She set off down the hall—the path Beth must have walked each day at work—her sensible shoes clicking like a march with each step.

And actually, wasn't this better than making an appointment? Especially if she had some news of Beth. He obediently followed, but if she had no leads, then this had better be quick.

∼

This time, Beth hadn't snuck around the back of the Boise Foundling Home and come in through the kitchen. She'd come boldly through the front door and asked to see Mrs. Martin. Without an appointment. And here she sat in her office, waiting for Mrs. Martin's return after a rather quick departure.

The door opened and in came—

"Timothy!" She started to rise, her heart urging her to race to him and be engulfed by his arms. But the shock on his face stopped her. No smile. No laugh of delight. And no arms opened for an embrace. He hadn't come here to see her.

"Beth!" He stopped mid-step.

"Timothy," Mrs. Martin said, "please have a seat. Beth, look who I found out front."

"Timothy, what are you doing here?"

He blinked, like the question—or maybe her presence—roused him from some far-off thought.

"I..." But he didn't say anything more, didn't look her in the eye, nor sit.

Beth swallowed down the last of her dreams. She'd hoped—oh so had hoped—that he would have missed her like she had him. That he'd had a change of heart. But hadn't she known all along that marriage wasn't meant for her? And now she had two children she was beyond blessed with. And she was welcome at home. That was enough. Really.

It had to be.

"Well." Mrs. Martin also remained standing. "I believe you two might have some matters to discuss. I'm going to go make my rounds. And when I return, I'll have Pearl bring in some tea."

Beth nodded at her. "Thank you."

Mrs. Martin left and closed the door behind her, and still Timothy remained silent, his head now bowed.

Beth stared at him. They were finally together—yet so far apart. And that's when a tear slid down his cheek. He was crying? Maybe also praying?

With one swipe over his face, Timothy raised his head and met her eyes.

"Beth. Oh, Beth." His voice was ragged, as if it pained him to speak. "I've been searching for you. And now...here you are."

Though he still didn't seem overjoyed at seeing her, at least he was speaking.

"I was such a fool, running away. And for my hatred of anyone German...that's what it was, hatred. But I was so wrong." The words seemed wrung out of him. "But I've asked God to forgive me, to give me another chance. And Beth..." He reached for her hand, then retracted his before they connected. "That's what I ask of you—plead with you—to forgive me and to give me another chance. A chance to prove my love to you. And to Elly Rose and Nicholas."

The words landed one by one in Beth's heart. He still loved her? "You...love my children?"

He nodded. "I do. They're a gift straight from God. I would love a life with all of you, if you'll have me."

She wiped her own eyes now. "I forgive you, Timothy McPhearson. And I love you too."

He took both her hands in his. "Beth, I know we have things to work out. But I want nothing more than to be your husband and a father to Nicholas and Elly Rose. And maybe"—he gave a shy smile—"a houseful of children."

And there, hopefully, was the answer to Beth's biggest question that she hadn't yet spoken.

She opened her mouth, but Timothy put a finger over her lips. "So I'm asking, whether you give an answer today or need time for me to prove myself, will you marry me? I promise to love you always and to strive to be a man of God to lead our family. And if we need to hide for the rest of our lives, I'll do that. Anywhere, as long as it's with my family."

"May I speak now?"

He nodded, a shadow dimming the earnestness in his eyes.

She jumped up and flung her arms around him. "Yes, oh yes, Timothy!"

"Beth. My sweet, sweet Beth." His lips moved over her hair. Her ear. And then he cupped her face between his hands and leaned forward and kissed her. Gently at first, then soundly.

Kissing her—Beth Calloway—who'd had no hope of ever having a family. And now his kiss sealed the promises he'd made, that he loved and wanted to marry her and care for Elly Rose and Nicholas and any other children they might have.

A moment later, a knock sounded on the door. They jerked apart as Mrs. Martin cracked it open. "May I come in?"

"Yes," Timothy answered and wrapped an arm around Beth's waist.

With a pleased smile, Mrs. Martin motioned for Pearl to enter with a tea tray. "Pearl even rationed us some biscuits. I hope in celebration?"

"Indeed!" Beth clapped her hands together.

217

"Yes, ma'am." Timothy grinned and pulled Beth closer against his side.

"Ah, so Timothy is in agreement with your news? That's wonderful."

"Um, I haven't told him yet. But we're celebrating it, anyway."

"I don't understand your riddles, child, but you're happy about something." Mrs. Martin gave a puzzled smile. "And I'm all for celebrating whatever we can in these times. Let's sit."

They took seats, and Timothy reached for Beth's hand. Pearl nodded at their joined hands as she poured the tea. "I do believe we'll have a lot more to celebrate in the days to come."

"What news do you have, Beth?" Timothy asked.

"News that I want you and your grandmother to hear at the same time." She turned to Mrs. Martin to see if she approved and received a nod.

"It's worth the wait." Mrs. Martin winked at him. "Let's eat and then be off with you two. Thank you both for stopping by today. Seeing God's goodness even during this war is something to celebrate."

Hopefully, when Beth shared her idea with Mrs. McPhearson and Timothy, they would feel the same way.

CHAPTER 24

Timothy had so many questions. But as soon as they stepped onto the foundling home's porch, the foremost one popped out. "Where are Elly and Nicholas? Are they safe?"

"They are. Safe on my parents' farm."

"That's where you went? But what about—"

Beth threw her arms out to the side. "It's so wonderful! Of course, I knew Elly Rose and Nicholas would be welcomed and loved. But, Timothy..." Her eyes filmed over with tears. "I was too. And Mama never blamed me. Here, all this time, I thought she did. So she was just as hurt as I was by the gulf between us."

"And how is Susannah doing?"

"She's so happy and energetic, and her scars are even fading a bit. She loves Elly so much."

"And Nicholas?"

She laughed, the sound he'd been afraid he'd never hear again filtering right into his heart. "I don't think he's ever out of sight of at least one of the boys—and Papa. They love having him tag after them."

"So tell me your news." With a hand on her back, he guided Beth off the porch and onto the sidewalk.

She grabbed his hand. "I told you—I'll tell you and Mrs. McPhearson together. But you can tell me how you ended up here at the orphanage."

"That's easy. I was looking for you."

"But you were up north at Farragut."

He winked. "I was, but I came back. To find you."

On the short bus ride, Beth seemed content just to hold hands with him, to have him next to her, to lean her head against his shoulder. And to think, this could be his life forever with her by his side—with Elly Rose and Nicholas. A real family.

Within minutes after getting off, they ran up his grandmother's steps. Timothy rapped, then opened the door. "Grandmother!"

She scurried from the kitchen. "Oh, Timothy!" She stopped, stared as Beth entered. "You found her! Oh, thank the Lord."

Beth engulfed her in a hug. "Mrs. McPhearson, I think you need to put on some tea. We have a lot to tell you." But she didn't wait for the water to boil before she blurted out her news. "Elly Rose, Nicholas, and I are safe. We can return home!"

But even once she made her announcement, Timothy wondered if this was home anymore. Or was Caldwell?

"What happened?" Grandmother sat. "The way you ran out of here, I worried I'd never see you again."

"It's all thanks to you, Mrs. McPhearson. The suitcase—if you hadn't reminded me it was here, I would have missed the treasure in it." Beth took a seat beside Timothy.

"The picture of Anneliese and her husband?" Timothy leaned forward.

"That, too—but Anneliese had stuck in an envelope from an attorney. I was shaking and was so scared to read it. It was an attorney I knew of through the orphanage. I was so afraid that

Judge Garrison was using him to track down Elly and get her back. That maybe the adoption papers Mrs. Martin gave me weren't good enough. But..." Beth stopped and took a breath. "When I read it, it was Anneliese's Last Will and Testament. She named me as the person she was giving Elly and Nicholas to. To raise."

"It's over—they're really yours!" Timothy squeezed her hand.

"Yes. I took a bus to the attorney's office and burst in—without an appointment—but Mr. McLaughlin agreed to see me. It's true. They're officially mine! And he showed me one other thing. Something I didn't see when I read it quickly here."

"What's that, dear?" Grandmother asked.

Beth laughed. "You won't believe it." The teakettle whistled, and she jumped up and turned the burner off. "You just won't believe it!" She poured the water into a teapot.

"Well, tell us." Timothy grinned at her.

"Yes, sir, Mr. Cookie Man."

"What?"

"Anneliese had told Mr. McLaughlin that the kind man who lived in this house had given her and Nicholas cinnamon rolls and a sugar cookie. And a cup of coffee. Nicholas called you Cookie Man, so she told Mr. McLaughlin she wanted Cookie Man in the will, to thank you for caring about them. And that Lord willing, he would marry me and become Nicholas and Elly's father. He said he told her it was unorthodox, but he did it. She didn't know your name—and she only knew mine because she'd had Nicholas grab my purse that day at the bus stop and found my name and address inside."

"Is that tea steeped yet?" Grandmother asked. "I'm more than ready for it. And cookies." She stood. "I have a whole batch to eat up, though there's mighty little sugar in them."

"I'll pour." Beth did so and passed the cups out, then sat.

221

"And what about Anneliese? How could she afford to hire an attorney?" Timothy couldn't fathom that.

"Did you notice the pearl choker she was wearing in her wedding picture? She gave it to Mr. McLaughlin in exchange for his services. She was going to sell it for food, but she heard Judge Garrison shouting out on the street after he left the orphanage the day he was denied Elly that he was going to get her. So Anneliese decided she had to make sure it was official that I was to have Elly."

"And where is Anneliese now?" Grandmother set a plate of cookies on the table and reclaimed her seat.

Tears filled Beth's eyes. "She's...she died two weeks ago. Now I am the children's mother in all respects."

"It's time to go get them, don't you think?" Timothy had missed them, his whole little family.

"I do. We can still make it to Caldwell today."

"Let's go, then." Timothy stood.

Beth turned to his grandmother. "Mrs. McPhearson...will you join us?"

"Yes, please come, Grandmother."

She nodded, finished her tea. "I'll go." She started to get up.

"Wait." Timothy motioned her back down and took his own chair again. "I need to tell both of you something first."

"Perhaps why you came back?" Grandmother asked.

"Yes. I didn't tell either of you the whole story of what happened in Germany. When I was discharged, I was a man full of hate. And that's why I ran off, because I was still a man so filled with prejudice toward anyone German." No matter what they thought of him, he needed to tell them the entire truth. He met their eyes, and both Beth's and Grandmother's held compassion, giving him courage to continue.

"I was a man unfit to even think of having such a lovely wife as Beth. There were two people I needed to track down. One was the German who stood over me with his gun in my chest and who I thought had murdered Stanley. I knew I had no chance of ever finding him. And the other was Roland Johnston, the first man to arrive from my unit. If I could find him, I could get the truth of what happened that day."

"And you found him while at Farragut?" Beth asked.

"I found both of them."

"The German man too?"

Timothy nodded. "The German man, the man I've hated ever since..." He swallowed. "Kristian. That's his name. Roland was about to stab him. It turns out that Kristian was not trying to shoot me in that apartment building. He actually helped save my eye. And it was Roland who killed Stanley." He shuddered, the thought sickening him.

"Roland, one of your men, did it?" Beth's face twisted with horror.

"Yes. One of our own." He shook his head, still not comprehending what drove Roland to do such a thing. He knew the reasoning he gave, but such hatred was beyond him. Or maybe not. "My thinking had gotten all twisted up. But I asked Kristian to forgive me and asked God to forgive me too."

"And both did," Grandmother said softly.

"Yes, and I ask that each of you might also."

"Of course," Beth blurted out.

"Yes." Grandmother nodded her agreement. "Forgiving and being forgiven go hand in hand."

"Thank you." Timothy stood again. "Now let's go pack."

"And call my family and tell them we're coming home." Beth stood also and wrapped her arms around Timothy once again. "I love you so much, Timothy McPhearson. So very much."

"Let's go get your children, dear ones," Grandmother said. "And I know just what to do with those cookies."

CHAPTER 25

Beth spotted Papa in front of the depot as the train slowed and jerked to a stop.

"There he is—Papa!" She pointed him out to Timothy and Mrs. McPhearson.

As soon as Beth's feet were on the ground, she ran into her father's arms, with Timothy and Mrs. McPhearson following behind.

Beth released him and looped her arm through Timothy's, pulling him close beside her. "Papa, this is Timothy McPhearson and"—she gestured to Mrs. McPhearson next to Timothy—"his grandmother, Mrs. McPhearson. Timothy, Mrs. McPhearson, this is my father, Josiah Calloway."

"I'm pleased to meet you, sir." Timothy held out his hand, and Papa shook it while he gave Timothy a cursory assessment.

Then Papa turned to Timothy's grandmother. "Mrs. McPhearson—"

"Bea, please."

"Bea, I'm also pleased to meet you. Come, let's get you all loaded up."

When they arrived at the farm, all the others were lined up across the porch, waving. The children surged forward, with Nicholas barreling straight into her arms. Mama stood on the porch with Elly.

"You came back!" Nicholas held her tight, not letting go. Oh, she hoped he hadn't fretted while she was gone.

Beth knelt and pulled him close. "Of course I did, sweetie. And I brought you someone." She pointed to Timothy just feet behind her.

"Mr. Cookie Man?"

Timothy walked up to Nicholas and ruffled his hair. "Hello, Nicholas. My grandmother made something special, which we brought for you to share with the others."

Mrs. McPhearson handed him a package. "Some cookies I baked."

His eyes lit up. "Danke. I mean, thank you." He turned to Beth. "Mama?"

"Yes, sweetie?"

Nicholas pointed back to the porch. "Elly missed you too."

"Then let's go say hello to her." She took his hand and led the way to the porch.

"Bethy! Bethy!" Susannah skipped up and took Beth's other hand. "Don't forget about me!"

Beth laughed. "Of course not. You're my best little sister."

And then she was on the porch and in Mama's arms, and Elly Rose was reaching for her.

The entourage crowded into the kitchen, and Beth stood by Timothy, Elly in her arms, Nicholas at her side, Mrs. McPhearson next to Timothy.

"Everyone, I want to introduce Timothy and Mrs. McPhearson, his grandmother." She grinned over at her parents. "They'll be part of our family very shortly."

Papa raised an eyebrow at Timothy but winked at Beth.

"With your permission, of course, sir." Timothy moved next to him. "I had wanted to properly ask you first to court Beth—"

Papa clapped Timothy on the back. "We'll talk later when things calm down."

"Thank you, sir."

Alfie grinned. "So you're getting married? If Papa lets you?"

"Yay!" Abe shouted. "When?"

"Yes." Mama grinned at Beth. "When? We have a lot to plan if he says yes."

Papa shook his head, his eyes twinkling at Mama, and kissed her.

Timothy raised his brows in question for Beth. "I think very soon, then, if Papa agrees. We need to give Elly and Nicholas not only a mother but a father too."

"Tomorrow?" Susannah hopped from one foot to the other, clapping her hands.

Timothy laughed. "That's a very good idea, Susannah. But I think your sister might want some more time to plan a really nice day. What do you say, Elizabeth Rose Calloway? Will you become my wife if your father gives his permission? Not tomorrow but very soon?" His eyes shone with hope. "You can have it as fancy as you want."

"Whatever day it is can't come soon enough."

"How about in six weeks? That'd be about the second Saturday in May. Is that long enough for you to plan?"

"Then that's our date." She kissed him on the cheek, and Papa cleared his throat. "If Papa gives his blessing, of course."

"Like I said," Papa reminded them, "Timothy and I will talk." But he was chuckling, and his eyes confirmed that, of course, he'd give his blessing.

The extra weeks and Papa's wisdom were needed, though, as he and Mama did need to get to know Timothy themselves, not just take her word that he was a good, godly man.

Her mother clapped her hands. "That gives me time to sew you a wedding dress."

"Oh, no, Mama. That's not necessary. I can wear one of my suits or pretty dresses you've made me."

"No. You're my first child to marry and my oldest daughter. You're going to have a lovely gown, one that you can pass down to Elly Rose one day. First thing tomorrow, we'll pick out the fabric, and I'll get started. The second Saturday of May will be here before we know it."

Too soon, if Beth didn't figure out quickly the details of the idea brewing in her heart of where they could live.

~

Now that he was going to be a husband and a father, Timothy needed a plan of how best to care for his family. Something he should have already started, but in the whirlwind of finding Beth and the trip to Caldwell, he hadn't gotten far, if at all. Until Mr. Calloway—Josiah—asked him his plan and goals out on the front porch. At this rate, Josiah wouldn't allow his daughter to marry him ever, and there would be no wedding that Beth was inside probably planning.

"Sir, I don't know what Beth has told you about me, but I'd like to tell you myself. And then if you have any questions or"—he swallowed against the words that would burn coming out—"objections, I'll honor your wishes." He sat stiffly.

"Go ahead." Josiah set his rocker in motion.

"I served in the army in the war and was medically discharged. My eye was wounded during a mission, but that wasn't the reason. My discharge papers say combat fatigue… due to the fact I attacked another soldier while in the hospital."

Josiah still didn't speak, just sat nodding to go on, and Timothy couldn't tell if he knew this part or not.

"My best friend was murdered, and a German was standing

over me with his rifle aimed at me. A shot went off, and flying debris landed in my eye, so I didn't see what happened, but a soldier from my unit had appeared. Roland was there and saw everything. It was him that I attacked in the hospital, begging him to tell me what happened to my friend Stanley. He refused, and I vowed to find out one day. I was a man of rage and prejudice, not a man you would have deemed worthy of your daughter." At that, Josiah's eyes widened briefly, but he continued just rocking, listening.

"I also held it against Elly Rose and Nicholas that they were of German heritage. But..." He looked Josiah in the eye, and Josiah met his gaze. "But God did something miraculous. He helped me to forgive this German soldier. And then..." Timothy choked up. "At Farragut, my path crossed with both the German and Roland. The German rescued me a second time. He had been helping that whole time I thought he'd killed Stanley. It was Roland who shot Stanley and let the German be arrested and sent over here to a POW camp. If it hadn't been for Kristian—amazingly, that's his name, the man I hated—I'd be dead too."

He bowed his head. "God did so many things for me, but most of all"—he caught Josiah's gaze once more—"He forgave me and set me free from this hatred."

Josiah rocked a moment longer, then stood and pulled Timothy up. "Son, you're a man I'd be honored to have in our family. As a son and as a husband to our precious Beth."

"Sir?"

Josiah tugged him into his arms, embracing him as a father would a son, and as man-to-man. "Welcome to our family."

"You mean—?"

Josiah grinned. "You have my blessing with my daughter."

"To court her?"

"To marry her. We trust Beth's judgment, and you've shown yourself to be the man of God we've prayed for her to find. Both

Lizzie and I see how much Beth loves you and how you love her and her children. Let's go inside, shall we?"

"But, sir—Josiah. What about a job and where we'll live and—"

Josiah laughed. "That, my son, is something you and Beth will figure out. Together."

CHAPTER 26

After going into Caldwell on Saturday and picking out wedding dress fabric with Mama and standing still for measurements, and church on Sunday morning, now Beth was back in Boise. Back in her side of the house, with the kitchen aired out and repainted a pale yellow.

"It's lovely, Mrs. McPhearson. So cheery." Nicholas clung to Beth's skirt as he took in his new home. "But do I owe you more money for repairs?"

"Nonsense. All the place needed was fresh air and paint and a new pot and pot holder. Though while I was at it, I sewed up some new curtains. I saved your money to return, as I don't need it."

"We'll see about that, but thank you." Beth twirled in the kitchen. "I'm just so happy to be back home."

"Speaking of home..." Mrs. McPhearson twisted her hands. "Have you and Timothy decided where you'll live? As this seems too small for your family already."

"We haven't, but I have an idea I need to discuss with both you and him."

"Certainly. Is now a good time? You gather the little ones

and come over. I'll pull out something good for our always hungry Nicholas, yes?" She tweaked him on his cheek.

"We'll be right there, then."

When she and the children arrived, Mrs. McPhearson was already puttering about in the kitchen. Timothy sat at the table, his eyes clouded.

"Is something wrong?" Beth took a chair next to him and set Elly in her lap.

"Not wrong, exactly. I'm just overwhelmed with the new responsibilities I'll have. I should have had a plan in place for providing for us. I have to find us a place to live. And a job. I don't know if the post office will take me back, and what can I do? You know how hard it was finding anything to do at all, and—"

"Shh. God will provide. Has He not already proven Himself more than capable? And Papa gave his blessing even knowing these things weren't planned yet."

"You're right. But I do still need a job. And we need a home. What would you think about living in Caldwell? You'd be near your family."

"We could. Or"—she motioned for Mrs. McPhearson to join them—"what if we stayed in Boise? This was once a boardinghouse. What if we could buy the house once we're married—and, of course, you'd still live here with us, Mrs. McPhearson—and we could open up the whole house again?"

"Oh, no, I couldn't impose." Mrs. McPhearson shook her head.

Beth patted her hand. "You're part of our family. Or we could just switch sides and you live in my smaller half if you'd prefer that. But we want you either with us or near us. Right, Timothy?"

"Right. Family. That's a possibility, Beth. A good one. But what would we do with all that space upstairs? Even we don't need that much."

"Oh, but we might. If we could take in more orphaned children."

"Really?"

"What do you think?" She took his hand and kept one around Elly. "Would you be willing to take in more orphaned children from the war—children like Elly Rose and Nicholas with German heritage?"

Shadows darkened his eyes a moment. Remembering the burned-out building in Germany and the little girl there? Kristian?

Then his eyes cleared. "Beth, sweetheart, you're so wise and compassionate. Other little girls like Kristian's? God rescued her, and she wasn't an orphan. Once the war is over, Kristian should be headed home to Germany, to her and her mother. But there are yet more children just like Elly and Nicholas here, those with German blood in them though born in America. Born to American servicemen. Born into families with hurting hearts." He drew her into his arms and kissed her with baby Elly cooing in his ear.

"Um," she mumbled from beneath his lips, "is that a yes?"

"Yes, it's a yes—yes, indeed! Lots and lots of children. We'll gather them from the north. And the south and the east and the west. From wherever God brings them to us."

Nicholas squeezed between them and tugged on Timothy's arm. "Yes, Nicholas?"

"Will Elly and me still be in your orphanage?"

"Oh, Nicholas." When his silent appeal to Beth for help was met with only a grin, he searched for words. "It won't be an orphanage—it'll be our home, and any children who come will come as our children. Just like you and Elly Rose. So, of course, you'll be there—in your home." Timothy tightened his arms encircling Nicholas, Beth, and Elly. "As soon as Beth and I are married, we'll be your and Elly's mother and father now, forever and ever. We may fill the house with other children, but you and Elly are our first ones. You are always loved. Do you understand? Liebe. You are loved."

Nicholas nodded, then smiled. "Liebe."

"Always."

~

Now with the where to live settled—aside from the details of the how—Timothy had hope. "All right, so since we'll be staying right here, then I can start hunting for a permanent job today."

"Me, too," Beth said. "Well, not permanent, but something at least until we get married and open our home." She turned to Grandmother. "Would you—"

"Of course I would," Grandmother said, reaching for Elly.

Nicholas took a seat next to Grandmother. "If we stay with you, do we get more cookies today?"

Grandmother patted his cheek. "We'll make some together, how's that?"

He nodded, already settling in.

Beth stood and kissed Nicholas and Elly. "I'll stop by and visit Mrs. Connor and let her know that Elly and Nicholas are safe. And see if she still can use me as a housekeeper. And if not there, I'll check with Mrs. Martin. Maybe I could help Pearl in the kitchen."

"Or with the babies?" Timothy winked.

Beth smiled. "Who knows? Maybe even with the babies. Should we meet somewhere?"

"How about at the bus stop by Brighton's Candy Shop? Or better yet, we could split a scoop of ice cream."

"I like that. Brighton's it is once we're both done. Whoever gets there first can wait inside."

So with the children happy, they set off.

Timothy first checked with the post office. Not surprisingly, they didn't want him back. Once again, he was back where he'd started when he'd arrived in Boise. No jobs available for anything that he was good at.

Maybe that was the problem—he didn't know what he was good at or even truly wanted.

He'd been good at advance scouting. Not as good as Stanley, but pretty good with him. Likewise at pushing a mop and broom at Farragut. And that's about all he had experience in except for his brief stint at the post office.

With discouragement hounding his steps, that scoop of ice cream with Beth was more and more appealing. When he arrived at Brighton's, Beth wasn't yet there, so he went on inside.

"Welcome to Brighton's Candy Shop, Boise's finest in chocolates, candy, and handmade fudge." Gideon stood behind the counter, grinning. "I was just remembering my greeting when I helped my grandmother as a boy. Except now I should add 'and ice cream,' I suppose."

Timothy could picture the red-haired man, maybe in his mid-thirties now, as a boy exuberantly calling out the welcome to customers. "It's the ice cream that I'm here for today. But I'm meeting my gal here, so I'll wait for her first."

"Have a seat, then." Gideon studied Timothy a moment, his green eyes now serious. "Weren't you in here looking for a job not long ago?"

"Yes, I was. Actually, that's what I'm doing again today, job hunting."

"Well..." Gideon tapped a pencil on the counter. "I've been thinking about hiring another person as I'm getting busier. With the war on and candy being shipped overseas to our fellas, we've been forgetting our own customers right here. But business is going pretty strong, getting a bit much for me to handle on my own now as I've joined the effort in making chocolates for our boys."

"What sort of help are you needing?"

"Watching the counter, helping with customers, keeping the store clean. Just making the fudge alone takes up a lot of my time, it seems. Manning the soda fountain. Any interest?"

Interest? Who should Timothy thank first—Gideon or God Himself? "Yes, I sure would be interested. I'm getting married soon. I think you know her—Beth Calloway."

"Calloway. Of course. Lizzie and Josiah's girl."

"Yes."

"Good family. Congratulations."

"But I need a full-time job."

"I can use you full time. So if you're interested, let's sit and talk before a customer comes in. When Beth arrives, I'll serve you ice cream sundaes—on the house, of course."

By the time Beth showed up, Timothy had a job. And by the smile on Beth's face, apparently, she did also. "Good news?"

She greeted him with a kiss. "Yes. Mrs. Connor will take me back for as long as I can help her. She sends her apologies to you too. She told me about you visiting her to inquire about me. But she didn't dare give out any information to anyone in fear of Judge Garrison finding me and Elly. She wants to meet Nicholas, and, oh, I'm just rambling, I'm so excited. How about you?"

Gideon walked over with two ice cream sundaes. "Hello, Beth. These are on the house for my new employee and his soon-to-be wife."

Beth's mouth fell open. "Timothy—does that mean—are you—"

"I'm a new full-time employee of Brighton's Candy Shop, Boise's finest in chocolates, candy, and handmade fudge. And ice cream."

"Oh, that's wonderful." Beth clapped her hands. "And thank you, Gideon, for our sundaes. They look delicious."

Gideon winked at Timothy. "Well, next time, Timothy will

be serving them up. Enjoy," he added as a customer walked in. "See you tomorrow bright and early."

Beth took a bite of her ice cream, then took Timothy's hand. "God has been so good. When Mama picked a bitterbrush branch for me to bring when I came to Boise looking for you, she was so right. Even though there was no beauty in it then, she said it still stood for the promise of God's faithfulness. That He would provide in His time and make something beautiful even when we couldn't yet see it."

Timothy couldn't argue with that.

CHAPTER 27

Beth's wedding day, the second Saturday in May, dawned bright and cloudless, as if God was shining His blessing down on them straight from heaven. Even without the lacy gown Mama had sewn or Grandma Eliza's earrings or the spring flowers Mama had gone out to pick, Beth would have been happy. Though perhaps the most treasured item she wore was the pearl choker around her neck. Anneliese's, which Mr. McLaughlin had given to Beth. One day she'd pass it on to Elly Rose, along with her little locket and her birth mother's story.

But Beth didn't need a bridal party all dressed up and a large crowd of well-wishers. She had everything and everybody she needed right here on the Double E Ranch.

Timothy stood grinning beside her on the porch, Elly Rose in her arms, and Nicholas in front of them. Her immediate family along with their grandparents—Grandma Eliza, Grandpa Caleb, and Mrs. McPhearson—and even Great-aunt Cora sat in the yard at the bottom of the steps on kitchen chairs.

Papa pulled out his harmonica and played "Blessed Be the Tie That Binds." When the music started, Cal gave Susannah a gentle shove. She stepped forward, climbed the stairs, and handed Beth her bridal bouquet—a branch of yellow bitterbrush blossoms in full bloom now. Beth inhaled the aroma of floral, spicy, lemony, and cinnamony scents mingled together, just like the blessings in her life had melded into richness, and handed them back to Susannah to hold as the little girl leaned up against Beth.

Timothy squeezed her free hand. She smiled up at her groom, at the joy radiating in his eyes, in his own smile.

Yes, she had all she needed for a perfect wedding.

The pastor opened his Bible to read the verses Timothy had requested, preceded by the two Anneliese had wanted her children to remember, making up one passage. "Beloved, these are the verses referenced on the engraving on Elly's locket given to her by her first mother, Anneliese. Psalm 107, verses two and three. 'Let the redeemed of the Lord say so, whom he hath redeemed from the hand of the enemy, and gathered them out of the lands, from the east, and from the west, from the north, and from the south.'"

Timothy wrapped an arm around her and Elly and laid a hand on Nicholas's shoulder.

"And now from those Timothy selected, also Psalm 107, verses four through nine. 'They wandered in the wilderness in a solitary way; they found no city to dwell in. Hungry and thirsty, their soul fainted in them. Then they cried unto the Lord in their trouble, and he delivered them out of their distresses. And he led them forth by the right way, that they might go to a city of habitation. Oh that men would praise the Lord for his goodness, and for his wonderful works to the children of men! For he satisfieth the longing soul, and filleth the hungry soul with goodness.' And one final blessing that Timothy requested in honor of his parents, who are no longer with us on earth, but who have left a lasting legacy. May God's grace walk with you."

What better blessing to start their married life?

"Let us pray. Lord, we gather here to thank You for Your goodness and Your wonderful works in how You brought this family here together. How You satisfy the longing soul and fill the hungry soul with goodness. May Your blessings be upon Beth and Timothy and their family. Please bless our gathering today to unite them in matrimony. In Christ's name, amen."

With each word of the ceremony, Beth's heart was full of praise to the Lord, for He had satisfied her heart and filled her longing soul with such goodness. Overwhelming goodness and blessings—from no hope of marrying and having children to the precious souls entrusted to her along with Timothy, whom God had returned to her from the north as a victorious man.

She could barely take her eyes off him. And her little family.

Amen and amen, her soul sang as the pastor closed the service and as Timothy kissed her—quite soundly, even in front of their families. As a husband in love would.

She pulled back from Timothy only when she felt a tug on the skirt of her dress.

"Yes, Nicholas?" She bent to his level.

"Is Mr. Cookie Man me and Elly's papa *now*?"

Timothy winked at Beth and knelt down to Nicholas also and gathered him into his arms. "I am, Nicholas. For every day as long as the Lord gives us, I'm now your and Elly's father. I hope to be half as good as your first papa. He's a man you should be proud of. But just like your mama wanted, I'm here now to love you and care for you, Elly, and your new mama. And you don't need to call me Mr. Cookie Man anymore. You can call me Father now. Or Papa, if you'd like."

"Yes." Nicholas nodded solemnly. "Papa."

Beth blinked back tears and laid a hand on Timothy's arm.

Her own father climbed the steps and pulled Beth up and into an embrace. Then he smiled at Nicholas. "And no matter how old a papa's children get or where they live, he always loves them." He turned his gaze to Beth's. "I love you dearly, my sweet Elizabeth Rose Calloway-now-McPhearson."

Mama approached and wrapped her arms around both Beth and Papa. "And that goes for mothers, too, Beth. I love you so much. And am so very proud of you."

"Thank you, Mama. Papa."

Grandma Eliza and Grandpa Caleb joined the group with their hugs and then stood with their arms around each other, eyes upon each other as if they were the newlyweds themselves. *May she and Timothy have a lasting love like that.*

And then Mrs. McPhearson—her new "grandmother"—and Great-aunt Cora enfolded them with more hugs and kisses.

"Hey!" Peter called across the yard. "Is it time for the cake now?"

"Pretty soon." Mama winked at him. "First, we'll enjoy the wedding feast. And then the cake."

His eyes got a hopeful glint. "But maybe this time we could just start—"

"No, Peter Calloway. The celebration meal and after that, the cake. And you may not have the first piece. That's reserved for our bride and groom."

"Yes, Mama. But maybe they'll want me to have the second piece."

"They just might." Mama laughed.

The Calloway and McPhearson families ate the wedding feast, and Beth and Timothy cut the cake and made sure Peter got a slice big enough to satisfy him.

The day ended as beautifully as it had started. Beth's father played his harmonica in the background as the sun set, with the table lined with bitterbrush blooms as a reminder of God's goodness and faithfulness to all generations.

Did you enjoy this book? We hope so!
Would you take a quick minute to leave a review where you purchased the book?
It doesn't have to be long. Just a sentence or two telling what you liked about the story!

∽

Love Christian Historical Romance?
Looking for your next favorite book?
Become a Wild Heart Books insider and receive a FREE ebook and get exclusive updates on new releases before anyone else.
Sign up for our newsletter now.
https://wildheartbooks.org/newsletter.

AUTHOR'S NOTE

Dear Reader:

I hope whether you're continuing this generational journey in the Blooms of the Bitterbrush series or joining in with this book, that this homefront story set during World War 2 touches your heart and life. The struggles of Beth and Timothy in wartime—of children needing good homes and the effects of prejudice—are still just as prevalent today. Whatever our circumstances, may our hearts turn to the Lord for hope and forgiveness.

In the final story in the series—*When the South Wind Blows*—you'll meet the elusive New York City family who for generations have wanted nothing to do with the Double E relatives. What could finally lure them to Idaho? This story will be a reunion of sorts, bringing the heroes and heroines of the entire series to the Double E for its climax.

And, as always, Elizabeth Roberts's legacy of the bitterbrush plant stands as a reminder of God's goodness and faithfulness through the generations.

May you, too, cling to His faithfulness.

Barbara

ACKNOWLEDGMENTS

Thank you to the many who, through the writing, editing, and marketing processes, have had a hand in this story.

As usual, thank you to Denise Weimer for her extra hard work on the editing of this story. To Susan May Warren, thank you so much for your help brainstorming and getting this story started at the 2012 Storycrafter's Retreat, which was a blessing to attend. This story has been in the works for that long but never given up on, and what a blessing to have it now come to fruition.

And again to Danielle Rafoss for continuing to enhance my website (BookwithBarbara.com).Thank you also to Sarah Sundin for her input at the 2018 American Christian Fiction Writers conference and for her advice in structuring the story and having Timothy start right out on the home front.

As always, thank you to each one who had a part in these books—those who offered encouragement, prayers, research help, and marketing aid. And to those who have said, "I've been to Caldwell"—or to Boise.

ABOUT THE AUTHOR

Barbara A. Curtis lives in Connecticut with her husband, and they have one grown son, a blessing to their hearts. She is a member of American Christian Fiction Writers and Novel Academy.

Reach her at https://www.bookswithbarbara.com/

Want more?

If you love historical romance, check out these other Wild Heart books!

A Not So Peaceful Journey by Sandra Merville Hart

Dreams of adventure send him across the country. She prefers to keep her feet firmly planted in Ohio.

Rennie Hill has no illusions about the hardships in life, which is why it's so important her beau, John Welch, keeps his secure job with the newspaper. Though he hopes to write fiction, the unsteady pay would mean an end to their plans, wouldn't it?

John Welch dreams of adventure worthy of storybooks, like Mark Twain, and when two of his short stories are published, he sees it as a sign of future success. But while he's dreaming big with his head in the clouds, his girl has her feet firmly planted, and he can't help wondering if she really believes in him.

When Rennie must escort a little girl to her parents' home in San Francisco, John is forced to alter his plans to travel across the country with them. But the journey proves far more adventurous than either of them expect.

~

Ranger to the Rescue by Renae Brumbaugh Green

Amelia Cooper has sworn off lawmen for good.

Now any man who wants to claim the hand of the intrepid reporter had better have a safe job. Like attorney Evan Covington. Amelia is thrilled when the handsome lawyer comes courting. But when the town enlists him as a Texas Ranger, Amelia isn't sure she can handle losing another man to the perils of keeping the peace.

Evan never expected his temporary appointment to sink his relationship with Amelia. Or to instantly plunge them headlong into danger. But when Amelia and his sister are both kidnapped, the newly minted lawman must rescue them—if he's to have any chance at love

~

A Heart's Forever Home by Lena Nelson Dooley

A single lawyer whose clients think he needs a wife.
    A woman who needs a forever home...or a forever family...or a forever love.

Although Traesa Killdare is a grown woman now, the discovery that her adoption wasn't finalized sends her reeling. Especially when her beloved grandmother dies and the only siblings she's ever known exile her from the family property without a penny to her name.

Wilson Pollard works hard for the best interest of his law clients, even those who think a marriage would make him more "suitable" in his career. And when the beloved granddaughter of a recently deceased client comes to him for help, he knows he must do whatever necessary to make her situation better.

As each of their circumstances worsen, a marriage of convenience seems the only answer for both. Traesa can't help but fall for her new husband—the man who's given her both his home and his name. But what will it take for Wilson to realize he loves her? Will a not-so-natural disaster open his eyes and heart?